For Susie, my eternal flame

Table of Contents

FACTORY WALL

ALLEY

9 Helen Smith	7 The Flahartys	5 The Gillinghams	3 The Bedfords	1 The Boscos SUNSHINE CAFE

LITTLEBROOK TERRACE (Paved)

10 Robert Ryan	8 The Denhams	6 The Staples	4 Mrs Pierce	2 The Khans HAMZA'S SHOP

ALLEY

SINGERBROOK ROAD

1

3 Littlebrook Terrace Sunday 8th of July 2012

Bethany ran downstairs and jumped over the bottom three, her thick plaits flying after her. 'Where d'you think you're going, it's late?' Lily, her mother, said tersely.

'Just to post this,' Bethany waved a red envelope, 'it's Jon's birthday day after tomorrow, and I've forgotten to send it.'

'Post it in the morning; you have to pass the box.'

'No, I might forget.' Bethany smiled winningly and slipped past her mother on the way to the front door. Lily aimed a swipe at the back of her head, and Bethany ducked before the half-hearted blow could land. She laughed, well used to her kind mom being playful.

'You've got five minutes, my girl, and then I want you in bed. School tomorrow as if you don't know.' Bethany opened the door. 'Are you listening to me, young lady?'

Bethany sighed. 'Of course, I'm only going around the corner, don't fuss.'

Lily turned away and walked into the kitchen. She cleared the dishes from their supper of cornflakes and sultanas, a favourite late evening snack. Minutes ticked by filled only with white noise in Lily's head. She often passed the time with no thought while doing mundane chores. It had been like this since Greg shared his secret with her shortly after they married. As she placed the clean bowls in the cupboard by the sink, Lily became aware that she was listening out for the sound of the front door.

She went into the sitting room, raised a corner of the white net curtains that she was proud of, and peered out. Their front door opened straight out onto the pavement. She lifted her hand and returned her neighbour, Zeta Flaharty's wave as she passed close by the window. Nosey bugger, she thought but without any resentment. They got on well. All the neighbours in this cul-de-sac did. It was a close community, and neighbours helped each other. The downside was they all knew each other's business or thought they did and often had something to say about it.

Lily let the curtain drop; there was no sign of Bethany. She turned from the window, walked to the mottled brown, tiled fireplace, picked up a packet of Benson's and flipped the top. Her mouth curled as she noted for the second time that only three ciggies remained. 'Damn,' she said aloud. She flicked her Bic lighter, lit the filter tip by mistake, broke it off and started again. Taking a deep drag, she blew twin plumes of smoke down her nostrils, knowing it would leave nicotine stains on her lip. It had become a habit. Yet another bad one, she thought for the millionth time.

Lily knew she wouldn't sleep unless she had something to damp down her early morning cough and felt mad at herself for not asking her son, Ryan, to buy cigarettes earlier. She'd meant to, but he was so difficult to talk to these days. She suspected it was the influence of his mate, George Denham, who lived at number eight. They were rarely apart; both were keen footballers who supported Aston Villa. Unless funds were short, they never missed a game.

I'll go as soon as Bethany's back, Lily thought and fetched her black padded jacket from the cupboard under the stairs. She shook her head and hung it back up. It was a hot evening, even for July and she would look silly just nipping over to the corner shop done up as though it was winter. Lily had a thing about coats. She felt undressed without one. She'd used them all her life to disguise her large boobs that she felt were provocative and unsightly. She would have had them reduced if she could have afforded the operation. However, it would have to be done secretly because Greg loved her breasts and would never agree to what she wanted.

Lily took a last drag, ran the cigarette under the cold tap, and gave the stub a hard look, disgusted at her lack of willpower; she'd been trying to quit for the last two months and was failing miserably. She trod firmly on the pedal bin lever and threw the stub onto the accumulated rubbish. The lid clanged shut, and so did Lily's mind on that particular subject.

She returned to the window and peered up and down the terrace; not a soul in sight. It only took five minutes to walk around the corner past the café onto Singerbrook Road. The post box was another couple of minutes to where it stood like a reassuring sentinel outside the post office. Bethany should have returned by now. Lily dropped the curtain and adjusted the folds. She liked it to appear just so from outside. She glanced again at the watch that Greg had given her for her thirty-eighth birthday last month and twisted her arm to catch the light. She hadn't yet become blasé about the sparkle from the cubic zirconium stones surrounding the dial. She'd told him who needs diamonds when he tried to explain that he would have liked to be able to afford them for her?

It was nine o'clock, and Hamza's shop shut at nine-thirty. Lily chewed at the skin surrounding her thumbnail. Another bad habit, she thought and pulled the offending digit from her lips, deciding to go and meet Bethany and give her a flea in her ear. She had to pass the shop and could kill two birds with one stone. The old sayings ran through her mind as she tried to dampen the worries assaulting her.

Lily opened the door and stepped out onto the narrow-paved area that separated her house from Mrs Pierce's opposite. She turned and locked the door, glad that cars were never allowed along this terrace that ended in the sweet factory wall. She began to hurry towards the grocery shop, expecting Bethany to appear any minute. Bethany was a good child but sometimes thoughtless and wouldn't appreciate the worry she could cause her just by dawdling.

4

2

4 Littlebrook Terrace Sunday 8th July 2012

Mrs Amanda Pierce tore her eyes from the TV as she heard the familiar sound of a door closing opposite. She leaned forward on the padded arms of her chair and carefully lifted herself to a standing position. Her back ached something wicked today, and the two paracetamol she'd taken an hour ago hadn't helped.

'Oh dear, Henry,' she said woefully. Henry licked her hand sympathetically as she drew her walker close, leaned on the handles and proceeded slowly to the shallow bay window where she peered through the vertical blinds.

Nine o'clock on a Sunday evening sounds carried in the usually quiet space. Nothing moved in the well-lit terrace, but Amanda knew her senses hadn't betrayed her. She had a good idea that Lily's door had banged and wondered where she had gone. Or perhaps it was Greg that had alerted her. 'What's going on, eh?' she asked Henry. 'Do you think they've had an argument, and Greg's gone to the pub?' She stroked down her dog's back, enjoying the feel of his soft fur. His ears flapped as he listened intently to his beloved mistress's voice.

Amanda leaned on the plastic grips with one hand and put her other one on the middle of her back where the pain was. She rubbed as vigorously as she was able in the hope of bringing hot blood to the area to ease the pain. Then, she stood still and gazed at her chair, which looked the worse for wear. Both arms were faded where her hands had rubbed away the pattern from the floral material. 'I swear I'll get myself a new suite one of the days,' she told Henry as she settled her bones into the familiar contours that fitted her so well. She knew she wouldn't be doing any such thing, but it was something to share aloud with her chocolate brown Labrador. He was her only full-time companion these days, and she shared everything with him. She'd had another Labrador before this one and had called him Henry too. Ever since she'd lost her husband when she'd been fifty-six, she'd been on her own. Her dogs were her life since she'd retired from teaching, and her biggest worry was that Henry would outlive her and be neglected. However, she didn't think her friend Robert would allow that to happen. She missed Robert when he was away in London or had flown across the Atlantic.

As soon as Amanda was settled and her knees appeared, Henry's head snuggled into his familiar place. He gazed up at her with liquid brown eyes trying to understand everything she said. He wanted nothing more than to please this person from whom he'd known nothing but kindness since he was a puppy.

Amanda turned her attention back to the television and tried to concentrate on the wildlife programme about gorillas that always fascinated her. She'd crossed a wish to travel and see them in their natural habitat off her bucket list as arthritis had curtailed her travels. Fifteen minutes later, she realised that she had stopped watching, and her mind had been dwelling on life with her husband. They had spent every minute possible together and been so happy.

Although a couple of men had invited her out over the years, she hadn't been interested. Roy had been the only man she had wanted to be intimate with. When he fell from the Copper Beech that he'd been pruning and broken both his legs, Amanda had taken time from her job as a Primary school teacher to look after him. It had meant that his job as a tree surgeon would no longer be possible, and they had decided to sell their house and use their savings to buy a small café at one of the popular seaside towns. While he was healing and they were getting over the shock of his accident, the first time he'd ever fallen in thirty-two years, he was diagnosed with a brain tumour. It had explained the fall, but no one expected that he would die before walking again. Amanda was devastated at her loss, and even now, twenty years later, reliving his death brought a physical pain slicing into her diaphragm, causing her breath to falter.

People had been kind, especially Roy's family. His brother Ray, who resembled Roy, still kept in touch with an occasional phone call. He was now a widower, and at one time, had asked her to go and have dinner at a pub with him, but Amanda declined. She liked him, but he could never replace Roy; no one could, and she wouldn't risk putting either herself or Ray in an embarrassing situation.

Amanda gently smacked the back of her hand. 'No one could replace him, Henry,' she said, 'and he'd have loved you.' She shook her head and kissed Henry between his ears. 'Right, enough of being maudlin, I'm going to make tea, and as you are a good boy, I'll put some in your bowl. We'll drink it together and then go up to bed; what do you think, eh?' Henry wagged his tail and followed her trolly into the kitchen.

She didn't hear Lily return and shut her door, but Henry did and barked once. 'Shh, you'll have Mrs Moanalot round in a minute to complain about your barking again.' Amanda held her hand over Henry's muzzle for a second and then let go and wiped moist fingers on her cotton skirt. 'Take no notice, love, and you can bark if you like. I forgot they wouldn't be back for another week.' She laughed. 'I shouldn't call Mrs Staples that; I might do it to her face, which would never do. We don't want trouble with neighbours, do we?' Amanda guessed why Henry had barked and wheeled her trolly, teapot, and all to the window as quickly as she could. Nothing stirred outside. 'Never mind, I'm just too slow these days,' she said sorrowfully. Henry whined. 'Ok, I know you want your drink,' she said and scratched his head before sitting down and pouring their tea.

If Amanda could have seen through walls, she would have witnessed Lily as she gave vent to her anger at her daughter. 'How dare you promise me you'd be five minutes and worry the life out of me. Where have you been? What took you so long to post a bloody letter?' She lit a cigarette with trembling fingers.

'I'm sorry, Mom, truly I am. I never meant to stop on the way back, but Bryn was in the chippy and called me in as I passed. I only meant to stay a minute, but she talked and… oh, I'm sorry, the time just went.' Bethany's face was white as she faced her mother. She hated to upset her and felt terrible about it. She'd run home when she realised she'd been out at least half an hour.

8

'That's no excuse for making me so worried. It's the last time you go out of here so late in the evening, and I've got a good mind to ground you.' Lily's anger fizzled out as she knew Bethany wouldn't worry her on purpose.

'I'm sorry, Mom,' Bethany said and wiped a tear from her cheek.

'Well, alright, but think on, anything could have happened to you. It's just as well you came running past the shop when you did; I was on my way to find you after buying my ciggies.'

Bethany hugged her mom, who hugged her in return after a slight hesitation. 'I wish I'd been a boy,' she said.

'So do I sometimes, but I'd have still worried about you, now get yourself off to bed. I'll be up later. Brush your teeth.'

'Aw, Mom, you don't have to remind me anymore; I always brush them.' She giggled and started up the stairs.

'Don't be cheeky,' Lily called, but she chuckled.

Lord knows what time Greg will be home; Lily thought as she carried out her usual struggle with the ironing board, determined to catch up with the never-ending clothes she'd been avoiding. She enjoyed ironing late at night; she found it soothing before bed, especially on Sundays when Greg had gone to his club. She liked to wait up for him even though he never expected her to.

Her thoughts switched to her son, Ryan, who was sleeping over at the Denham's. It was all or nothing these days. Either she had her son and George, his friend staying at her house, or both were at the Denham's. It was ok either way; they were good kids. She turned the TV on without sound. It didn't matter what was on; it was just company. She yawned as she pulled Bethany's favourite shirt from the basket and listened as the steam hissed its willingness to smooth the creases.

3

3 Littlebrook Terrace Monday 9th July 2012

Lily visually checked Bethany over as she came downstairs. 'Ok, you'll do.' She smiled approvingly. 'Got your lunch money?'

Bethany rolled her eyes. 'For the second time, yes, you gave it to me while I was eating cornflakes, remember?'

'Less cheek,' Lily said distractedly and walked into the kitchen, where she continued to stuff laundry into the machine and tip powder and softener into the appropriate compartments. 'Never bloody ending,' she spoke her thought aloud.

'What is?' Bethany didn't expect an answer. She'd helped her mom collect and sort laundry from everyone's bedroom after her dad and brother left the house. She picked up her hessian schoolbag that she'd decorated with graffiti in rainbow colours. 'I'm off now, Mom, see you later,' she called.

'Hey, kiss please,' Lily answered from the kitchen. She pressed a button and listened a second to the water flow before hurrying into the hall and hugging her daughter. Lily needed to embrace all her family before they left the house.

She had a deep-seated dread that something would happen and she would never see them again. She didn't share this fear but thought they probably knew anyway.

As Bethany opened the front door, Rita Gillingham walked past, holding Tilly's hand. Lily thought how soon they grew; it seemed two minutes since Rita had given birth to her, but here she was, an energetic six-year-old. She had springs in her legs as usual on her way to school.

Lily stuck her head out the door. 'D'you fancy coffee and toast at the café when you return?' she asked her friend.

'Sounds like a plan; I'll give you a knock,' Rita said and crossed the pavement to follow Bethany.

'Hey, wait for us,' Tilly called, but Bethany either didn't hear or chose to ignore her. They went to the same school, but at nine years of age, Bethany saw Tilly as too young to be seen in her company by her friends, even though she liked her.

Lily closed the door and returned to the kitchen, where she cleaned all the surfaces with Dettol spray. She loved Monday's and always got up early to get chores out of the way. She worked at the local Aldi store Tuesdays and Thursdays and an occasional Wednesday. Then Friday was get ready for the weekend day. Monday was her day of freedom to do as she liked. She loved her family fiercely but sometimes felt swamped by their needs. Most Monday's she met up with Rita, her friend and neighbour, at the café. She knew that some people would think it was silly as it was situated next door. The side entrance where the Polish couple, who owned the café, Alek and Maja Bosco, lived was at number one Littlebrook Terrace. The main entrance was around the corner on Singerbrook Road. It was called The Sunshine Café, and Maja had certainly ensured it looked the part. The tables had yellow and white check cloths, and each chair back had a small yellow or white crocheted blanket over it. The walls were painted white, and the white crockery had a tiny daisy pattern. It was a pleasure to sit in the window, and people watch even on a winter day. Lily liked to find characters and spin stories about them.

Rita asked her once what constituted a character, but Lily answered after thinking about it, 'I can't say exactly; it's just something about them that catches my eye.'

It was ten o'clock when Rita rapped on Lily's door, and the friends went to carry out their Monday morning ritual. 'Morning ladies,' Maja called brightly as the doorbell clanged, announcing their presence. 'What can I fetch for you?'

'Coffee and two rounds of buttered toast.' Rita raised her brows enquiringly at Lily, who nodded. 'For us both, please, Maja. Where's Alek this morning?'

'At the wholesalers, you'll have to put up with my toast this morning.' Maja laughed, and so did Lily and Rita.

Lily had another reason to like meeting in the café. She couldn't smoke there, and funnily enough, she didn't get the urge to do so. She thought it was perhaps because she left all her baggage at home and became more relaxed in the happy atmosphere. Lily suggested to Maja once that she should move in there. Just a joke, but Lily would like to be permanently free from her responsibilities sometimes. She loved Greg, but he worried her lately.

'Have you heard that Robert has leased number nine to someone called Mrs Smith? She has a little girl and will be moving in sometime this week,' Rita said. She nodded like a wise owl and raised her eyebrows as Lily shook her head.

'How d'you know?'

'Straight from the horse's mouth. I saw Robert last week over at Hamza's when I was buying some skimmed milk, and I asked him straight out if he was ever going to let it or was he thinking of selling it. He teased me a bit and said I was nosey but then told me about Mrs Smith. I asked him where she was from, but he laughed and told me it was her business, and I could tell he meant it. He's a nice guy, and he's not a gossip. Let's face it; we know very little about him other than he's a pilot,' Rita said.

'Well, it's a good income for him. When his parents died, I think he inherited numbers seven, nine and ten, and I do believe a couple more houses in Bell Terrace as well,' Lily said, taking her purse from her bag and counting out the change for their meal. It always came to the same, and she had the right money.

'It's my turn to pay?' Rita said and reached for her bag.

'No, go on, it doesn't matter. You can pay next time.'

'Thanks, love,' Rita said as Maja brought their order and pulled out a chair so she could have coffee with them, as often happened on a Monday. The three women enjoyed each other's company. As soon as Maja sat down, Rita brought her up to speed with the gossip about Mrs Smith and other news. Monday morning became Monday lunchtime, something else that often happened when they all got together, and the café wasn't too busy.

Alek's arrival from the wholesale company broke up the laughter. Then, shortly after two o'clock, the friends parted company.

'See you next Monday or before,' Maja called and waved.

Rita said she had ironing to do and headed for home.

'Laters,' Lily said with a smile.

14

Rita nodded. 'Tarra love.'

Lily went in the front door, picked up a shopping bag, went out through their garden into the alley, and got into her black Toyota Yaris. Her head was buzzing but not with its usual white noise. She couldn't stop thinking about Mrs Smith and wondering what she was like and where she'd come from. Minutes later, she glanced at her watch as she pushed the trolly around Asda and hurriedly tried to concentrate on shopping for the evening meal. She wished she'd bought something from Hamza's, he sold most things, but everything was more expensive in his corner shop. It was alright for the odd thing, but working at Aldi had made her very price-conscious, not that she shopped there when she wasn't working.

Lily's house wasn't pristine, but she took pride in their matching light oak furniture, which she frequently waxed with solid polish and treasured the few expensive ornaments she'd bought. Her home always smelled of lavender, which even her children occasionally commented on. She thought about what it would be like for Mrs Smith to come to live in a fully furnished property and felt sad for her. I would hate it, Lily thought, and as she drove home, wondered if she had anything to give to their new neighbour without it looking like charity. She decided the least she could do was make a casserole and perhaps bake some muffins for her, maybe ice them with smiley faces. It had been a while since she had taken pleasure in baking, and it would be a traditional welcome to the neighbourhood. Yes, that would be ok, she decided, and her thoughts flipped to making her own family welcome home. She smiled to herself. She'd enjoyed her Monday and was ready to settle back into being mother and wife again; it was her life and one she loved even with all its problems. While Lily was peeling potatoes with her vegetable knife that no one else would touch because it was sharp with a pointed, curved blade, she suddenly realised she hadn't had a cigarette since early in the morning. 'Right, that's it, no more death sticks for me,' she said aloud and crossed her fingers.

4

10 Littlebrook Terrace Monday 9th July 2012

Robert Ryan garaged his BMW and let himself into his house through the conservatory. He'd returned that morning from a long-haul flight into Heathrow and was tired even though he'd managed a couple of hours sleep on the return flight from Las Vegas. He'd usually spend at least a couple of nights in London, but he needed to drive home and check on the house opposite before his new tenant moved in.

He wasn't on duty again until next Friday, but Mrs Smith had indicated via the estate agent that she'd be moving in on Wednesday. As she already had the keys, Robert thought all would be well. However, he needed to check the boiler and give the place a bit of a spruce up as it was two months since the last tenant had left, and he'd only been inside the property briefly to take away the bedding. Sometimes Robert wished he could sell all his houses and move to London, where he had a comfortable flat, and these days, he spent more time there than in his childhood home. However, he had tried to sell up before, but the minute the advert had appeared in Right Move, he'd changed his mind. He'd felt that he would be severing all links to his parents, and the thought had brought him sobbing to his knees. It had been five years since they died in an accident with a drunken driver on the M6, but he hadn't begun to come to terms with their loss. He had no one else except Amanda and considered his lifestyle precluded him from having a family of his own, much as he would love to be a father.

Robert threw his Maxwell Scott brown leather bag onto the Ikea Ektorp sofa and noticed that the red covers could do with changing. He dismissed the thought as he filled the kettle in his outdated but functional kitchen. He'd altered nothing. Even the pictures on the walls and his bedding were the same as when his mother was alive. He could hear and feel her presence in every room of this house. He heard his father too on occasions but more often, his mother, and it comforted him. While he lived here, he thought he would never truly lose them. Robert had been thirty-two when they died, but he missed them. An only child, they had meant everything to him. The only other person he cared about was Amanda Pierce, whom he intended to visit later.

Waiting for the water to boil, Robert ran his fingertips along the surface of the glass and kissed his parent's photo. 'Hello Mom, Hello Dad,' he said, 'I'm home, wish you were.' Pushing back the tears that always threatened him when he spoke to them, he made tea and took it upstairs to his bedroom. The familiarity soothed him as he drew off his shoes and folded his trousers neatly over the back of a chair. He continued to undress as far as his grey boxers, propped himself up on the pillows and, holding the tea bag string aside, quenched his thirst, then lay back and slept.

Robert opened his eyes, and it was seven o'clock. He'd slept well. Sometimes after a long flight, he didn't, and it pissed him off. It had taken a few years of fighting his body clock after becoming a long-haul pilot, but these days, he usually managed to adjust within twenty-four hours. This morning he was up, showered and eating a breakfast of bacon and egg sandwiches by eight-thirty.

He'd been grateful when he opened the fridge yesterday to find that Cathy from next door had not only bought him the loaf and milk that he'd texted a request for but had done a comprehensive shop and obviously run the duster around, making the house smell of lavender. He was fond of Cathy and David and their family. He'd known them a good many years and spent hours in their house when he was young. His mom had liked a good gossip, and she and Cathy had kept up with all the talk, good and bad, from the terrace and Meltoners Classics, the sweet factory where they had both worked. Cathy still did work there, but she had recently moved into sorting to enable her to sit down and take the pressure off the varicose veins that troubled her and at times made her wish she could chop off her legs. She knew it was possible to have them stripped, but she wasn't brave enough to have elective surgery.

Robert leaned against the sink and admired the garden while he wondered what his new tenant was like and what he needed to do at number nine. He watched two fat bumblebees as they flitted from rose to rose, collecting pollen. He didn't have the inclination to garden himself these days. However, his dad had been keen and had planted deep pink climbing roses that softened the red brick along the high factory wall. Robert remembered how small the plants were when he'd helped his dad dig the holes. He loved this time of year, high summer his parents called the middle of July when all the flowers were blooming profusely. Robert smiled as he took in the small lawn's neatness and well-kept pots of geraniums and begonias. He paid George and Lewis, Cathy and David's two sons, to look after all three of the gardens belonging to his houses on this terrace. They did a good job too. The long-term tenants of his two properties in Bell Terrace were enthusiastic gardeners, so he had no worries regarding their upkeep.

Robert sipped a cup of coffee, swallowed the last mouthful of his sandwich, then turned away from the window. He was pleased the lads had done such a good job and wondered if they had been as conscientious at numbers seven and nine. If they had, then he considered he probably wasn't paying them enough.

Taking the keys with their blue tags from a kitchen drawer, Robert crossed the pavement, unlocked the navy blue painted front door of number nine and went in. He sniffed deeply and thought that the place needed airing. He started at the top of the stairs and looked in all three bedrooms, inhaling deeply as he opened the wardrobe doors. The double divans and a single seemed to be as good as new. Neatly folded bedding that he'd paid Lewis to take to be dry-cleaned ready for the next tenants was in the walk-in cupboard in the small bedroom where he knew Cathy had left it. The bathroom's water supply was sufficient; he flushed the toilet a few times and allowed the cold water tap to run for a few minutes. So far, so good, he thought and checked downstairs.

It took a while for Robert to light the boiler, but everything seemed to be in decent condition. Not perfect, but certainly more than adequate. The garden was similar to his own, with roses on the factory wall and perennial shrubs and a few flowers dotted about. All was neat and tidy.

Robert peered over the lowish fence into the garden of number seven where Mr and Miss Flaharty were his tenants and found that their garden was pleasant too. He decided that the lads deserved a raise, and he would make sure they had one. His house and number nine had small conservatories, but number seven had a summer house butting up against the alley wall. He knew that the Canadians were at work most of the time and thought their home was sufficient for their needs.

Walking back indoors, Robert wondered if Cathy would give number nine a bit of a vacuum and polish if he paid her. She had done as much before the Flahartys moved into number seven, and he didn't think she would mind. The saying "strike while the iron's hot" ran through his head as he crossed the pavement and knocked on the front door of the house next to his own.

5

10 Littlebrook Terrace. Tuesday 9th July 2012

Robert listened with his head tilted as the *ratatat tat* echoed through the empty house. He glanced at his watch and smiled at his foolishness. Of course, they weren't in. Cathy and David would be at work and the youngsters at school or college or wherever they went now. He had a vague idea that Lucy, the eldest, was doing a degree at Birmingham University. I'm growing old, and I could probably do with a small pick me up, he thought as he glanced up at the factory wall where his father had fixed a hoop so many years ago. Its sturdy metal rim was rusted, but he would have used it if he'd had a ball. He knew that Lewis and Penny often had fun and some exercise the way he and his mates used to, despite having devices that took up much of their free time.

A little later, Robert chuckled aloud as he poured himself a tot of Jack Daniels. He wasn't a drinker, just the occasional social drink, but it was what he needed right now. He wondered if he was beginning to feel his age. Thirty-seven wasn't supposed to be old, but he felt ancient when he thought about the children from next door.

The Child in the Window

He opened the conservatory doors and settled in his favourite chair, savouring the perfumed air which immediately assailed his nostrils. His eyelids felt heavy, and he nodded off, but as he relaxed, the heavy crystal glass fell from his fingers and smashed on the marbled cream tiles.

'Fucking hell!' he exclaimed as he found himself on his feet. A piece of glass was sticking out from between his trainer and sock. He bent and teased the offending shard out. His sock felt wet, and it took him a couple of seconds to realise that he was bleeding. He swore a few more times as he hopped into the kitchen after divesting himself of trainer and blue sock, stained crimson on one side. The cut wasn't deep, and it stopped bleeding after Robert used some kitchen roll to put pressure on it for a few minutes. The box of plasters was where it had always been, and to his surprise, the pink strip stuck well to his foot even though it was a few years old. He threw the offending sock into the bin, knowing his mother would have told him off had she seen him do so. He grinned and said, 'Sorry, Mom.' Then removed his other trainer and threw the left sock into the bin to join the bloody one. He thought, must remember to take out the rubbish before I lock up.

Robert cleaned the broken glass up carefully in his bare feet, carried his trainers upstairs and donned clean socks. Pink this time, his favourite. A little later, he went to the café to have lunch. He often ate there when home. He couldn't be bothered to cook for himself and enjoyed the meals that Alek concocted. He ordered steak and kidney pie, mash, broccoli, and coffee, but when Maja brought it and tried to persuade him to have a sweet, he declined. 'I have to watch my weight, can't take excess baggage aboard my plane now, can I?' he said with a chuckle and patted his flat stomach.

'Go on, one slice of lemon meringue won't hurt you, and it's your favourite,' Maja said and gave Robert a winning smile.

Alek poked his head through the plastic strip curtain that covered the arch into the kitchen. 'Leave Robert alone Maja, he knows what he wants,' he said tersely and disappeared.

Maja's smile faded, and her nostrils flared as she rolled her eyes. 'Just being friendly, dear,' she called, then winked at Robert and went back behind the counter.

Not the happiest of relationships, Robert thought and shook some white pepper over his broccoli. Not his problem. He liked to eat their food, but he didn't wish to be drawn into their relationship issues, and if Alek thought he fancied his wife, he was mistaken. Robert was the type of man who turned heads, tall, clean-shaven with stylish dark hair, but not many people turned his. His thoughts focused on someone who had made him look more than once recently. It was the main reason he planned to return to London as soon as he'd sorted things out with Cathy and the boys.

Robert paid Maja and said, 'See you soon.' Then, he left the café and walked across the paved area to Hamza's shop.

'Hello, my man, what can I do for you on this bright day?' Beaming, Hamza came from behind the counter and clasped Robert's hands in his own smaller ones. 'I wondered if you were coming home this week, but Cathy said you were when she bought some shopping for you. So how long are you here this time?' Hamza let go and went back behind the till as Robert returned his greeting.

'Only until tonight when I've seen Cathy, but I want some flowers for Amanda. How's Nazia and the twins?' Robert asked while selecting a bunch of pink roses from a bucket by the counter.

'Oh, my goodness. Nazia is spending all our money in town.' Hamza laughed. 'Aleeza is settling down now, and we are getting less frantic messages from her. I think she is becoming used to marriage. We all do, don't we?' Hamza frowned and shook his head. 'Ramis is still with his grandparents in Bangladesh. He will be there for at least another couple of months. I miss both of them, and so does Nazia, but I think she enjoys her freedom. That's the second time she's been to town this week.' Hamza smiled indulgently. 'When are you thinking of settling down here instead of enjoying yourself?' He grinned. Robert flipped him the finger, which made them laugh, as he left the shop clutching tightly closed roses that dripped cold water down onto his jeans.

'Come on in love,' Amanda Pierce said as soon as she opened the door. 'Oh, you've brought me some flowers again.' Amanda put her face up, and Robert kissed her cheek gently, then hugged her as she held on to her walker. 'You are kind, isn't he kind, Henry?' She turned around and went into her sitting room. Robert patted Henry and followed her, shutting the front door behind him.

'How are you, lovely?' Robert asked and folded his length into the chair opposite his friend, who had loved him like a grandmother since he'd been a small boy. Amanda had been friends with his mother and babysat whenever his parents went out. Robert had sometimes spent overnight and, on a few occasions, whole weeks with Manda as he called her. She understood him, and he loved her in return.

Amanda smiled. 'Oh, you know. Good and bad days, and now today is a good day. It is so nice to see you and thank you for my flowers. Will I make you a cuppa while I put them in some water?'

'No, I'll do it. Which vase shall I use?' Robert got up and strolled towards the kitchen as Amanda told him to use the blue one, which he'd used many times before.

'When are you flying again?' Amanda called after a while.

'Not until Saturday but I have to get everything ready on Friday at the flat. Pack my flip flops and shorts etc.' Robert laughed and carried two mugs of tea in one hand, and the flowers arranged artistically in the blue vase in the other. He shut the door with his hip and placed Amanda's tea on the table by her side. 'Where would you like these?' he asked with raised brows.

'On the fireplace where I can enjoy them, please,' Amanda said, 'they are lovely, Robert. You think so, too, don't you, Henry?' Henry's tail thumped on the floor.

Robert looked serious and said, 'Tell me properly how you are doing? Are you managing shopping and cooking, ok?'

'Yes, you don't need to worry about me; we're fine, aren't we, Henry? Hamza brings anything round if I phone him, and you know Lily and Bethany, and of course, Rita will always do a supermarket shop for me. Sometimes I still like to walk to the shop, not that I can carry much, but Henry doesn't like it when I shut him in. He whines, so I haven't been at all this week, but that's ok.'

'Good. You seem to be pretty well stocked up. I checked the cupboards and fridge while I was out there. Is there anything else that you need, my friend?' Robert smiled tenderly at Amanda. 'Have you seen anyone lately? Has Roy been in touch?'

'No one's been in, but I talked with June only last weekend. They are all doing well and thinking of a holiday here next year. That would be something to look forward to, wouldn't it, Henry?'

Henry rested his chin on Amanda's knee. She automatically took a cloth from where it tucked down the side of her chair, wiped his muzzle, and then replaced it. 'Roy and I don't keep in touch so much these days,' she sighed.

'I don't think people do as much as they used to. There are so many ways they communicate; they don't need real people,' Robert said seriously. 'I'll try and stay in touch more love, I really will, but you know I'm out of the country most of the time. I tell you what; I'll get you a mobile phone which will make it easier. I'll be able to call you from anywhere, and I won't need to worry that I'm making you get up.

'That would be good, but I wouldn't know how to use one.' Amanda smiled wistfully.

Robert laughed. 'I'll teach you next time I'm home, ok?'

Amanda nodded. 'You're so good to me, Robert.'

'Well, you've always been good to me.' He stood up and took the mugs into the kitchen, swilled them and left them to drain. 'Now, are you sure there's nothing else you need before I go to see Cathy?'

'No, really, I have everything I need.' Amanda placed her hands on the arms of her chair.

'No, don't get up; I'll pull the door shut behind me as I leave.' He bent forward and kissed her, patted Henry, waved and left. Robert wished she wasn't on her own but didn't see what more he could do.

6

8 Littlebrook Terrace. Tuesday 9th July 2012

Cathy sank into the chair and hiked first her left leg and then her right onto the pouffe. She sighed, leaned back and closed her eyes. She felt exhausted, and the ache in her legs seemed to be getting worse.

'Fetch us a couple of paracetamol will you love?' she said to Penny, without opening her eyes.

Penny looked in the drawer in the kitchen where her mom kept the painkillers, but the blue and white packet was empty; she threw it into the bin in disgust.

'There's none there, Mom. Shall I fetch some from Hamza's?'

Cathy's eyes flew open. 'I only saw the packet in the drawer this morning, love; look again, will you?'

'Packet's empty; I've binned it. Shall I go to the shop?'

'Yes please, love.' Cathy shrugged her shoulders irritably. She guessed it would have been David or one of the boys because they often put empty containers back in the fridge too. Perhaps it's a man thing, she thought, determined to tell them off for the thousandth time. Her legs

29

ached so much she knew she'd say nothing this minute, even if they were standing in front of her.

Just over an hour later, when the pain killers had done their work, Cathy sent Penny to the chippy on Singerbrook Road. She couldn't face standing to cook, and everyone needed feeding. George, her eldest son, had texted to say he was eating and probably sleeping over at Ryan's, so it was only Lewis and Penny having their tea on their knees in front of the TV as usual. Cathy didn't know why they had a dining table anymore; they rarely used it.

Cathy dipped a chip into the curry sauce and shoved it around her white plate for a few seconds before eating it. She didn't usually feel dispirited, but tonight she did. She wished David didn't work such long hours taxying, but every penny counted. He'd left the house that morning at eight o'clock, but she wasn't expecting him home before nine. He took advantage of as many early morning and late-night commuters as possible. They both wanted to give their four children a decent start in life which was more than they had had. But it didn't come cheap.

'Where's Lucy tonight, Mom?' Lewis broke into Cathy's thoughts as he stuffed three chips together into his mouth.

'There's a group of them going for a drink after the last lecture and the library, so she's staying over at Philip's flat tonight. He's in court tomorrow defending some burglar or something. She has a lecture first thing in the morning, and then she'll be home. It's quiet without her, isn't it?' Cathy took a swig of Pepsi. Lucy was her eldest and, at twenty, was doing a degree course in Forensic psychology. She was nearly through her second year and loved it. However, some of the things that Lucy told Cathy about made her shudder.

It wouldn't be something that she could do. The smell would be enough, never mind the sight of bodies and blood.

'Hope you'll miss me when I go to Uni.' Penny laughed and sent a forkful of peas skittering onto the carpet.

'I won't mind missing you while you clear that lot up,' Cathy said and turned the sound up on the series they were watching about a boy and his dog.

Penny picked the peas up and stepped over Lewis's sprawled legs. She took a white envelope from on top of some books and handed it to her mother. 'I nearly forgot; Robert left this for you before he had to go back to London.'

'Thanks, love.' Cathy placed her almost empty plate on the floor and looked carefully at the envelope before tearing it open. She gasped as five twenty-pound notes fell onto her lap. She took the sheet of lilac paper out and read the neat writing.

Hi Cath,

Sorry I didn't get to see you this time, I've had to hurry back to London. I wanted to ask if you would pop over to number nine before Mrs Smith moves in on Wednesday and give it a once over with the vac and polish as you did at the Flaharty's. It's ok over there but needs a bit of airing to make it smell better. If you can't, will you get one of the kids to, pretty please? I've left the boys gardening money. They have done such a good job I've upped their wages to twenty-five each. The other fifty is to say thank you to you. I appreciate all you do Cath. Well, you know I do. Hope your legs are feeling better. See you soon, I hope. XX Robert.

'What's it say, Mom? Doesn't he want us to d-d-do the gardens anymore?' Lewis stumbled over the words; it was his dread. He loved gardening and did nearly all the upkeep on the four gardens himself because George made excuses most of the time. Without Robert's money, he'd only have a couple of quid each week. He'd saved nearly three hundred towards the Epiphone Les Paul guitar he was desperate to buy. Lewis knew his parents couldn't afford to buy it for him, and he hadn't even told them how much he wanted it.

'No, he's more than happy with the work you do. In fact, he has put your wages up to twenty-five pounds each.' Cathy smiled at the delight on her young son's face. 'And what is more, I know who does most of the work, and I'm going to give you thirty pounds, and your brother can stay at twenty. I know what you're saving for, and you'll be able to buy it quicker.'

'George will be mad.'

'You leave George to me. You deserve to have the lion's share.' Cathy turned to Penny. 'How would you like to earn some money tonight?'

'Yeah, how?'

'Come and help me get number nine ready for Mrs Smith to move into tomorrow. Shouldn't take long. I'll wipe surfaces in the kitchen, and you can do the vacuuming and bathroom?'

'Ooh yeah, when?'

'Wait until your dad's home, and then we'll go. You'll have to do a good job, mind, and I'll give you twenty pounds.'

Penny's cheeks were flushed as she thought of earning so much money. She jumped up and took the plates into the kitchen, and Cathy could hear her scraping them and placing them into the dishwasher. 'Cup of tea, Mom?' she called.

'Thanks, love,' Cathy said.

While the tea was brewing, Penny sorted out the cleaning things they would need to take over to number nine and put them by the front door. She knew there was already a vacuum cleaner on the property.

'I hope you haven't left those where your dad could trip over them,' Cathy said and took the mug of tea from her daughter.

'Course not d'you think I'm a baby still?' Penny said and rolled her eyes.

'No, I know how sensible you are.' Cathy said.

Penny made a disbelieving noise.

'Really, I do. You are probably the most sensible one out of my lot anyway,' Cathy said.

'What about me?' Lewis grumbled.

'You're sensible too sometimes; look how well you do Robert's gardens and ours. I'm proud of both of you.'

'Does that mean we are better than George and Lucy?' Lewis laughed.

'Ok, enough. Here's your dad now.' She watched the door. 'Hello, love,' Cathy greeted her husband, who walked into the room and dropped a kiss on her head.

'Pour us a beer, would you, son?' Lewis got up and went to the kitchen.

'I would have done that, Dad,' Penny said, looking disappointed.

David chuckled. 'I know you would, love, but he needs to get up off his lazy arse occasionally.'

'I heard that,' Lewis called from the kitchen making everyone laugh.

7

1 Littlebrook Terrace. Tuesday 9th July 2012

'Hurry up, Maja; it's been a long day.' Alek spoke sharply as he looked around the café where everything was ready for the next day's customers.

'I'll be with you in a minute, just putting cloths to dry.' Maja said and hung several tea towels over a rack by the food preparation area. She glanced around, then flicked the light switch off before joining her husband.

Alek locked the door behind them and stood back out of the way of three passengers who alighted from the bus that stopped outside the café. He recognised Mr Flaharty and his attractive daughter, but they hadn't noticed them. Good, he thought; he was tired and had no wish to talk to anyone.

Alek and Maja followed the Flaharty's around the corner into Littlebrook Terrace, where they continued along to number seven while Maja unlocked their door at the back of the café and climbed the stairs to their home. Their sitting room was situated above the café kitchen and storage area, and Maja kept the pleasant space neat and tidy. Fortunately, they had ceased to notice the ever-present cooking smell that pervaded every piece of furniture they owned.

Maja went into their small kitchen, poured red wine for them and carried it to Alek as he stared silently into space. 'Here, love,' she said and handed the crystal glass to her husband. 'Shall we take it to bed with us, or do you want to watch TV?'

'Bed.' Alek strode into the bedroom and placed his wine glass on the bedside table while he used the connecting bathroom. He had almost finished his drink when Maja slipped into bed by his side. She tilted the bottle and topped them both up. As she drank, Maja ran her free hand caressingly downwards from his groin to his knee, kneading a little more firmly with each stroke. Gradually she felt his muscles relax. She drained her glass, placed it on her bedside table, turned off the lamp, and slid her body a little further down the bed. Taking his now erect penis in her hand, she began to move it slowly until Alek's breath deepened. He disposed of his drink and turned to face Maja.

'We try again; perhaps tonight, you are ready,' he said and kissed her, exploring her shapely body that he knew so well.

Maja sighed. 'Perhaps it will happen tonight; I love you, my darling,' she said as he positioned himself above her and thrust deeply. Please, God, please God, Maja repeated to herself until she knew it was time to pretend to climax as he wished her to. He had often told her she needed to enjoy their lovemaking; he believed it was the best way to ensure she became pregnant. Maja had lost the ability to relax and rarely had an orgasm, but she had become adept at putting on a convincing performance. She sadly thought that men were so easy to fool as Alek told her to lie still while he went to the bathroom. Maja didn't move a muscle, but she had no great hope that this time would have a better ending than all the other frustrating times when they had tried to conceive. When they arrived in England six years ago, Maja remained on the pill until their business was established. They both wanted to start a family now and had been trying to make their wish come true for the last two years. Maja wanted to have tests, but Alek refused; he couldn't bear the thought that there was something wrong with either of them. The constant frustration put a strain on their marriage, affecting their relationship with their customers and friends. Alek was becoming increasingly gloomy, and Maja didn't know how much longer she could go on like this. She loved her husband and didn't want to go against his wishes, but she secretly considered seeing a doctor.

Alek returned to bed and pulled Maja towards him, gently cradling her on his shoulder. 'We need some sleep, or I shall be dropping the crockery,' she said. After about ten minutes, when neither said anything, Maja kissed Alek's cheek and extricated herself from his strong arms.

'I'm going to have to be up earlier than usual I'm meeting John before we open. He's got some gear for me.' Alek turned onto his side.

'Not more knock off, I hope?' Maja said as she pulled her pillow into a comfortable position.

'No, not at all,' Alek said, 'trust me.'

'Well, you know what happened last time; some of the stuff had maggots. John's not to be trusted.' Maja wriggled her legs, trying to relax them.

'Just leave it to me; I'll make sure it's ok before I hand over any money this time. Let's get some sleep.'

Alek was snoring gently in no time, but Maja's brain refused to follow suit. She was missing her family and her daughter. Alek had no idea that she had a child; he thought

Alina was her fifteen-year-old sister. Only her parents knew. They had been so shocked when she became pregnant at fourteen and had sent her away to a small convent where she gave birth to her daughter. Her father had fetched the baby and taken it home, leaving Maja to continue being schooled at the convent. During the time away, Maja's mother had pretended that she was pregnant and then supposedly given birth to Alina. Maja had not returned home until Alina was two years old. The family perpetuated the deception even after Maja had met and married Alek.

Maja knew that she was fertile, but she wasn't sure that the pill hadn't altered her hormones, and she wanted to know. She thought that Alek would be badly affected if he found out that he was infertile. If that were the case, it would be another secret she would carry, but she wanted a child so desperately that she convinced herself she had reason to deceive her husband again. Maja eventually fell into an uneasy slumber, waking with a thumping headache and a plan to make an appointment with her doctor.

The space on Alek's side of the bed already felt cold to the touch when Maja ran her hand across the dip in the mattress. She felt concerned about the arrangement he had mentioned last night regarding John, an unscrupulous man. Maja thought he would sell his mother if it gave him a profit. Alek was too trusting and too anxious to keep their business a success, even if it meant doing things that would be classed as criminal were he found out. He wouldn't listen to her advice; he never had. Maja had seen Alek's flaws when she married him, but she had her faults too, ones that weren't criminal but some she thought her husband could never forgive.

Maja forced herself to stop thinking about the past. She showered and dressed in a pretty floral top and white cut-offs, ready for the day ahead. Wednesdays were usually busy, and she wanted to make that doctors appointment before the café opened. The thought brought a slight frisson of excitement into her belly.

8

5 Littlebrook Terrace Wednesday 11th July 2012

Steve Gillingham waved his hand to his father, Andrew, left the disability lounge, and walked briskly to his office. Just another typical day at work. Check-in with his dad before sitting behind his computer updating information for all trains entering or leaving New Street Station.

Andrew, a retired train driver, was in charge of accessibility for disabled travellers. He loved his job and enjoyed seeing his son at the start of each day. A few times each week, they met up again for lunch, but Wednesdays were special. They caught the bus together at five o'clock and met up with Andrew's wife, Anna, back at Steve and Rita's house in Littlebrook Terrace.

This Wednesday was no exception; when Steve and Andrew walked from the bus stop around the corner, Tilly waited for them in the window. Anna let them in, with Tilly jumping up and down excitedly.

'Calm down, love,' Anna said and laid her hand firmly on Tilly's shoulder, but it was like trying to calm a small puppy. Tilly held out her arms, and Steve picked his daughter up, swung her around and deposited her headfirst onto the sofa, where she promptly rolled off onto the floor and giggled.

Anna tutted. 'You need to watch her neck when you throw her about like that.'

'Oh Mom, she's alright, aren't you, love?' Steve said and scooped Tilly up onto his knees.

'I've told him before, he's too rough with her,' Rita called from the kitchen.

'No, he's not; I like it,' Tilly exclaimed.

'Hush now and calm down. Come and help me lay the table,' Anna said to her granddaughter.

Andrew and Steve sat watching the BBC news until sausage and mash with onion gravy drew them to join everyone seated at the table.

Rita said grace as soon as everyone settled. She wasn't very religious and seldom went to church, but she believed in saying thanks for their good fortune. She often compared their privileged life to poor people in places like India and Africa that she'd seen on TV. Steve once told her that she should see some conditions people endured in places like Brazil, but Rita barely knew where Brazil was and didn't take him seriously.

Steve winked at his father, then said, 'Amen.' Anna gave them a frosty look as she intercepted the wink. But as with most Wednesday evenings, the family's love and care for each other was almost tangible. It filled the room as serving dishes emptied and plates became loaded.

Anna paused with her fork by her mouth when there was a lull. 'It's nearly our holiday, Tilly. Are you looking forward to going to play on the beach again?'

'Yes, but I'll miss my friends,' Tilly said and pulled a silly face.

'Have you booked the same cottage again?' Steve asked his mother.

'Well, you all said last year that you wanted to come back, so I have. Is that ok?' Anna frowned uncertainly and looked at each adult to gauge their reaction.

'Of course, it is, and we're glad you're so thoughtful. I'm looking forward to it, and I need a change,' Rita said.

Steve smiled. 'Don't we all, love?'

'Might as well enjoy your freedom before you go back to work,' Andrew said. 'You did get the job, didn't you?' he added and bit into a plump, well-browned pork sausage.

'I did. I start as soon as school opens in September, and I can't wait. I'll be looking after the reception class. How could anyone not love all their little trusting faces?' Rita said with a wide smile.

Anna laughed. 'Well, I hope it goes well for you. I remember Steve's first day. He cried for an hour before he'd let me leave him. He was still snivelling when I eventually had permission from the teacher to go. Then he came home in different trousers.' She nodded her head at her son.

'Mom, do you have to tell that story to everyone?' Steve's face was scarlet.

'Oh, get over yourself. You weren't on your own; most kids are upset on their first day at school.' Everyone, including Tilly, laughed good-naturedly.

'New York cheesecake and strawberries for dessert. Who wants some?' Rita said to take attention off her husband.

Everyone did, and Steve and Andrew promptly cleared the table before Rita dished up the second course, which quickly disappeared.

Rita collected the empty bowls and put them in the dishwasher while everyone else made a fuss of Tilly.

41

Wednesday was her favourite day of the week. When the people she loved gathered together, it made her feel secure. Rita described her own family as being rough when she had to speak about them. Something she avoided if possible. They had never been supportive. One of her earliest memories was something that she kept firmly hidden even from Steve. She felt too ashamed to let anyone know how her father had been so abusive.

Myra, her mother, had three children, Rita being the eldest, then Simon and Belinda. She had almost died when Belinda was born, and the doctors had advised her not to have any more children. Consequently, Myra had refused to sleep with Gilbert even when using condoms unless he forced her to. The arguments and fights it had caused had worsened, escalating into physical beatings the more he drank. Rita had tried to reason with him as she grew older, but she became the object of his fists. Rita came to hate her father and grew to hate her mother for not defending her. She had seen neither since she left home at the age of fourteen and squatted with a group of youngsters who were similar in age. She had hoped that her sister hadn't taken her place in their father's twisted behaviour, but she could no longer cope with it herself.

Rita spent her teenage years living with friends, a month here and there or at the squat. She learned to lie, cheat and steal to survive, but she had not agreed to have sex with anyone until she met Steve at a friend's house when she was sixteen. It was an instant attraction, but Rita trusted no one. They didn't date for another six months, although they had met up a few times at gatherings. Rita had become quite aggressive in her dealings with men, and it took her months to begin to have confidence in Steve and allow him to get close.

Eventually, his patience and care allowed Rita to shed her tough exterior, and they married at the registry office on the fourth of September nineteen-ninety-one. Steve was twenty-one and Rita nineteen. From sharing a flat with friends, they saved hard and were able to buy the house in Littlebrook Terrace before Rita became pregnant. They were delighted initially, but Rita miscarried, and it was two thousand and six before she gave birth to Tilly. They both decided that one child was enough, and Steve chose to have a vasectomy.

Rita had explained her hatred of her parents to Steve by only saying that they were verbally abusive. He could never get her to say more, but when they were married for two years, and Rita felt secure, he persuaded her to contact her mother. They occasionally wrote to one another, but Rita's feelings never changed. Then, in twenty-ten, Myra phoned to say her dad had died. Rita said, 'Good riddance.' She didn't tell Steve or mention that she drank a bottle of wine on the day of the funeral and whispered, 'Rot in Hell' into the ether.

Although Steve was aware that Rita had siblings she hadn't seen since she left home, she'd told him that they didn't exist for her when he asked about them. He had accepted that and never asked her again. Strangely, it made him feel closer and more protective towards her. He suspected that there was more to Rita's earlier years than she had let on. However, he was disinclined to delve deeper, thinking that whatever had happened was not affecting their happy life together, and he didn't need to know more than that.

9

10 Littlebrook Terrace Wednesday 11ᵗʰ July

Helen Plester locked the heavy oak door and got into her packed red Toyota Yaris. Then, without a backward glance at the chocolate box cottage that had been her home for the last twelve months, she started the engine and left that life behind, both physically and mentally. She was already Helen Smith.

Helen had been planning the next stage of her disappearance ever since the man and his wife, who lived nearby, had become intrusive. She thought of them as nosey old gits but knew they were only acting neighbourly. Well, the woman, Brenda, was anyway. Nigel had been giving her some odd looks recently. Nothing that she could make a fuss about, but she knew where it was leading.

When Brenda had knocked on her door for the third time in a week, enquiring if she was alright and would she like company, Helen decided it was time. She had gradually withdrawn most of her remaining money from her account at Santander and opened a new one in the name of Helen Smith at Lloyds bank. Helen had lived on the rapidly dwindling capital from the sale of her house for the last three years and needed to find a job soon. It had taken nearly three months to make the changes and rent the fully furnished house in Birmingham, where she was now heading. Another new life.

As she drove, Helen thought briefly about her childhood in Scotland and Lincolnshire, where her sister Jean now lived; she had no regrets that she'd broken all ties with her family. As soon as she knew she was pregnant, Helen moved to Nottingham, where she gave birth on her own. Then, a few weeks after, she moved to Devon, never letting anyone know where she went. However, she had registered the birth as she didn't wish to be troubled by the authorities and knew that she would need proof that Emma was her daughter sometime in the future.

'Mommy, I'm tired,' Emma said, 'we go home now?'

Helen glanced in the driving mirror that she had set to show her daughter in her car seat. 'We're going to a new home darling, go to sleep; we'll soon be there.'

Emma was an obedient child; she'd learned early not to upset her mother. She placed her thumb back into her mouth, cuddled Mrs Mouse and shut her eyes.

'There's Mommy's good girl,' Helen said. She was still miles from her destination and didn't want to stop at the services unless it was to give her daughter a drink. She'd brought coffee in a flask for herself, but she'd heard the clunk as Emma's cup had dropped onto the carpet. If she became thirsty and cried, she would have to stop.

Helen tuned the radio to Smooth and concentrated on the road. The traffic seemed to be extraordinarily heavy. She felt aggrieved to find so many lorries driving so close together. 'Bloody lorries,' she said aloud as an Eddy Stobart passed her in the middle lane. She had seen three so far, and much as she liked to see if she could spot their name, she wished they would piss off. Helen again remembered the green lorry from a few years ago when Tony was alive. She always kept an eye out for it. It had a painted sign behind the cab saying —It's Wavy Davy The Candyman With His Golden Balls—. She had thought it might have been carrying sweets, but she never found out any more about it.

Thinking about the lorry brought her husband, Tony, to mind. She shuddered and felt the familiar taste of bile in her mouth. Three years after the accident that had almost sliced him in half, his memory still caused her to have a physical reaction. She touched the ridged scar on her cheek where his belt buckle had cut into her face. Flashing images appeared, and tears spurted, blurring her vision.

She dashed them away with her hand and wiped them on her jeans. She felt the moisture on her leg through the fashionable tear. The crying ceased, but she continued to think about the abuse she had known all her life. First, her father and then the man she had thought she could trust to love and protect her. She'd been so wrong. After the first three months of marriage, the first blow had hit her out of the blue. She still thought sometimes that perhaps she had deserved the smack across her face. She'd washed a pair of Tony's white socks, he always wore white, with a pair of her new red knickers, and the colour had run. The whole washload had become pink.

Helen remembered holding the socks up to show him how silly she'd been and had laughed at her mistake. He had lost it. He smacked her hard, making her head ricochet off the kitchen door frame. She could still feel the slight dent in her scalp when she washed her hair and remembered the way her cheek had throbbed for some time before the stinging calmed down. The hurt to her psyche did not calm down, and it went deep. She was now certain that she was worthless.

He had said, 'You won't make that mistake again, will you?' and walked calmly into the sitting room.

When Helen had plucked up the courage to follow him, he hadn't mentioned the assault, and neither had she. Their lives had continued as before, and Helen still believed that Tony loved her and would, as he'd promised, protect her from her father's drunken rages when he showed up occasionally. A couple of months passed before Tony hit her again when she said she would like to book a holiday abroad. He had become red in the face, and a vein pulsed angrily in his forehead as he said, 'We're not made of money, you stupid bitch.'

Helen had turned to look out of the window and said quietly, 'But I could go to work.' She hadn't seen the blow coming and barely felt it initially as he knocked her to the floor, then dragged her up by her long, dark hair and raped her.

Although she remained and tried not to provoke him, he now permitted himself to abuse her when he wished. If there was no reason, he invented one. Other than going to the shops when necessary, he expected her to be at home. Helen had never had many friends, and after a visit from Valerie, who she'd known since schooldays, he told her not to invite anyone again without his permission. Gradually Tony restricted Helen's life until she didn't know who she could confide in and lost the will to try and leave her tormentor. He wouldn't allow her to go to work, and as he was a self-employed painter and decorator, he could check up on her at any hour of the day or night. Helen grew to hate men, and her hatred exposed feelings that had been dormant since childhood. She could feel the screams building when she watched TV and sometimes had to hide in the bathroom where she would pinch herself to stop giving vent to her tangled emotions.

Initially, Helen's sister, Jean and her husband, Bill, visited a couple of times, but they had never been close. Jean was ten years older than Helen and had left home as soon as possible, so they had little in common, and Helen suspected that Jean was more than a little afraid of her sister's acting out. From an early age, Helen had displayed behaviour that eventually caused her to be diagnosed as being on the autistic spectrum. She had tantrums and would laugh, cry and scream for no apparent reason. There had been several occasions when Helen had deliberately inflicted damage to herself if she managed to get hold of a knife or other sharp implement. Still, her doctor had insisted that she would grow out of it and by the time she reached ten years of age, she had calmed down. However, Helen had always been referred to as mentally unstable by her father, an alcoholic who sometimes used drugs. Growing up in a home where fighting and abuse were frequent, Helen thought her continued abuse was the norm. So, when Tony died, Helen felt nothing but relief even though she had no idea how to look after herself or what would happen to her. However, the relief faded when she had missed three periods and realised that she was pregnant.

Lost in thought, Helen almost let go of the wheel when a car blasted angrily as it almost rear-ended her, swerved and then raced past in the fast lane. She had begun to lose concentration and hover over the dividing white line. Perhaps I should have a break, she thought, and a couple of miles later, when she reached Michaelwood services, pulled in.

When she opened the rear door and undid the harness that kept her daughter safe, she said, 'You've been such a good girl; do you want a wee-wee now?'

Emma nodded and looked up at her mother. 'Drink please, Mommy,' she said, her eyes huge with unshed tears.

'Toilet first,' Helen said and was surprised when Emma started to cry.

'Are you very thirsty darling, don't cry; I'll bring your juice.' Helen gave her daughter a quick hug and her tippy cup.

Minutes later, they were on the road again. Finally, after just over an hour of uneventful driving, Helen arrived at her destination. Grateful for the estate agent's explicit directions, Helen pulled into the alley and parked by the back garden gate of number nine.

10

9 Littlebrook Terrace Wednesday 11th July

Helen stretched her arms above her head and stamped her feet to get the blood flowing as soon as she left the car, then opened the back door quietly and surveyed her sleeping daughter, who had her thumb in her mouth. She paused for a moment before deciding to leave her where she was until she had unpacked the car. She clicked the door shut and opened the boot. Her heart sank as she gazed at all the bags and boxes piled up on top of a large suitcase. She looked around and rubbed the back of her neck. She thought, better get on with it and searched in her rucksack for the keys to the property. Mr Ryan had texted to say that all was ready for them. It had bloody well better be, she thought.

As she walked up the path past the small, wooden shed and unlocked the conservatory doors, she heard a man say, 'Welcome, Mrs Smith, would you like a hand to unpack your car?'

Helen looked up at the bearded man next door who stood head and shoulders above the fence. 'Thank you; I'd appreciate some help. I've left my daughter asleep, so I need to unpack quickly,' she said and smiled. She didn't have to think about how to react; she had already worked out her strategy for living in what she knew was a small community. She had to appear friendly to fit in but remain as aloof as possible. Anyway, a strong pair of arms would be welcome. She pushed open the doors and looked around. The conservatory was small but neat, with two cane chairs next to each other, a table and a bookcase. She explored no further, everything could be deposited right there, and she need never invite anyone further inside. She returned to the car and was met by the man who introduced himself as Claude Flaharty and his daughter Zeta. Zeta resembled Claude in some ways but was considerably smaller and her features more refined. She had the highest cheekbones Helen ever remembered seeing and wondered how she managed to make her face up so perfectly. Her skin looked flawless, and her eyes sparkled as though with mischief as she smiled at Helen.

'Come on then, let's do it,' Zeta said and picked up two large bags. 'Where do you want them?' she asked as she started to walk up the path.

'I'm going to put everything in the conservatory so I can bring in my daughter. Please put them just inside.'

Helen grabbed several bulky, black bin bags and Claude some boxes marked kitchen in black ink on the side and ferried them to the house. By the time the three of them had made a couple of trips, only the suitcase was left. Helen took hold of the handle and felt her hand brushed aside as Claude said, 'No, you get your daughter, and I'll carry this.' Helen bristled at being ordered about but managed to hold her tongue and stood back as Claude lifted the case and placed it on the ground while he shut the car boot. He picked it up and began to walk. 'My goodness, this is heavy,' he said.

But Helen had turned away and was undoing the straps that held her daughter, who was now awake and wide-eyed, taking in the unfamiliar surroundings.

Instead of allowing Emma to wake completely and walk, Helen carried her as quickly as possible to the conservatory, where Claude and Zeta hovered and put her down on the beige carpet.

'Hello little one, what's your name? Zeta said and stooped down in front of Emma. Emma scooted on her bottom as far away from this stranger as possible and said nothing. Zeta stood and took a step back away from the pretty child.

'My daughter's name is Emma, but she is shy with strangers. Thank you so much for your help. I appreciate it. We are both tired, so I'm going to make beds up and get some sleep.' Helen smiled and gestured towards the door.

'Are you sure I can't help you make beds up or anything else?' Zeta asked.

'That's very kind, but no thanks, I'll manage, and I need to get my bearings,' Helen said and held the conservatory door open for her neighbours to leave. They took the hint and waved as they made their way down the wide path that followed the line of the fence. Helen locked the door behind them and surveyed all her possessions.

Leaving Emma by the conservatory wall, she dragged the suitcase through the kitchen, pushed it slowly upstairs, and then hauled it into the main bedroom. She surveyed the empty fitted wardrobes and then a cupboard in the room next to the sweet factory wall, which contained bedding. She piled it up on the single bed, then hauled in the suitcase, and quickly transferred the bundled contents into the closet as she heard Emma call to her in a panicky voice.

Helen retraced her steps and said, 'What's the matter darling, I haven't left you, do you want a wee-wee?'

Emma nodded tearfully; she hadn't moved an inch. Helen took her hand and pulled her up from the floor. 'You've been a good girl, and when you're comfortable, I'll make us something to eat and drink,' she said and went quickly to find the bathroom.

Emma sat still on the cold tiles and smiled with relief as she waited for her mother to use the toilet after her. 'Is this where we live now, Mommy?' she asked quietly.

'Come and wash your hands. Yes, you must forget all about the cottage and the seaside. We don't want anyone to know where we used to live. Remember what I've told you, my good girl.' Helen gazed unsmiling into her daughter's blue eyes that were so like her own. 'You will, won't you?'

Emma nodded vigorously. 'We lived in a big city, but I don't know where. Is that ok?'

Helen smiled. 'Yes, just right. Did you like the people who live next door?'

'Are they nice? Will we be friends with them?' They helped us, didn't they, Mommy?'

'Yes, they did, and we will be friendly, but we won't trust them to know anything about us so remember never tell them anything.' Helen's eyes lost their smile, her lips narrowed, and Emma began to cry.

'It's ok, and you haven't done anything wrong; it's just something you need to remember, understand?' Helen took her daughter's still wet hand in her own and squeezed it affectionately but just a little too hard.

Emma pulled her hand from her mother's and swiped tears from her face. Her expression should have been beyond her years. 'I remember Mommy,' she said in a monotone that satisfied Helen.

'Come on then, let's get settled in. I'm hungry; I'm sure you are too.' Helen led the way downstairs and into the conservatory, where she found the box containing kitchen equipment and carried it through to the well-appointed blue and white room that overlooked the garden. She felt satisfied that she had made a good choice in renting this place. Even though she had neighbours next door, the sweet factory wall bordered the other side of the property. Helen thought there wouldn't be too many prying eyes and people wanting to be intrusive. She ate her piece of cheese on toast and carefully placed a second one in a plastic bag, ready to take upstairs. Helen gazed at her daughter and watched how her blond curls bobbed while she ate. Emma was pretty, and everyone who saw her admired her looks and quiet behaviour, making Helen feel proud. No one would ever believe how close Helen had come to killing her daughter as soon as she was born. She had tried but just couldn't do it. Now even though Emma caused problems, Helen felt glad that she had kept her.

11

***London** Thursday 12th July 2012*

Robert took his tumbler of long island tea through the sliding doors and set it down by the nearest Adirondack style chair. It was sweltering; he could feel beads of sweat rolling down as far as his bushy eyebrows. He stripped off his vest top, scratched gently through his chest hairs and sat clad in khaki shorts and flip flops. If anyone cared to look up, they would have seen him, but no one did. As usual, the street bustled with shoppers minding their own business.

He sat for a while, taking frequent sips of his drink. The ice had all but melted by the time he'd emptied the glass. He debated whether to get a refill and decided against it. He wanted to be alert when he went to meet his date later that evening. He felt what was becoming a familiar jolt in his midriff when he pictured Guy again. He hadn't been this nervous when he had his first inevitable encounter as a teenager. A handsome older man had been more than willing to show the newbie the ropes, and Robert remembered him with affection. Many men from all over the world had shared his bed since then, but no one else had made him feel this way. The first time he saw Guy as they

55

passed in the doorway of Compton's in Soho, he had been in a hurry and had no chance to speak with him. But his face had become such a fixture in Robert's mind that he had gone to Compton's hoping he would see him again as soon as he returned from Birmingham.

Robert sucked in his breath jerkily as he recalled how he felt when the search had been successful and the man he was looking for appeared. He had caught his eye from across the opposite shank of the horseshoe-shaped bar and smiled. He was beautiful. No other word came into Robert's mind as he pictured again the blond hair that looked as though sunshine was buried in its luxurious depths and the golden tan that enhanced this man's even features. Just thinking about him caused Robert's penis to stiffen.

Younger than Robert, by a few years, he had strolled slowly but confidently around the base of the bar and said, 'I'm Guy Meredith. Can I buy you a drink?' When he smiled, and he did so a lot, his perfect white teeth and soft lips had mesmerised Robert.

Robert found it difficult to reply but eventually said with a quaver in his usually steady voice. 'Hello, I'm Robert Ryan, and let me buy you one.' He felt out of his comfort zone for the first time in years.

Guy had laughed. 'Hello Robert Ryan, I asked you first.' He laughed again. 'What do you like?' He paused, and his twinkle said it all, but he added slowly, 'To drink, I mean.'

Robert shook his head and grinned at his reaction to this Adonis, who stood a few inches taller than his own six feet. His smile lifted crinkles around his eyes which also smiled. 'I'm only drinking lemon and lime, I'm working tomorrow, and I can't risk a trace of alcohol.' He tapped his full glass. 'Now, what can I get you?'

'Ok, you win. Just a pint of speckled, and then I'm afraid I have to run,' Guy said.

'Wife and kids expecting you home, are they?' Robert said playfully as he ordered the drink.

Guy laughed. 'What about you, married?'

Robert shook his head and said, 'Not my scene; I can't afford attachments.'

'Sounds interesting.' Guy downed his pint in a few swallows and returned the glass onto the highly polished bar. 'Thanks, Robert, but I really do have to go. I'd like it if we could get together, though. You free tomorrow night?'

'After five o'clock, I will be, then I fly out to Vegas on Saturday morning.' Robert could have met Guy earlier, but he didn't want to seem too eager.

'What takes you there?' Guy raised dark eyebrows that contrasted with his hair.

Robert had regained his usual aplomb and said with a grin, 'My plane, I'm a pilot.'

'I see, now that is interesting. I'm boring. I work for the government.'

Robert touched Guy's arm. 'I'm sure you aren't boring. Tell me more?' The skin around his eyes crinkled attractively again.

'I'm so sorry, but I must run. Can you meet me at Jerry's? I'll buy you dinner, and we can get to know each other a little better?'

'I'll look forward to it, Guy. Eight suit you?'

'Yes, I'll be there.' Guy had grinned, run his fingers lightly across Robert's hand and was gone.

'Oh, for God's sake, get a grip,' Robert admonished himself aloud, but yesterdays' scenario played over in his mind until he forced himself out of the chair, took a second shower, dressed and left the flat.

He killed time by wandering from shop to shop until he eventually tried on a sports jacket he liked in Debenhams. As he turned this way and that, checking his reflection in a cheval mirror, a woman said, 'Suits you, you should buy it.' Robert smiled as she continued along the aisle towards the café and glanced back at him a couple of times with a wide grin on her pleasantly plump face. Robert noted her smart appearance and liked the way her auburn hair bounced in time with each step, but she aroused him not one whit. However, he appreciated the waft of Daisy perfume that lingered in the air. Robert had several women friends, and one wore that scent, but they were just that: friends he felt comfortable with, and he cherished their company.

Robert replaced the coat on its hanger, he had enough coats, and he'd only tried it on to pass the time. His thoughts turned to Mrs Smith, wondering if she had moved into number nine successfully. He sent her a text message and received one that just said. All's well, thank you. That will suffice, he thought. He had no wish to be an intrusive landlord but decided to ring Cathy and ensure that all had gone as planned. There was no reply, so he left her a message to call him and continued to window shop.

Before returning to his flat, he bought coffee in Starbucks and phoned Amanda just to say hello. She was delighted to hear from him as always. He had to speak with Henry and listened to his heavy breathing as Amanda held the phone first to his ear and then his mouth. One of their silly but affectionate rituals. Minutes passed, and Robert remembered that he intended to buy a phone for Amanda. He didn't need it yet, but he finished the coffee and continued shopping. The only purchase that Robert made in three hours was the mobile phone. Knowing that the phone would enable him to speak with the woman he cared about more than anyone, he bought the best one the salesman recommended as it was arthritis-friendly. He knew she didn't always tell him everything in order not to worry him, but he worried about her anyway. He didn't think he could bear her loss as well as his parents.

As soon as Robert made the purchase, he returned home and showered for the third time that day, made himself a ham and cheese sandwich, decided he didn't want the smell of cheese on his breath and removed it. He ate slowly, now unable to stop excitement from making his stomach churn. He'd eaten nothing since breakfast and hoped the sandwich would calm him even though he would be having a meal at the restaurant. He felt relieved when an hour later he showered again, changed into dark slacks and an open neck, short-sleeve, blue shirt and took a black cab to Jerry's.

12

3 Littlebrook Terrace Saturday 14th July 2012

Bethany's phone pinged. She stopped shuffling the pack of Tarot cards, last year's birthday present from her dad. She shut her eyes and remembered that he'd laughed uproariously when she'd returned from school and torn the paper off the box he'd handed her. She'd gazed open-mouthed at the picture of a knight holding a sword. 'What, why?' she'd said.

His laughter had gradually faded. 'I thought you were into witchy things and spells and such like, aren't you?' he asked, frowning.

Bethany had pursed her lips and then chuckled. 'Oh, you. Just because I said, I'd like to go to Hogwarts.'

'Well, I bought you this as well.' He'd handed her another gift and sat back quietly watching his daughter's face as she opened a framed picture of Dobby, the house-elf and a long box with a wooden wand inside. He was no longer sure of his choices.

Bethany's eyes had danced with amusement as she'd said, 'Thanks, Dad. I might have known you'd buy me something unusual.'

The Child in the Window

'Well, you can tell my fortune when you've learned how to read the cards and hex your brother when he eats all the biscuits out of the tin. He's like a bloody locust.' Greg had laughed.

'I'll put them on my wall.' Bethany waved the picture and wand as she had danced to her dad and planted a smacker on his cheek. 'I think I will learn to tell fortunes.' They had both laughed. But true to her word, Bethany studied the cards on YouTube and was becoming quite proficient at spinning a good read.

Bethany glanced at the picture of Dobby on her wall and returned to the present. She picked up her phone from the nearby table and read the message from her friend, Penny, who she knew had borrowed her mom's phone.

Hey, I'm bored come visit.

Ok, see you in five.

She put the cards back into the box, wrapped them in a scrap of red velvet, and then hid them behind a cushion in case her brother returned home. Bethany liked her own company, but her mom wouldn't be home until four o'clock, and the day was dragging, so she was glad of Penny's message. Ryan was probably already at number eight with George, his friend, but she hoped the boys had gone out. It wasn't that she didn't like them, but they delighted in teasing her. She preferred it if only Penny and Lewis were home. Taking a minute to braid her long hair, Bethany left the house, ensuring she locked the door behind her. As she turned to walk down to Penny's, Mrs Pierce beckoned to her from her window. Bethany loved Aunty Amanda as she had sometimes called her when she was tiny and skipped across to see what she wanted.

Amanda met her a few minutes later at the door. 'Be a darling and pop to Hamza's, will you love? I need a fresh loaf. Were you going to see Penny?'

'Yes, but I'll fetch the bread first. Is that all you need?' Bethany asked while stroking Henry, who licked her hand each time she stopped doing it.

'Yes, darling, it is. Hold on; I'll get my purse.'

Henry stayed on the doorstep with Bethany while Amanda went to fetch her money. It must be awful, Bethany thought, not for the first time, to have to do things so slowly. She was somehow convinced that she would never be like that. 'It's not nice getting old, is it Henry?' she asked quietly and gently scratched his ears which twitched every time she spoke to him. She gave Henry a final stroke as Amanda passed her the purse as she had many times before. There was never much money inside, but Bethany felt very trusted and grown up to be given this responsibility.

Minutes later, Bethany handed a seeded brown loaf and the purse to their owner. 'Thank you, Beth, you're a good girl. Did you see Nazia?'

'No, only Hamza,' Bethany replied and blew Amanda a kiss before she ran two doors down and knocked on the rose etched glass section of the front door.

'Took your time, didn't you?' Penny exclaimed as Bethany followed her into the empty sitting room.

Bethany ignored the grumpiness. 'Where is everyone? I thought that Ryan was here.'

'They've gone to football practice in the park. Where they usually go. Bloody morons.'

'What's up with you. Have they upset you?'

'Not really, but I'm fed up with George assuming I'll do the jobs that Mom has asked us to do. Lewis is as bad; he's gardening as usual.' Penny's voice took on a lighter tone as she said, 'That Mrs Smith has moved into number nine.'

'Have you seen her?' The girls flopped down onto the sofa.

'No, but I think her little girl's called Emma. Mom said Emma was cute but very shy; she never said a word even though Mom spoke to her. Mom took them a casserole and some muffins on Thursday, but she never got invited in.'

'Well, listen to this then,' Penny leaned towards Bethany, 'Mrs Smith told Lewis that she doesn't want him in her garden even if Robert pays him to keep it tidy. She said she would do it. She was very sharp and abrupt with him, Lewis said, and he won't be going back there even if Robert has a word with her. Shame because Robert has just increased his wages. Now Lewis thinks he'll lose some money, and you know he's saving every penny he gets towards that guitar he wants.'

'Oh, that's not fair; why should he lose out because she's spiteful? I bet Robert will tell her off. She did thank Mom for being kind, but Mom said she wasn't too friendly. Perhaps she won't fit in around here. It must be that house. The last people who lived there were a miserable pair of bleeders. Do you remember they were mad at us every time we used the hoop?'

Penny nodded. 'Yes, and perhaps she will be funny too when we use it again.' Penny's face took on a mischievous look. 'Shall we find out? I'll need to blow the ball up, though.'

Bethany giggled. 'Ok, let's do it and see.'

Both girls raced into the kitchen, where Penny retrieved the bicycle pump from under the sink, pleased because it still had the adapter attached. Penny went into the garden and fetched the blue-green and black ball from where Lewis had kicked it towards the shed. As Penny picked the ball up, Lewis came in the back gate carrying a pair of secateurs and a trowel.

'Oi, what you doing with my ball?' he shouted.

'It's not yours; it's mine. You lost yours up the park, remember?' She scurried into the house and heard Lewis come chasing after her. He burst into the kitchen but pulled up short when he saw Bethany.

'That ball's mine; hand it over,' he said calmly.

'No, we're going to play shooting hoops and see if Mrs Smith gets mad at us,' Penny said.

Bethany nodded. 'Back off, Mr Grubby hands.'

'After the way she's been with you, you should come and join in,' Penny said.

'Great idea, I'll just wash my hands.' He stuck his tongue out at Bethany. 'The ball needs blowing up,' Lewis said.

'Duh, we know. What's this for?' Penny wagged the pump at him. Lewis smiled as he ran the cold tap.

Fifteen minutes later, the three began taking turns to throw the ball to each other and then shoot at the hoop making whooping noises each time the ball clunked on the metal. They were even louder in their exuberant cries when the ball went through the ring.

13

4 Littlebrook Terrace Saturday 14th July

Amanda Pierce sighed as she saw her neighbours, Pat and Eric Staples wheel their bikes past her window. They were dressed in matching khaki shorts and blue tee shirts, and Pat had a bandana covering her throat. They appeared to be fit and healthy, but Amanda didn't trust people as skinny as this couple were; it wasn't normal. Neither was Pat's tightly permed grey hair that was plastered to her red forehead contrasting with Eric's bald head that looked the same colour as the stockings Amanda had worn when she was young. She recalled the name American Tan and smiled at her judgmental foolishness.

Amanda held on gently to both of Henry's ears as she whispered her thoughts aloud. 'They're back, so you'd better remember, no barking now. I don't want to start Mrs Moanalot off. I've kept the note she pushed through the letterbox before they went on holiday after hearing you bark at the postman.'

Henry's sleepy brown eyes now gazed intently into Amanda's as he made small chuffing noises. Finally, he seemed to understand what she was saying and rested his head on his person's knees. 'There, I know you don't bark unless you have to. We'll take no notice if she carries on moaning. Robert said he would have a word with her if she sends nasty notes again.' Amanda stroked Henry's silky fur flat, ruffled it up and stroked again. 'Lewis will be here later to take you for your walk and clean up the garden for me, so we'll have lunch now, and then you can poop while you're out.'

Amanda rose awkwardly from her chair, leaned on her walker and made her way into the kitchen, followed by her hairy best friend. He knew the word lunch and his tail never stopped wagging, smacking off every piece of furniture they passed. As she took three slices of bread from the packet that Bethany had fetched for her, she said, 'I must remember to close my bedroom window tonight. We don't want to be kept awake again by their bedroom antics, do we love?' She laughed aloud, startling Henry, who answered with a small bark. 'Shhh, remember, no barking.' She couldn't help herself as she laughed again when she thought about Pat and Eric, in their late sixties, getting up to sex games. It had taken her a long while listening to rhythmic slapping noises before she realised that what she heard a couple of times each month when the windows were open was spanking. Amanda wasn't prudish, but once she had identified the sounds, she shut them out. She thought that private fantasies were one thing but having to share them, quite another.

'What's the matter, what can you hear, eh?' Amanda placed a hand on Henry's collar to calm him. He'd begun to pace from one side of the small kitchen to the other making tiny whimpering noises. She looked out of the window to see Lewis open the back gate and stride purposefully along the short, crazy paved path towards the shed. He is a good boy, always reliable, Amanda thought as she watched him take out the bucket and spade and begin scooping up Henry's mess.

Pat's head appeared wrapped in a towel above the fence the next minute. It always ruffled Amanda's tolerant nature that her nosey neighbour kept an old green milk crate close so she could look into Amanda's garden. Sometimes she would find something to take umbrage over and come knocking on the front door. Amanda couldn't hear what was being said now, but Lewis didn't look pleased as Pat gestured with both hands, indicating both sides of the garden. Amanda longed to open the door and tell Pat to mind her own business but resisted. It paid to keep on good terms with neighbours, especially ones like the Staples.

She turned away and finished making her's and Henry's lunch. It was ham sandwiches today, and even though Amanda knew she shouldn't feed Henry with human food, she always made him one. The chore didn't take long, and she had no sooner put the plate and a mug of coffee onto her walker seat and ferried them into the sitting room than she heard the back door open and water running into the stainless-steel sink. Lewis was washing his hands.

Minutes later, Lewis brought the orange drink she had prepared for him into the room and sat opposite as usual. Henry whined and leaned against his welcome friend. The three of them enjoyed the routine that happened several times each week, usually after school finished.

'And what did she have to say this time?' Amanda said and frowned.

'Oh, you know, same as always. Ensure I don't miss any poop and dispose of it properly in the bin. She doesn't want the smell or the fly's buzzing about.' Lewis shrugged, then grinned at his friend. 'I told her that I always did, and would she like me to tidy her garden for her?' He laughed. 'She hesitated and then asked how much I would charge. I told her that she couldn't afford me at a hundred pound an hour.' Lewis's eyes twinkled, and he laughed again.

Amanda joined in his merriment. 'You didn't say that, did you?' she asked incredulously.

'No, but I did say twenty pounds an hour, and Mrs Staples disappeared, but I bet she'll have something to say to Mom about me being cheeky.'

'Well, I wouldn't worry too much; your mom knows what she's like. Now tell me what you've been doing lately.'

Lewis told Amanda how Mrs Smith had behaved over her garden and said he was disappointed as Robert might reduce his money. Amanda 'ahhed,' sympathetically and wondered if she could afford to give him an increase in the small amount she paid him to help with Henry. She didn't know and said nothing but decided to check her bank account.

Lewis fetched Henry's lead from the cupboard in the hall when the mugs were empty, with Henry jumping around excitedly. 'Sit,' Lewis said firmly and felt pleased when Henry obeyed instantly. 'See you later,' he called to Amanda and pulled the front door shut behind him.

Amanda always felt slightly sad as she watched them turn the corner into Singerbrook road and out of sight. She remembered when Henry had been a puppy, and she'd been able to take him walking in the local park. Amanda wasn't one to feel sorry for herself, but she sometimes did where Henry and walking were concerned. She sat back in her chair and thought about Pat and Eric. Something she often did. They had been together for many years, but she didn't understand how two people could be so miserable and stay married. Whenever she'd seen Eric on his own, he'd seemed happier, but Amanda wondered what made them tick. What had happened to make them dour? She speculated as she had before if having no children had soured them.

Amanda turned on the TV and deliberately put her neighbours out of her mind. She had better things to occupy herself while waiting for Henry's return after Lewis tired him out fetching sticks ensuring the dog had enough exercise. And so, she ceased to muse and concentrated instead on the quiz that she enjoyed watching; it gave her brain the exercise that she thought helped prevent its atrophy.

14

Benton Hill Group Practice. *Wednesday 18ᵗʰ July 2012*

Maja walked briskly along Singerbrook Road, admiring the Mountain Ash trees spaced every fifty yards or so. She was on her way to keep the ten o'clock appointment that she'd had to fight for with the pinched face receptionist, who sat behind her screen as though it allowed her to speak with impunity. Without a seeming thought regarding patient privacy, she had asked what the appointment was for in a voice that carried. Maja had told her that it was private and personal. According to her badge, the receptionist's name was Diana, and she had twisted her lips and made a snorting noise but did as requested.

Maja had a suspicion that her Polish accent had caused Diana, who certainly didn't resemble a goddess, to be unhelpful, but she didn't care. She knew that getting time away from the café without telling Alek where she was going would be even more difficult. So, after worrying about it for a couple of days, Maja asked Rita Gillingham to cover for her for a few hours. Rita jumped at the chance to earn the few pounds offered, and Maja told Alek that she needed to go shopping for new underwear. Something special she'd said and winked. She had no qualms about lying; she'd proved to be good at it when necessary.

Alek had surprised Maja when he smiled and said, 'Why don't you have lunch in town. I'll manage on my own after Rita leaves; you deserve a day off.'

Maja had placed her arms about his neck and kissed his cheek; an intense wish to protect him overwhelmed her. She didn't feel guilty about her deception; she needed to know why she wasn't becoming pregnant and knew that Alek would feel vulnerable and hurt if she told him the truth. Of course, it was too late in the day to talk to him about her daughter, but Maja half hoped that the problem would lie with her. Perhaps then she could tell him that it wasn't his fault.

Maja glanced at her watch as she sat in the waiting room. She was on time, but she waited another fifteen minutes watching a screen that informed her of signs of impending health problems that she would prefer not to know. Maja was usually an ostrich where unpleasant knowledge was concerned. Eventually, after having too much time to rehearse what she was going to say to the doctor and wondering if she might have something seriously wrong with her, she was relieved when her name and the room she should go to appeared on the screen.

Dr Mott had greeted her, and as she took a seat, he looked into her eyes and said, 'What can I do for you today, Mrs Bosko?'

Maja's mind was in turmoil; all her careful planning had disappeared, a lump came into her throat, and hot, noisy tears coursed down her pale face.

Dr Mott sat quietly then handed her a tissue from the box on his desk. After a few minutes, Maja's sobs subsided, and she mopped at her eyes. 'I'm so sorry,' she gasped while thrusting the wet tissue into the shopping bag at her feet.

'No need, no need, please tell me how I can help?' He leaned back in his brown leather office chair and waited.

'I'm sorry, I didn't mean to make a fuss, but I want a baby,' Maja blurted out.

Dr Mott smiled. 'Why don't you start at the beginning. Aren't you able to conceive?'

Maja took an unsteady breath. 'I am, I have a daughter, but my husband doesn't know that. He doesn't know I've come here today either. He doesn't want us to have tests, but he does want children. He hasn't said, but I think he may feel something is wrong with him.'

Dr Mott nodded. 'You have a daughter. Was the birth uncomplicated?'

'Yes.'

'How old were you?'

'I was fifteen, and my parents have brought her up as though she is my sister.'

'Well, I think we should do some tests to see if anything has changed.'

'But---'

'Let's take it one step at a time, Mrs Bosko. Hopefully, we'll be able to solve the problem.' When is your period due?'

'In about two weeks. I'm a little irregular.' Maja blushed and glanced out of the window.

'Excellent, excellent.' The doctor had then taken her blood pressure and pulse before he turned away and began typing into his computer, and following many whirring noises, the printer spat out two forms which he handed to Maja. 'Take these to the nurse, and I'll make another appointment to see you in a week when I'll have some results. Same day and time?'

Maja nodded, took the forms, thanked the doctor and, feeling comforted, headed for the unisex toilet. She looked in the mirror above the sink; her eyes were red-rimmed and puffy. She splashed cold water on her cheeks and gratefully went to have blood taken. As ever, it was not an easy thing for her. Her veins weren't prominent, and she winced as the nurse attempted to find a cooperative vein on the third try. Eventually, the plump nurse filled three phials successfully, and Maja breathed a sigh as she rolled down her sleeves. 'Not so bad, was it?' the nurse said and smiled reassuringly. Maja couldn't agree, so she said nothing, merely smiled.

It wasn't until she was on the bus on her way to the city centre that Maja began to worry about how she could keep the next appointment without Alek becoming suspicious. He wouldn't expect her to go shopping again so soon. As she watched the passing cars through the window, she began to wish she had left well alone. If she was still fertile, she had no idea how to persuade Alek to see the doctor. He'd been so set against it. She didn't know how she would tell him what she had done but dreaded seeing the disappointment on his face every time her period made an appearance each month.

As the bus neared town, Maja remembered what the doctor had said about taking a day at a time, and determined to take his advice, gave herself over to a rare feeling of freedom as she wandered around the shops. First, she bought a colourful, butterfly printed polyester blouse before choosing new underwear, which she didn't need. Then in Debenhams, Maja purchased a blue shirt that had caught her fancy. The blue was just the colour of Alek's eyes, one of the first things she noticed about him when they met by chance at a friend's house.

After treating herself to lunch in Debenhams café, Maja sat for a while on a bench in St. Philip's churchyard, sunning herself and watching squabbling pigeons as they searched to see if manna had fallen from their heaven.

Maja had to pass an Ann Summers shop on her way to the bus stop. She stopped and looked in the window, then grinning inwardly, went in and bought herself a lilac and black thong that she thought Alek would appreciate. She planned to surprise him one night as she'd never worn such a provocative anything before. Maja allowed her bedroom fantasy to develop when she was back on the bus and felt a flush come to her cheeks as she imagined what her fellow travellers would think if they could see her thoughts. Perhaps if she could relax and enjoy herself instead of worrying about conceiving, there might be nothing wrong, and it just might happen, she thought.

15

5 Littlebrook Terrace Saturday, 21ˢᵗ July 2012

Rita sat on the side of the bed and picked up her brown, uninteresting, elevated shoe. She turned it this way and that. It was one of a pair that she had bought five years ago, two years after the stupid accident that had caused her to break her tibia plateau. Not just break it, smash it, the surgeon, who had carried out an operation which called for two long bolts to be inserted and bone slurry used to fill in gaps, had told her.

Rita eyed the shoe with dislike and remembered how it had become such a necessary part of her life. Her leg had healed, and she could walk unaided after three months, but it had left her right leg shorter than her left. Steven had tried to persuade her to seek help, but Rita had refused to talk to her doctor about it. She wasn't in pain, but she walked with the rolling gait of a sailor and was very conscious of the disability on occasions. Eventually, a friend had advised her to get built-up shoes, and they had helped, but they were expensive, so she managed with one pair and a pair of trainers. Rita didn't mind very much, vanity had never been one of her deadly sins, and she always acknowledged the accident had been her fault.

It had happened in the flat they rented before buying this house, and Rita was reminded of it every time she saw a spider. She had told the story many times. How she'd visited the bathroom in the night, and a small spider had started to trek across the white floor tiles towards her bare feet. Ordinarily, Steve dealt with unruly crawlies that made her shudder, but it was two in the morning, and he had to be up early. So, she had plucked up courage, threw a piece of toilet tissue on top of the spider that had halted and heart-pounding, stepped on the tissue. The spider had run, the tissue slid, and Rita could still feel the shock as she had landed with her leg twisted under her. Her scream had woken Steve up as the spider continued to crawl slowly towards her. Paramedics arrived quickly, and she was taken to hospital. An experience that she had not forgotten. Rita now left spiders or any other annoying insect alone, removing herself from the scene.

Rita shook her head and slid her foot into the shoe just as Steve came from the shower with a white towel wrapped around his nether regions. He strolled to where she sat and dropped a kiss onto her silky hair. Although her hairdresser gave the long strands a helping hand to be a honey colour, Steve thought it was beautiful and often ran his fingers through the tresses, sometimes protesting when she tied it into a ponytail.

Rita flashed her husband a wide smile showing her beautiful white teeth that had never known even a filling. Something for which she was grateful to her parents.

'Come on, stop daydreaming. Mom and Dad will be here soon; you know what a stickler Dad is for timekeeping.'

Rita laughed as she held on to a corner of his towel as he passed, and it obligingly exposed his bare bum, which she gave a light smack.

'Hey, you,' Steve exclaimed and laughed.

Rita stood up and snuggled into his embrace. 'Sure you don't want me to make us even later?' she giggled into his chest.

'No, evil woman. Get dressed. We need to get a move on; it's ten to,' Steve said, 'good job we packed last night.'

Less than ten minutes later, they heard Tilly answer a knock on the back door and greet her grandparents excitedly. Rita hurried downstairs to find Andrew and Anna perched on the edge of chairs by the kitchen table.

'Morning, would you like a drink before we set out? 'Rita said.

'No, thank you,' Anna answered decisively, 'I'll be needing a pit stop before we leave Birmingham if I drink anymore. I've already had two cups this morning. Are you all packed and ready?' She attempted a smile.

'Yes, Steven's just bringing the cases down to put in the car. Come here, you,' Rita said to Tilly. Tilly skipped over to her mom, and Rita retied the blue ribbon hanging down by her daughter's shoulders. Rita wondered if Tilly's hair needed some taken off the length that looked somewhat straggly but said nothing; now wasn't the time to cause a fuss. She was aware that Anna's long, pink-painted fingernails were tapping impatiently on the table.

Rita inwardly heaved a sigh of relief as Steven brought the cases to the conservatory door, and Andrew helped to carry them out. 'I won't be a minute; I want to say goodbye to Lily and give her my key so she can water the plants while we're away,' she said.

She headed for the door, leaving her mother-in-law to talk to her granddaughter. As she went, she heard Anna say to Tilly, 'Have you been to the toilet? We're not going to stop for at least an hour, be a good girl and try to squeeze one out.'

Rita smiled as Tilly said something unintelligible and then bounded up the stairs. By the time she returned, everything was tucked away, and they were waiting for her. She made them wait a little longer while she made sure that she wasn't the one requesting an early pitstop. Then they all trooped down the garden to the minibus that Steven had hired for their holiday. Despite Anna's often disapproving and bossy behaviour, they'd had such a good time the previous year that their spirits were high as Steve filtered into the traffic on the M5 south and headed for the cottage in West Bay.

Their good humour gradually faded away as they became stuck in a traffic tailback just before Bristol. After half an hour at a standstill, Anna became anxious. 'I told you we needed to set out earlier, but you wouldn't listen to me; we'll never get there at this rate,' she said and, unzipping her capacious handbag, delved into its depths, bringing out a blue inhaler. Anna inhaled deeply and held her breath. Then she did so a second time before shutting her eyes and leaning back in her seat.

'Are you alright, Grandma?' Tilly asked worriedly.

'Of course, she is, don't you fret, little one. It's just her asthma. Sometimes when she's upset, you know it's difficult for her to breathe.' He turned to his wife. 'You're alright, aren't you, love?'

'Would you like a mint, Anna?' Rita asked, pursing her lips.

'No, take no notice. I'll be ok in a minute.' Anna didn't open her eyes.

No one took any more notice of her histrionics. She frequently behaved like this if something didn't please her. It worked most of the time, and she managed to get whatever she wanted, but no one could do anything to help the situation. A few minutes later, the traffic started to move slowly and everyone, even Anna, cheered noisily.

'I'll have that mint now,' Anna said.

Steve caught Rita's eye in the mirror, and he grinned as she handed his mother, who he loved despite her silly behaviour, a mint. Then she unwrapped one for him, leaned over the seat and popped it into his mouth.

'Thanks, love,' he said, knowing that Rita would understand why he was really thanking her. He loved his wife's good-natured tolerance and expected them to have a great time again this year.

As the traffic speeded up, he began to sing the old ten green bottles song, and everyone joined in until it was replaced with raucous laughter when Anna said, 'Andrew, you dirty bugger that fart is stinking the bus out.' She held her nose with one hand and wafted the other in the air.

16

7 Littlebrook Terrace Sunday, 22nd July 2012

Claude sliced the top off his soft-boiled egg with a knife. He had perfected the operation. One swift cut a third of the way down exposed the yolk without splintering the shell. Most mornings, Zeta watched admiringly as he did this. She had tried to follow suit with never a good result.

Claude smiled at her rueful face. 'I've told you, it's a sharp knife and confidence.' He laughed as she stuck out her tongue at him. 'Hmm, very ladylike.' His eyes twinkled lovingly at her, deepening the creases that radiated out from the corners. 'Have you any plans for today, dear?' He dipped a finger of toast into the golden yolk and popped it into his mouth. Although it was Sunday morning and he wasn't going to work, he had dressed in his usual immaculate fashion. White shirt and grey waistcoat buttoned, shiny, bright blue tie knotted neatly and his well-behaved salt and pepper hair looking good.

In contrast, Zeta was still in her aqua silk pyjamas covered by a matching dressing gown cinched in at her slim waist. Her luxurious reddish-brown shoulder-length hair was untamed. Even without make-up, which she expertly used each day, she was a striking woman. She took a bite of dry toast, trying to settle her stomach, which kept making unbecoming growling noises. She'd been reluctant to tear herself out of bed, but a search for some paracetamol to soothe her abused body had won. She'd had more than enough alcohol the previous evening to expect the hangover, and each spike of pain in her head reminded her that she'd had a good night at the White Lion pub on Singerbrook Road.

Claude had accompanied her on a couple of occasions, but he preferred to stay home with his beloved books, and Zeta didn't try to persuade him that he needed some fun. She knew that, unlike herself, he didn't need other people to enhance his contentment. Since his wife Suzette had died from melanoma four years ago, Claude preferred his own company. But Zeta often went for a drink after work and usually found one or two people there that she knew and liked. She rarely overindulged, but there had been a bit of a party going on to celebrate one of the men's birthdays the previous night. The birthday boy had introduced himself as Brien MacDade and spent a good bit of the evening peering down her cleavage. She'd never met him before, but his behaviour didn't faze her. She knew the attraction of one of her chief assets and dressed as she pleased to suit herself, not to gain the attention that was a consequence. But she happily accepted the complimentary glasses of white wine that seemed to appear as if by magic.

Zeta liked men's company. She found them easier to talk to than most women, who she thought showed their claws far too readily. She was always pleased when Eric Staples, who she'd sometimes heard described as a miserable bugger, spent an hour or two there. He made her laugh, as did his next-door neighbour David Denham. Occasionally David's wife Cathy joined them, but she hadn't met Eric's wife even though they lived almost opposite. Zeta had seen her in the supermarket a couple of times, but she avoided speaking to her. She did look miserable, Zeta thought but didn't allow herself to dwell on Pat's behaviour.

Zeta took a last bite of toast and stood up. 'See you later, Dad; I'm going back to bed for a bit.'

'Ok, love, but it's a beautiful day, and I might go for a walk along the canal later. Do you fancy keeping me company?'

'Perhaps. I'll see how I feel,' Zeta said.

They both looked up, startled as something hit the wall between their house and Helen Smith's. 'Bloody hell, what was that?' Claude exclaimed.

'Don't know, sounds as though someone fell down the stairs. Shall I go and make sure no one's hurt, d'you think?' Zeta looked worried and, without waiting for an answer, headed for the front door. She knocked at Helen's, but there was no answer. She waited a minute and knocked again. Zeta felt a little panicky, her mind conjuring a vision of Helen lying unconscious at the bottom of the stairs. She peered through the window and was about to knock again when the door opened, and Helen stood there po-faced.

'Can I help you?' Helen said sharply.

'Oh, you're alright. Thank God. We heard a bang and thought you might have hurt yourself on the stairs. Is Emma ok?'

'Yes, of course, she is. She's in her room playing. Did you want to see her?' Helen's chin jutted forward as she gave Zeta a fierce look.

'No, oh no, I just thought I heard her cry out,' Zeta said and stood her ground.

Helen's somewhat aggressive attitude changed in an instant as she said, 'Well, thank you for being so caring, but we are all good. I just dropped a box, and Emma was startled.'

'Ok, see you then,' Zeta said and gratefully shut her door as Helen closed her's simultaneously but none too quietly.

She went into the kitchen where Claude sat gazing out, watching sparrows as they breakfasted from a transparent box that he had attached with suckers to the kitchen window. 'Everything alright?' Claude asked as he folded a newspaper that he had been looking at before the birds' pecking grabbed his attention. He placed his reading glasses on his book and waited until Zeta sat back down at the table.

'I think so, but she's a funny bugger, in my opinion. She says she dropped a box down the stairs, and Emma was upset. I thought she was quite defensive when I asked after Emma.'

'Defensive?' Claude took on a quizzical expression.

'I don't know, perhaps my imagination, but I got the impression that she didn't like me being there. Have you spoken to her again since they moved in?' Zeta asked with a puzzled frown.

'No, why?' Claude shook his head.

'Never mind.' Zeta stood up again. 'I'm going to have a shower. My head feels better. What time are you thinking of going out?'

'After lunch. Shall we eat at the café?'

'You paying?' Zeta grinned.

'Don't I always. You should appreciate me more.'

'I always appreciate everything you do, and I love you up to the top of the museum,' Zeta said, and they both laughed. Next door's drama already forgotten for now.

Later while Zeta and Claude were sitting at their favourite table by the window in the café, they overheard Cathy telling Maja about how Bethany, Lewis and Penny had been screamed at by Helen when they were shooting rings a few days earlier. It caused them to recall Helen's earlier unpleasant behaviour.

'Why did she, did they let the ball hit her house?' Maja asked doubtfully.

'No, but she said they shouldn't be making noise outside her place, and it was making her nerves bad. Mind you, in fairness, they were making a lot of noise to see what she would do. I think they were pretty shocked, though, to hear someone swear at them. She used the F-word more than a few times. David was all for going and having a word with her, but I wouldn't let him. He has a temper when roused and isn't above using a few choice words himself. I could imagine the slanging match. I'm not sure she will fit in here, but I suppose time will tell.'

Zeta felt tempted to tell them what she had experienced but thought better of it. She had to live next door to Helen, and she felt sorry for Emma. Best not to add to gossip. She caught her father's eye, and he placed an index finger to his lips and shook his head.

17

9 *Littlebrook Terrace Sunday 22ⁿᵈ July*

Helen stood with her ramrod straight back pressed against the inside of her door and listened as Zeta closed her front door quietly. Her eyebrows almost met under the frown lines on her forehead. Her lips were a hard straight line. Impossible to tell where the upper and lower met. Nosey bloody neighbours she seethed inwardly; it's started already. They had better learn to keep their sharp noses out of her business; otherwise… she didn't finish the thought. Instead, she took a few deep breaths, exhaled hard and glanced upstairs to where her daughter lay curled in a ball on the red carpet. She ignored her, and stepping away from the door, began picking up laundry that was strewn about the hall. She stuffed it back into the hamper that had skittered across the tiles ending up by the living room, then calmly strode into the kitchen, where she sorted it and programmed the machine to heat to thirty degrees. Then having given Emma enough time to think about what she had done, she began to climb the stairs.

Emma was now kneeling and watched her mother warily. She knew she was in trouble and had wet her knickers. Fear clawed at her mind, her face as pale as the paint on the bannisters; she waited to see what her punishment would be.

Helen climbed slowly, taking one step at a time while holding her daughter's pleading gaze. Emma tried to make her eyes close, but they wouldn't obey her wish to shut her mother's looming face out. She was terrified. She knew it was her fault that her mother had fallen downstairs. When she dropped her red piece of Lego on the landing, she should have picked it straight up, but Harry had called to her, and she went to see what was upsetting him. When her mother had left the bathroom, she stood on the Lego and cried out, bringing Emma onto the landing from the bedroom. As Emma watched, horrified, her mother had tumbled downstairs, unable to stop the forward momentum as she carried a hamper of washing. Halfway down, she smacked her head on the neighbouring wall, allowing the hamper to spill dirty laundry into the hall below.

As soon as Emma saw the offending piece of Lego in her mother's hand, she began to sob.

'What have I told you about these damn pieces, eh? You are a bloody nuisance,' Helen hissed.

'Harry---'

'You and your bloody pretend friend. I could have been killed; then you would have had to manage on your own. You'd starve to death, do you understand?' Helen's hand fell heavily across Emma's bare legs twice, leaving a welt of finger marks that reddened immediately.

'Now get in your room and stay there until I say.' Helen turned and stomped down the stairs.

Harry was lying by the bedroom door where Emma had left him. Trying to stem her flow of tears with her hand and wanting to retch, Emma alternately swiped her eyes and wiped the wet saltiness on her legs where the imprint of fingers sent pulses of pain to join other memories lodged deep into her psyche. Finally, she grabbed Harry and dragged him into his room, then shut her mother out.

Emma carefully tucked Harry back into his cupboard and then lay on her bed, gently rubbing her leg. Her tummy rumbled, and she began to cry quietly again, sure that she would now go without breakfast and probably lunch. It had been her fault; she should have been more careful. She knew that her mother liked to keep secrets, and she had made the pretty lady from next door appear and start asking questions. She didn't want her mother to die and leave her to starve to death. She had sometimes gone without food for a couple of days when her mother felt furious about something she hadn't meant to do. It was hard to remember everything she was forbidden to do and say. Emma remembered the hunger pangs. She shut her eyes, placed her thumb in her mouth and tried to sleep.

Downstairs, Helen ceased to think about her daughter. Instead, she made herself some toast and honey and sat at the kitchen table drinking coffee and eating. She was becoming worried about money. She needed to set about finding work the next day and tried to think about where to go. It had been years since she'd worked, and it wasn't going to be easy now she had her daughter to think of. She needed to find someone to mind her. Helen pulled at her lip, where the hot drink had left a tiny sore spot. She had considered locking Emma into her room while she worked but knew the neighbours would soon find out, and there would be consequences. Investigation from any official body was the last thing she wanted. Her life would not stand up to scrutiny even though she had moved house three times after selling the one she had lived in with Tony.

Helen stood up and took a fork from the cutlery drawer. She pushed up the long sleeves that she invariably wore, turned the fork over and over in her hand, then scraped it from top to bottom of her arm. The sharp tines brought blood spots to the surface as they pierced her skin, leaving four new lines beside the scars she had inflicted before. It calmed her to see them. She tore a piece of kitchen paper from the nearly new roll and dabbed while leaning on the sink, looking out of the kitchen window. Helen could see Claude as he walked down to the garden shed carrying a tin of paint and an old sheet. Her lip curled. She hated him. He had been kind on the surface, but she knew that he wanted only one thing from her underneath that smile. The same thing all men did. She wouldn't let him get close enough to dominate and force her to do anything. No man ever would again.

Helen tore her eyes away and felt bile in her mouth as she lived again the nightmare childhood filled with abuse from her father and her uncle on a few occasions. When she'd married Tony, her mother had tried hard to advise her not to. 'There's something in his eyes, love,' she'd said, but Helen hadn't listened. She had seen Tony as a way to escape her evil father and her pathetic excuse for a mother. A mother who had suffered from her husband's brutal controlling behaviour for more than twenty years and did not attempt to protect her two girls from his deviant violence. Helen grew to hate her and her older sister, Jean, who had run away as soon as she left school and landed a job in an office as a junior clerk. She wanted to kill them all and had often thought about doing so before she married.

Afterwards, Helen had only thought about killing Tony if she could, but he had died before she could work out how to do so. Her brain had always become foggy when she had tried to make a plan, and it had been the same when she had been unable to kill after giving birth secretly.

Helen did not recognise her behaviour as being abusive towards her daughter. She only considered that she had been kind enough not to kill her and thought Emma would one day be grateful for the love and guidance she felt she showered on her.

Helen emptied the washing machine, took some pegs from under the sink, went into the garden, and hung it out to dry in the bright sunshine. A chore she didn't relish, but it was necessary, and Helen always did what she saw as necessary. Tomorrow I'll see if I can talk to the woman in the café and see if she can help with advice or perhaps the woman from number three who had brought them some food, she thought and felt her spirit's lift. Maybe it was time to forgive her daughter and allow her to come downstairs. She missed her company. She hummed an old tune as she returned to the house and shut the world out.

18

9 Littlebrook Terrace Monday 23rd July

Helen rubbed a fist over her eyes that felt sore and full of grit. She glanced at the clock on her bedside cabinet; it was six-fifteen. She'd only had about three hours of sleep, but she was wide awake. She sighed. She'd attempted to settle down at eleven, but the more she tried to clear her mind and relax, the more memories had assailed her. She invariably stayed up watching whatever she could find on the TV until she could no longer keep her eyes open, but her brain nagged the minute she got into bed.

Bed had never been her friend or refuge since a time when she was six years old. She lived that night repeatedly, and last night the scenario had kept her from sleeping yet again. Helen's memory always took her back to the first time her body had experienced the abuse that had made her hate men. All men. She had woken into a pitch-black room and opened her mouth to call her mother because her night light had disappeared. Instead, a hand was quickly clamped across her mouth. She became rigid with fear as she smelled alcohol and could hear the harsh breathing of her father as he knelt by her side. She felt his fingers as they pushed into her vagina. She had been too petrified to speak or move. Helen had felt tears spring into her eyes. She wasn't sure what was happening but knew it wasn't right. He wasn't hurting her exactly, but her mother had told her she must always keep her private bits covered, and now they weren't. Suddenly her father groaned, and her duvet once again covered her body. She heard a click as he left her room. She lay still for a long time, thinking she must have done something wrong. Eventually, she cried herself to sleep.

The next morning, she wasn't sure if she had had a bad dream as her father sat eating his breakfast and told her to hurry up or she'd be late for school. It had been a few nights before it happened again, but it rapidly became the pattern of her nightmares. Helen was never quite sure why she hadn't told her mother what had happened; she just somehow didn't seem to be able to talk about it. The frequent abuse continued, and Helen gradually realised that it coincided with her father's alcohol abuse. Helen loved her mother and tried not to hear the rows between her parents, and as time went on, she didn't want to add to her mother's distress, although sometimes she would find herself behaving in a rebellious way, screaming and shouting without seeming cause. She couldn't help herself.

Time passed in this vein until Helen's ninth birthday. Her mother had organised a party for her which she didn't want. Helen had tried to hide in the garage, but her aunt had found her and coaxed her out. Helen watched her father as he drank all evening heavily, so she expected him to come to her room. She kept herself awake as long as she could, determined that she would tell him to get out. However, she fell asleep, and when she woke, it was to find her father climbing into bed beside her. That night the assault on her body escalated. Throughout this time, neither Helen nor her father ever uttered a single word to each other. By the time Helen became a teenager, she'd convinced herself that it was normal behaviour until she mentioned it one day to Beryl, a girl she'd become friendly with. They had been sitting on a bench at the front of the school, somewhere they weren't supposed to be, and Helen felt they were partners in crime. After talking and laughing about boys that they liked, Helen asked Beryl if she enjoyed what her father did to her at night when he came into her bedroom.

Beryl's reaction had horrified Helen as she had laughed nervously and said, 'What do you mean? My dad never comes into my room. Mom has always put me to bed, and now I go on my own; I'm not a baby.'

Helen immediately knew that what she suspected was wrong, was undoubtedly something that shouldn't happen. She had made an excuse and left Beryl open-mouthed. Two days later, Mrs Baxter, the headmistress, had sent for Helen to go to her office. Helen had only been in there briefly on one occasion when she had taken a message. However, this time was different. She had a good idea why she'd been sent for and had stood on the swirly patterned green carpet before a large mahogany desk feeling trembly inside. After a moment or so, Mrs Baxter had put down the pen she'd been busy using and asked her kindly to repeat what she had said to Beryl.

Helen's insecurity faded, and she became sullen. 'I don't remember what I said, and it wasn't important. Can I go now?' she said truculently.

The headmistress had studied Helen's scarlet face. Then she nodded. 'Yes, Helen, but I want you to know that your father nor anyone else should touch you anywhere that makes you feel uncomfortable.' She'd paused then said, 'You may go, but I'm always happy to listen to anything you may wish to tell me; I might be able to help. Do you understand?' She smiled, and Helen had opened her mouth to confide in her but thought better of it. The fact that she now enjoyed the sex that had been forced on her initially kept her quiet. She hated her father but not how he made her feel, even if it was wrong.

'Yes, I understand, but there is nothing to tell,' Helen said and managed a smile as she turned and fled from the room. Later that day, Helen caught up with Beryl as they walked through an alley between some houses. She punched Beryl hard in the face and walked calmly home, feeling satisfied as she saw the blood pour from her erstwhile friend's nose.

The incest between Helen and her father had continued without it ever being discussed until she met Tony. Then Helen had found the strength to tell her father to get out and stay out, and he hadn't argued.

Helen remained in bed for another few minutes then, shaking off her nighttime memories, showered, and went into Emma's room. Emma was, as always, lying wide awake waiting for her.

Helen leaned over and kissed her daughter. 'Good morning, my good girl, time to get up and have your shower.'

Emma obediently shoved the duvet off and headed for the bathroom, where Helen had set the shower running for her. 'Can I shower Harry today, Mommy?' she asked as she hoisted herself onto the toilet seat.

'Not today, lovely girl, I'm busy today, and I'm taking you out to find someone to mind you while I get a job. So, hurry up and shower, and I'll sort some nice clothes out for you.'

'Mommy, I'm done,' Emma called minutes later, and Helen helped her to dry off and took her into the bedroom where she had laid out a pretty yellow dress and white socks for her.

'Stand still while I brush your curls; you have to look pretty today.' Helen used the hairdryer and admired her daughter as she gave her a twirl. 'So, there you are, all done and beautiful. I'm proud of you. Now I want you to listen carefully. You must remember what I've told you to say about where we used to live.' Helen waited and peered intently into her daughter's wary eyes. 'Do you remember?'

'Yes, Mommy. We used to live in a big city, and I don't know where that was. I mustn't mention the beach or the cottage, and I can't tell anyone about Harry. I remember.' Emma's eyes filled with tears as she repeated what Helen had impressed on her.

Helen reached for Emma's hand. 'That's right, my good girl. You must remember that Harry is only your pretend friend, and people would think you very strange if you talked about him. He doesn't really exist, does he?' Helen squeezed Emma's hand until she winced and tried to pull away. 'Does he?' Helen's voice took on a threatening tone.

'No, Mommy, I remember. I won't talk about him.' This time Emma managed to pull her hand from Helen's grasp, and tears spilt down her pink cheeks.

'There's my good girl. Now don't get messy before we go out. Shall we have some breakfast?' Helen went downstairs, and Emma followed.

19

3 Littlebrook Terrace Monday 23rd July 2012

Lily dried her hands on the Mickey Mouse tea towel Rita had brought her from Disney Paris a few years ago. She was still struggling with the temptation to smoke, and the only thing stopping her from rushing over to Hamza's and buying a packet was her daughter. She had agreed to quit if Bethany gave up eating chocolate. They had made pinky promises, and now that school holidays were here, she wouldn't be able to hide if she gave in to temptation. And, of course, she didn't want Bethany to eat chocolate either.

Lily had struggled all her life with a tendency to put on weight easily, and Bethany had recently begun to pile on the pounds. Lily thought that giving up smoking could mean she would replace ciggies with chocolate herself. And so, she didn't want it in the house. She thought how lucky Greg was; he never put on a pound no matter what he ate. Mind you; she thought he would never overeat; because he had a horror of being unable to fit into his fancy clothes. Lily had a sudden vision of the clothes he changed into when he went to his club and grimaced. She tried not to mind but couldn't quite understand the need that seemed to have escalated recently. But she recognized it was a compulsion that drove him, and she loved him fiercely and protectively.

Lily walked towards the mantel shelf where her cigarettes usually were and then laughed aloud. You can do it. Stop torturing yourself, she thought and glanced out of the window to see Claude and Zeta as they hurried to catch the bus to work. She liked the Canadian couple and wondered how they were getting on with their new neighbour, who didn't seem too friendly. Perhaps she would go to the pub one of the nights and possibly meet up with Zeta and get the gossip. She admitted to herself she had an unusual, for her, curiosity about Mrs Smith ever since she had tried to welcome her to the neighbourhood and been rebuffed.

Walking to the bottom of the stairs, she stood with her hand on the cream newel post and called, 'Beth, come on, you lazy bug. The streets are aired. I'm going to start breakfast, poached egg, so hurry up.'

Bethany hurriedly finished off her morning routine and jumped her way downstairs and into the kitchen, where she pulled out a chair from the small table and parked her jeans-clad bottom. 'Aren't you going to the café this morning?'

Lily handed her a white, heart-shaped plate with two pieces of buttered toast and a couple of poached eggs, then sat down opposite with a duplicate. She immediately stood back up. 'Forget my head if it was loose,' she said and placed a mug of coffee beside each plate.

'Café?' Bethany repeated.

'Daft question, I wouldn't be cooking breakfast if I was, would I?'

Bethany shrugged. 'You always go on Mondays.'

'Well, no point while Rita's away, have you forgotten?'

Bethany laughed. 'What about Maja? She'll miss you, won't she?' She stuck her fork into one of the golden yolks and followed it with a piece of toast.

'I'll pop in later for coffee. You coming with me?'

Bethany shook her head. 'Why would I want to listen to you old uns?' She grinned as her mom flicked her with the tea towel that was still over her shoulder.

'You get cheekier, my girl. Bloody hell, who's that!? I haven't combed my hair yet.' Lily exclaimed as a knock sounded at the front door.

Lily hurried into the sitting room, patted ineffectually at her hair in front of the wood-framed mirror over the fireplace and went to open the door. She heard Bethany's laughter as she said, 'You're beautiful, Mom.'

To Lily's surprise, the person she'd been thinking of stood there with her hand on Emma's shoulder.

Recovering quickly, she smiled and said, 'Hi there, what brings you here on this bright sunny morning?' She inwardly cringed; she knew she was babbling to hide her embarrassment.

'I hope you don't mind, but I need some advice, and as you were kind enough to welcome us to the terrace, I thought you might be able to help.' Helen said and smiled.

'Of course, I will try. Why don't you come in and tell me what you need?' Lily held the door open and stepped aside.

Helen's heart sank; she didn't want to become too friendly but had no option. She stepped inside and took the seat Lily indicated.

'Would you like a cuppa?' Lily asked. 'And what about a drink for you, Emma?'

Emma clung to her mother's knee and didn't look up or answer as Helen refused for them. 'I don't want to take up your time, but I need a job and a minder for Emma while I work. I thought you might know someone.' Helen raised her pencil-thin eyebrows and gazed fixedly at Lily.

Bethany came in from the kitchen, nodded at Helen and then knelt by Emma. 'Hi there, Emma,' she said, but Emma hung her head and pushed closer to her mother.

'She's shy,' Helen said, 'say hello to,' she turned to Bethany, 'I'm sorry I don't know your name.'

'It's Bethany.' She smiled and held out her hand to Emma. 'Would you like a drink, or perhaps an ice cream; we've some in the freezer?'

'Thank you, but no.' Helen said firmly. She turned to Lily. 'Can you help me?'

'Well, erm, I work at Aldi, and they are looking for staff. It's hard work, but the pay's not bad. What did you do before?'

'I didn't need to work before, but I do since my husband was killed.' Helen held up her hands and shrugged. 'I'm not trained to do anything and have no experience, but I'll try Aldi and perhaps other supermarkets. So, thank you, but what about someone for Emma? Is there a local childminder, do you know?'

Lily stuck a fingernail into her hair and scratched. 'Hmm, the only person I know who might look after Emma is Amanda Pierce over at number four. She's a retired teacher. Have you met her? She used to mind Bethany. In fact, she has minded several of the young ones who've lived on the terrace at various times. She's lovely, isn't she Beth?'

'Oh yes, she really is, but that was four years ago, and her walking has become worse recently. Shall I nip over and ask her for you?' Bethany said.

'Would you? It would take away a worry.' Helen sat back in her chair, reached out and moved Emma away while crossing her legs. 'Sit on the floor by me, Emma,' she said, and Emma sat down obediently close by her feet.

After a few minutes, Bethany returned to find the room in silence with her mother peering through the net curtains. 'That was quick; what did she say?' Lily asked.

'She said she wanted to talk to Mrs Smith and meet Emma.'

'Now?' Helen stood up, then pulled Emma to her feet. Emma staggered but grabbed onto her mother's skirt.

'Yes, I've left her door open for you. Just call out to her as you go in.'

'Thank you,' Helen said and, without a backward glance at Lily, left and walked to the other side of the terrace with Emma trailing after her.

'Strange woman,' Lily said as the door closed behind their awkward, unexpected visitor.

'Emma's like a scared little kitten, isn't she?' Bethany said.

'Mmm, she is a bit, but perhaps she hasn't mixed much with anyone. Her mother is hardly sociable. I wonder where they come from and if they have any family nearby; I didn't like to ask. Strange woman,' Lily said again.

'Come on, let's forget about them and go and have a cuppa with Maja.' Bethany said.

'Give us a minute; I want to get some chewing gum from Hamza. If I can't smoke, I need to chew.' Lily replied and went to fetch her jacket. 'I don't care how warm it is; I need it,' she said as Bethany grinned at her.

'You're too sensitive. Your boobs are just right. I wish mine would hurry up and grow.' Then, laughing, they left the house together.

20

The Sunshine Café *Monday 23rd July*

'Hello Lily, I missed you and Rita earlier. You must be missing your friend too.' Maja said as she hastened from behind the counter.

Before Lily could answer, the doorbell clanged, and Bethany joined her mother at their usual table in front of the picture window. 'Ah, but you've company now that school is finished for the summer.' Maja smiled at Bethany. 'What can I get you? Coffee? I have just cut up a lovely marble cake that Alek baked this morning if you'd like a slice?'

Lily tapped Maja lightly on the back of her hand. 'No, don't tempt us. We're both trying to lose a few pounds.' Then she glanced at the Perspex cover over the cake, keeping insects from their sugary treat. 'It does look lovely, though. Perhaps a small piece for me with my usual coffee.'

'What about you, Bethany?' Maja directed her smile at the young girl she was watching grow into a young lady. She reminded her of her daughter that she had missed seeing so much since coming to England.

'Mmm, yes, please, I'd like a slice but not too small and some sparkling water, please.' Bethany grinned, and they all laughed.

'Not too big, eh?' Lily said.

Maja grinned as she went to take an order from two women who had alighted from the bus outside and walked straight into the café. They had settled at a table at the opposite end of the bright, welcoming room. In minutes she had served them toasted teacake, a pot of butter and one of jam before returning to Lily and Bethany with their order and her own coffee.

'It's been very slow here this morning, I've only had a few people in, and two only wanted a sausage roll and a can of Pepsi to take on the bus. I think they may have been going for the whole journey. I believe the bus route goes in a circle,' Maja said.

'Mmm, yes, it does. People often used to do that on the number eleven when I was young. I did it with Greg once, but I was bored halfway round, and we caught one back the way we came,' Lily said.

'Whatever floats your canoe, you say, don't you?' Maja joined in their laughter as they corrected her saying. 'It'll pick up later though, it always does. Especially since Alek added some Jamaican dishes to the menu.'

'Oo, let me see.' Bethany picked the menu from its holder and began to study it while her mother and Maja talked about the weather and the outrageous price of a leg of lamb Lily had bought at the weekend.

Bethany's ears tuned in to their chatter as her mother said, 'Alek at the wholesalers, is he?'

'Yes, he was late going this morning, but he'll be back soon.' She seemed worried and looked up sharply as the bell sounded, announcing that the couple at the other table was leaving.

'What's up? You're jumpy today, aren't you?' Lily teased.

'Well, I was hoping you'd come in. I have a favour to ask before Alek returns, but,' she looked at Bethany, 'would you be kind and give us a minute to speak private, love?'

'Sure, I intended to go and see what Penny is doing, so if it's ok, Mom, I'll go now.' Bethany stood up, pushed her chair under the table, and picked up her phone. She wished again that Penny had a mobile so that she could text her, but her parents had other more important things to buy. Penny didn't seem bothered and said she hated using phones anyway, although she sometimes used her mother's.

'Are you sure you don't mind Bethany?' Maja patted her arm and handed her something wrapped in some paper napkins. 'There are two pieces in there, don't eat them both though they'll go straight on your bum.'

Amid laughter, Bethany said thank you and turned to leave. 'See you later, Mom, but I'll be back and let myself in if she's not home.' She blew a kiss to each of them, and the bell clanged noisily as she skipped out.

'You are lucky; she's a lovely girl,' Maja said as her gaze followed Bethany past the picture window.

'Are you ok? You sounded so serious,' Lily looked concerned as she tore her eyes from her daughter's vanishing form and faced Maja.

'It is serious, and Alek can't know what I need you to do.' Maja visibly worried the inside of her cheek with her somewhat pointed teeth.

'Frankly, I don't like deceiving people, and there are some things that I wouldn't be prepared to help with, but if

I can, of course, I will. So, what is it, and why can't Alek know?' Suddenly Lily's eyes widened, and she shook her head as a possibility entered her thoughts. 'Are you having an affair?' she asked bluntly.

As Lily asked the question, a picture of Hamza the last time she'd seen him popped into Maja's mind; he had often been kind and listened to her woes, and Maja had come to realise that they were attracted to each other. So, she avoided shopping there whenever she could. Feeling her cheeks flush, Maja quickly shook her head. 'No, don't be silly. I would never do that; you know I love my husband. But wait, I'll explain.' She placed her hand on Lily's arm and, leaning forward, spoke quietly about going to see the doctor for tests. 'And I have to go again this Wednesday at ten for results, and I can't tell Alek I want to go shopping again so soon; he'd never believe me.'

Lily swallowed hard. The word cancer had entered her head. 'Why? Can you tell me and how can I help? Are you ill, Maja?'

'No, it's nothing like that. But I'm hoping you can give me an alibi, something personal you've asked me to do with you so Alek won't ask questions.' Maja replied quickly.

'Well, what is it then? For goodness sake, spit it out.' Lily sounded a trifle irritated now.

'I trust you to keep my secret; you will, won't you?' Maja swallowed a mouthful of cold coffee too quickly and began to cough as she hastily put the mug down unsteadily.

'Of course, I will; I won't breathe a word to anyone. Now come on, tell me what's the matter.'

'We want to start a family, but it's not happening,' Maja blurted out.

'Ok,' Lily spoke slowly, 'what's the problem?'

The Child in the Window

'It needs to be secret because Alek doesn't want us to be tested, and I've been for one. I think he's afraid that the fault might be his, and he can't face it.' Maja's eyes begged Lily to understand.

'But lots of men are like that; they can't bear their manhood to be called into question.' Lily smiled reassuringly.

'Well, I thought if I found out that I was still able to become pregnant, I might try harder to get him to seek help. Or if not, then perhaps we could adopt. But, if Alek finds out what I've done, he would be so angry with me. I'm not sure he would forgive me.' Maja looked anxiously at the door as the bell sounded. She smiled as a woman came in and sat down. 'I'll have to see to her, can you wait?'

'Yes, no problem.' Lily said then a thought occurred to her. 'Were you going to ask me to say you were accompanying me to the doctors?'

'Yes, how did you guess?' Maja stood up. 'Will you? Do you mind me asking?' Then she called over her shoulder. 'I'll be with you in one moment.'

'Well, lucky for you, I'm on a late shift on Wednesday. Did you say ten o'clock?'

'Yes.' Maja nodded.

'Ok, don't worry, you can say I need support. It'll be alright. Now see to your customer before she walks out.' Lily began to walk towards the door.

'Thank you, I'm so grateful,' Maja said as she hurried to placate the customer.

Lily strolled home feeling glad that she and Greg had never had any such problems. She was pleased she could help Maja but doubted that anything good ever came out of such deception.

21

4 Littlebrook Terrace Monday 23rd July

As she rounded the corner into the terrace, Bethany's phone buzzed. She stood still, and Amanda said, 'Please will you pop in when you can? I need to talk to you.'

'Yes, Nan, I'll come straight over. Is the door on the latch?'

Bethany was used to calls from Amanda. She often shopped for her, and she had such lovely memories of the kind and amusing person who had treated her like she was one of her grandchildren since minding her frequently from an early age. Bethany crossed the terrace and called, 'Only me, Nan,' as she pushed open the door.

Henry greeted Bethany joyously, jumping up and trying to lick her face, almost knocking her off her feet. 'Get down, silly boy,' Bethany said and fussed him while holding on to his collar.

Amanda said, 'Hello, love.' Then firmly, 'Behave yourself, Henry. Come and lie down!' Reluctantly Henry did so and made small protesting chuffing noises as he sprawled on the small, red hearthrug.

The Child in the Window

Bethany hugged Amanda and kissed the top of her sparse white hair. As she did, she remembered how thick it used to be when she was small. Bethany had loved to watch Amanda coil the long tresses that she dyed auburn into a bun worn towards the back of her head. She'd never asked Amanda where all her hair had disappeared to, but she wondered.

'What do you need, Nan?' she asked and perched on the arm of the chair opposite Amanda.

'I don't need anything, love, thank you. I just wanted to talk to you. And how many times have I told you to sit properly on that chair? You'll have the arm off.' Amanda tried to look stern but failed abysmally. They both laughed as Bethany slid over the arm and sat squarely on the chair cushion.

'What d'you want to talk about?' Bethany said when the laughter had died down.

'It's not important, and I don't want you to think I'm prying, but I wanted an idea of how well your mom knows Mrs Smith?'

'I know you don't want gossip, Manda, but I couldn't tell you anything anyway. Mom took her a welcoming casserole the day after they moved in, and we haven't seen her since. Oh, and she shouted at me and Penny and Lewis for being noisy when we shot hoops. Then she turned up at our house this morning wanting help, so Mom thinks Mrs Smith's a bit strange. I think she's mad and I'm sorry for Emma. Oh, and she won't let Lewis do her garden anymore even though Robert pays him. But that's all we know.'

'I thought Lily might have known her before she moved here. Do you know where she's from?' Amanda ran her tongue inside her cheek and across her dentures and picked a crumb from her tongue.

'No, she has a bit of a funny accent, but Mom said she didn't like to ask. Why? Are you going to mind Emma?'

Amanda nodded. 'Yes, I've decided I will. I wasn't thinking I should until I met her, but I think she needs me.'

'I thought she was like a frightened little rabbit or kitten. She wouldn't even look at me when I spoke to her. Did she talk to you?' Bethany asked.

'Not a word. Emma clung to her mother the whole time they were here and took no notice of Henry, although she didn't seem to be scared of him even when he sniffed her.' Amanda sighed. 'You're right, I wouldn't say I like gossip, but I think your mother's description fits the bill. Abrupt and very reserved and indeed a little strange. I'd like to know more about her. But then again, she may be more forthcoming as she gets to know us. She hasn't been here five minutes, and I'd hate to think we were unfriendly and judging her harshly.' Amanda frowned. 'We don't want to be unkind, do we, Henry?'

At the mention of his name Henry stretched, yawned and came to the side of Amanda's chair. She automatically dropped her hand down and petted him.

'She actually scares me a little bit. Well, not exactly scares, but she makes me feel uncomfortable. I wonder how well Robert knows her?' Bethany said.

'I don't know, but he phoned yesterday, and I think he will come home soon. I do miss him when he goes, and I know he worries about me.' Henry gave a small bark and his ears pricked up. 'Yes, he misses you too, you attention-seeking dog.' Amanda laughed.

The Child in the Window

'Ah, but you're lovely, aren't you, Henry?' Bethany said. Then her face took on a serious expression. 'Will you be able to look after Emma on your own, or would you like me to pop in and help while I'm on holiday. I could take her to the park sometimes when she gets to know me?'

Amanda nodded thoughtfully. 'I know what's worrying you, but she's hardly a willful little girl, and I would have to ask her mother how she feels about the park. I suppose she could play out in the garden, but if Lewis misses a day, he sometimes does, Henry's mess might be about, and she might step in it. That would be awful for her, and I might have a job cleaning her up.' Amanda scratched her head. 'Mrs Smith seemed desperate to have her settled before she got a job, so I expect she will be ok with what I suggest. Thank you, Bethany; we'll see.' Amanda looked tenderly at the child, who was growing fast. She was so grateful for the way she was always willing to help. Amanda pictured the days Bethany used to play in the garden on a swing that she'd bought for her and wished that her legs were still as spry now as they had been then. She would have liked to be able to take Emma to the park herself.

Bethany cut across her thoughts and said, 'Manda, shall I make you a cuppa before I go and see what Penny's doing?'

'No, thank you, love. I've held you up long enough. Get yourself off to see Penny but give me a hug before you go.' She held her arms out, and Bethany did just that. She loved Amanda and knew that, just like Robert, she would always look out for her and never forget her kindness. In a way, she felt slightly jealous that Emma would spend time with this lovely lady that she often called Nan as well as Manda. But as that thought hit her, so did gratitude that she didn't have Mrs Smith as a mother.

Penny wasn't home, and Lewis told her she'd gone shopping with her grandma. He had offered to have a game of cards or monopoly with Bethany, but she refused and went home to find her mother had beaten her to it and was sitting with her feet up watching TV.

Bethany joined her on the sofa and said, 'Nan is going to mind Emma starting tomorrow so that she can get used to it before Mrs Smith goes to work.'

'Has she got a job already then?' Lily asked.

'I don't think so; perhaps she wants to make sure that Emma will be alright with Nan before she does. I expect she will find work easily enough. She doesn't seem to mind what she does.'

'Hmm, strange woman, let's forget about her and watch the rest of this episode, shall we?' Lily said and tucked her arm into Bethany's.

22

Benton Hill Group Practice *Wednesday 25th July*

Lily took a book with a lurid picture of a girl walking along a deserted lane out of her capacious bag and, removing her bookmark, began to read. She'd been trying to get into it for the past week and was considering giving it up as a bad job. She had no empathy with the protagonist, and she needed to care about the main characters before enjoying reading about them.

After a couple of pages, she reinserted the bookmark, a strip torn from the last packet of Benson and Hedges she'd bought. She thrust the book back into the depths of her handbag and tried not to watch the intrusive TV screen on the wall. Lily tapped her foot impatiently. As soon as she'd seen the bookmark, it had prodded unmercifully at her wish to smoke. Well, you can't, the small voice in her head said and repeated all the reasons that she needed to stick with her promise to her daughter.

After a few more minutes, the door to Doctor Motts room opened, and Maja appeared. Lily jumped up and went to meet her. 'You ok?' she asked.

Maja didn't smile a greeting merely nodded and walked briskly to the exit. Lily immediately assumed that she'd had bad news and followed her out feeling very concerned.

Maja's steps faltered as she reached one of the benches positioned just before a bus stop on the main road. She sat, and Lily joined her. They silently watched the traffic as it stopped at the lights allowing an elderly man and woman to cross. After a few minutes, Lily realised that Maja's shoulders heaved with sobs that brought tears coursing down her pale cheeks.

'Oh, love, I'm sorry the news was awful. But please don't lose heart. You said you can always adopt, or perhaps Alek would agree to a surrogate,' Lily said and placed her hand on Maja's shoulder in an attempt to comfort her. While Lily spoke, she realised that she had no idea what surrogacy or even the adoption process involved. Lily thought her words were empty even though her intention hadn't been. She wished she knew what to say for the best, but she'd never encountered anything similar before.

Maja gave a heavy sigh and mopped her eyes with the sleeve of her cardigan while Lily gave a cutting look to a woman who had stopped just past the bench and was openly staring at Maja. The woman intercepted the look and moved on, and Maja turned to Lily. 'You are so kind, and I'm sorry, but I've misled you. The doctor told me that I could still have children and suggested again that I ask Alek to come in for tests.' Maja's knuckles showed white where they gripped her colourful crocheted bag. She gazed intently across the road at a Shell garage where a small man in a grey suit was at the pump, hose in hand.

The colours red, yellow and white stood out for Lily, but she wasn't sure that was what Maja was seeing and sat quietly as seconds passed. Then Maja shook her head and said, 'I'm upset because even if I told him what I have found out, I know he wouldn't agree to be examined. I think it would destroy him; he's very proud.' She paused and hung her head. 'And I think it would destroy our marriage too. He'd never forgive me for knowing that he couldn't father a child and going behind his back.'

Lily had no idea what to say, so said nothing. Instead, she patted Maja's arm sympathetically.

Maja leaned forward and kissed Lily's cheek and then said, 'I trust you, Lily; I've never heard one word of gossip from you about anyone.'

Lily's eyebrows almost reached her hairline, and she gazed wide-eyed at Maja, wondering what was coming next and hoping it wouldn't involve her having to be deceitful again. She pursed her lips. 'I don't like malicious gossip, and I wouldn't like anyone to talk about me behind my back, so yes, you can trust me. I won't tell anyone that I came with you today.'

'Thank you, Lily, but I want to tell you something that no one except my parents knows and certainly not Alek.' Maja's mouth took on a wry twist, and she seemed to have difficulty uttering her following words. 'I have a daughter who lives in Poland, but everyone thinks she is my sister.'

'Oh,' Lily exclaimed softly.

'I'm sorry, perhaps I need to explain. When I decided to go and see Doctor Mott, I hoped that something had happened when I had Alina. I thought that perhaps I had been damaged somehow and that damage might prevent me from becoming pregnant again. But I was only fifteen, and I don't remember much about her birth.' Maja stared into Lily's startled eyes for a moment and said in a small voice,

'I hope I haven't shocked you, Lily,' she sighed deeply. Then Maja's expression became animated as she blurted out, 'It would be so much easier for Alek to accept our lack of children if the fault was mine.'

Lily was a trifle shocked, but she wouldn't let Maja see that and said, 'No, I'm not shocked; these things happen. But I'm so sorry you've had to carry that secret with you all these years. If I remember rightly, you told us that you lived in a small community, so it's not so surprising, but in this country, even fifteen years ago, single motherhood was no longer a big issue,' she said and held onto Maja's slim hand. 'Do you ever see her?'

'Only on skype occasionally since I left Poland, but I miss her every day. Sometimes we write letters. And I know my Matka, sorry Mama encourages her to do this. I think my parents hope that we will be able to tell her the truth one day. But Alek would never understand, so I don't think that will ever happen. I should have been honest with him before we married, but I was a tch... I mean coward,' Maja said.

'And you've never told anyone until now?' Lily said and shook her head in amazement.

'No, I've never trusted anyone enough before, but it feels good and lightens my heart to know that you will share my secret and I can talk to you about Alina. I can, can't I?' Maja looked unsure.

'Of course, you can. We're friends, and perhaps I can share a secret that I'm keeping one day?' Lily smiled.

'I'd like that,' Maja said. 'And now I'd better get back to the café. One more favour, please will you come in with me and have a coffee so Alek can see we have been together?'

'Yes, but I can't stay long. I've things to do before I go to work.' Lily and Maja stood up simultaneously and grinned at each other, somehow knowing they would be that rare thing; friends for life. They both felt happier than they had for some time and chatted inconsequently until the bell rang as they entered the café, and Alek put his head out of the kitchen.

Alek barely glanced at his wife or Lily when he spoke. 'Glad you're back, kochany. It has been busy. Hello Lily.' he said and promptly disappeared into the kitchen again.

'I told you he wouldn't ask you any questions,' Maja whispered as Lily sat down and Maja quickly donned her apron. She checked that the other customers were served and didn't need anything else, then brought coffee and a piece of cake for Lily. 'Thank you again,' Maja said quietly, waved away the money Lily offered and then went into the kitchen.

As soon as Lily had finished her lemon drizzle cake, she grinned and waved at Maja as she left and hurried around the corner to make sure that her youngsters were ok. Even though it was almost lunchtime, it was evident that Ryan and his mate George had just crawled out of bed and were eating bowls of cornflakes for breakfast.

'Where you been, Mom?' Ryan asked and ran a hand through his unruly hair. George grinned at her around a heaped spoonful of cereal.

'None of your business, nosey.' Lily laughed. 'But if you must know, I've been for a walk with Maja to give her a break from work. Not that you'd know anything about work, either of you,' Lily said and smirked at their pained expressions. 'Where's Bethany?'

'She said to tell you she'd done the vacuuming, and she'll be at Penny's if you want her.'

'I hope you've both made your beds,' Lily said as she left the room, thinking how hard it would be not to be able to acknowledge your child.

23

6 Littlebrook Terrace Friday 27ᵗʰ July 2012.

Pat hung Eric's blue denim jeans over a coat hanger and hooked it over the kitchen door handle. She wasn't feeling well, and resentment lay heavy in her chest as she continued removing laundry from the dryer that repeatedly squawked if she ignored its warning that items were in danger of creasing. She didn't see why it was her job always to do the chores.

She sat down heavily at the table and stroked her forehead with her fingertips, wishing the headache that had troubled her for the last three days would go. It wasn't a thumping headache that would make her take paracetamol, but the pressure over her eyes had lowered her everyday unhappy mood to a worse point. She felt miserable and had been glad when Eric had gone to the pub as he often did lately a few times each week.

'For God's sake, take some tablets, can't you and see if they help,' Eric had exclaimed as he left the house. Pat had bent his ear over trivialities for the third time that day, and he'd had enough. Was it his fault that Amanda's dog had barked several times, asking Amanda to open the back door and let him back into the house? Or should he have noticed that Pat's library books were overdue? They'd taken books out on different days last time, and his weren't due to be returned for another week. However, Pat had blamed him for both these things. The final straw was when she'd moaned about him going to the pub without her. She'd only been on a couple of occasions and said it was too noisy for her. So, he'd never asked her to go since. However, he wouldn't let her moodiness prevent him from seeing other people and enjoying a pint. If anything, it made him determined to shut his ears to her admonitions.

On his way to the White Lion, Eric found himself thinking of their lives together. When had Pat become so miserable? She hadn't always been like it. Although he was losing patience with her outbursts, Eric loved his wife. He had appreciated her since they met at the Land Registry in Liverpool, where they had started work on the same day. He'd always been awkward where women were concerned, so it had been such a relief when Pat had made it easy for their relationship to develop.

Eric was just about to have a bit of a party to celebrate his twenty-first birthday on the tenth of November, and Pat had turned twenty-three earlier that month. It gave them something in common to talk about, and Eric had invited Pat to the party at his parents' home. He'd considered that he'd been quite good looking then and thought Pat was well within his league. He thought she was pretty enough and a very confident person but certainly not a beauty.

During the party, Pat told him that she thought he was a bit of a dandy, but she liked him, and Eric had never looked at another girl after that evening. They'd married on the fourth of December the following year at Wallasey Town

The Child in the Window

Hall just across the Mersey from where they worked. A sizeable gold-framed photograph of the two of them taken as they walked down the fabulous wide staircase after the ceremony still took pride of place above their fireplace.

Although Eric knew they still cared for one another, he sometimes wondered, as he did now, if they'd made a mistake when they agreed not to have children. Their decision had given them the freedom to live their lives as they wished. They'd travelled and holidayed worldwide and seen wonders that tourists raved about and some unspoilt scenery, but it hadn't brought them the happiness they thought it would. On the contrary, returning home after each holiday to an empty house had always brought them down to earth with a bump. Even more so after both sets of parents died, and retirement had made their social life as a couple dwindle. Not that they'd ever had a vibrant social life. He pictured the one couple he felt were genuine friends, James and Kirsty, who kept in touch. They would arrange to meet up midway between Banbury, where they lived in a small bungalow and Birmingham and have a meal together two or three times a year. They had holidayed as a foursome on several occasions when Kirsty wanted to see America and India. But they weren't into biking holidays, and for the last few years, that is what had suited Pat and himself. Although Eric secretly thought that as Pat was now seventy-one and he was only two years her junior, perhaps they should consider taking things easy. He'd wanted to talk to Pat about it after their last holiday, but she'd been so down and moody that he hadn't broached the subject.

Eric's troublesome thoughts ceased as he pushed open the heavy oak door and entered the brightly lit, welcoming pub. He glanced over to where he usually met up with David and sometimes Steve, but he didn't expect to see them there. It was too early for them, so Eric went to the bar then carried his pint over to an empty table. He looked around at familiar faces and tuned in to the many conversations that flowed around him, feeling contentment steal over him. Yes, it is noisy, he thought, but he loved it, and Pat wasn't going to make him feel guilty about being here.

Eric sipped at his beer, smiled broadly, then waved as Zeta appeared, returned his greeting, and began to wend her way between tables towards him. His smile died away as a man stepped away from the bar and intercepted Zeta. They began to talk, then he placed a hand beneath her elbow and steered her to a barstool. Eric watched as the man ordered a drink for her, and the way she smiled as she accepted it and took a sip made him feel a pang of jealousy deep in his stomach. He'd been hoping that Zeta would arrive before the others, and he wanted to be the recipient of that smile. He told himself not to be so foolish as he glimpsed a dim reflection of his bald head and sunburned wrinkles that spidered his face, but just a smile from the young woman who sometimes haunted his dreams would have made him feel young again, he knew.

Eric drained his glass and contemplated leaving the pub before David arrived. He decided against it and ordered another pint after saying hello to Zeta, who was deep in conversation with the unknown man. Feeling somewhat flat, Eric returned to his table, aware that David would appear soon if he were coming. Minutes later, he felt a lightness in his chest as Zeta slid down from her perch on the stool, picked up a drink, spoke and smiled at the man who had bought it and walked purposefully to join Eric.

'God, he was boring,' she said with a grin as she deposited her bag and short-sleeved jacket on the bench seat beside her.

'More boring than me?' Eric asked casually.

Zeta smiled. 'You're not boring,' she said without suspecting how her words affected Eric's heartbeat.

All thoughts of his wife left Eric's head as he enjoyed chatting with Zeta until David turned up five minutes later.

But thoughts of her husband hadn't left Pat's mind as she got ready for an early night. She pulled the no-frills black polyester nightdress that had sweet dreams printed in white over her head and arched her back for a couple of minutes, hoping it would help untangle the knots that tension in her shoulders and neck had tied. Instead of the movement helping, it made her feel worse, and she began to cry, something she seemed to do frequently lately, she knew. She had no understanding of what was happening to her. She'd been fit and strong until recently, and constantly feeling under par was beginning to grind her down.

Even though she thought they wouldn't help, Pat reached into the bathroom cupboard and, taking out a packet of paracetamol, pushed two tablets through the silvered foil. She tipped her toothbrush and tube of toothpaste into the sink from her glass, filled it with water and swallowed the pills. As she did so, Pat saw the small white box of Zopiclone her doctor had prescribed the previous year. She'd only taken them for two weeks after a fall, which had hurt her back. They had helped her to sleep. She didn't hesitate as she pressed two out of the blister pack into her hand and sent them after the painkillers. Then she walked into the spare bedroom and drew back the bedspread. She slid in under the duvet, shut her eyes and waited for the tablets to work. She didn't care what Eric would think when he arrived home and found their bed empty. As she drifted off, she thought he just hadn't better wake me up,

24

The Corner Shop Friday 27th *July 2012*

'I'm going, with or without your permission,' Nazia said and smacked her tiny hand off the counter next to the till. She turned, and head held high, strode into the stock room, leaving her husband mouth open, ready with a retort that she thwarted.

Nazia hadn't been home since she had left her parents' house to come to England and marry Hamza. They'd been discussing Nazia's possible trip to Bangladesh to see her mother, Fatima, before she succumbed to terrible cancer that was eating her alive. She was feeling desperate to go, but Hamza refused to hear of it.

Every time Nazia brought the subject up, Hamza left the room and, on occasions, vacated the apartment where they lived above the shop. However, this morning Nazia's father, Akram, had phoned and told her she needed to come home soon if she wished to see her mother alive. 'She is becoming frail, and I have been told she hasn't very long. I also need you to come. I need the support of our only daughter. Please come,' he said.

The call had brought things to a head, and Nazia had cornered Hamza in the shop. Usually, they would only discuss personal matters when the shop closed, but Nazia knew what she had to do. She was determined that Hamza should listen to her. So, when Hamza stacked the shelves with tins of red beans in the aisle away from the door, she turned the open sign to closed and dropped the latch.

Head held high, feeling that she had grown taller by another few inches, she walked determinedly around the shelving. 'I'll help you with those,' she said and picked a tin up in each hand.

'No, it's not needed. You need to be at the till for when a customer comes in.' Hamza didn't look up, expecting Nazia to obey him as she invariably complied with his wishes. When she didn't move, he looked hard at his diminutive wife. 'Didn't you hear what I said?'

'There won't be any customers coming in right now; I've closed the shop. I need to talk to you, and you have to listen to me this time.' She paused as Hamza took a step backwards and surveyed her handiwork in disbelief. They never shut the shop in the daytime unless it was an emergency. He began to walk towards the door, intending to change the sign, but Nazia stopped him as she threw the tins she was holding onto the wooden boards, where they bounced noisily and rolled under the shelving.

'What are you doing? Have you gone mad?' Hamza roared. Nazia calmly watched as he continued towards the shop front. She again drew his attention as, using her arm, she pushed all the tins that he had stacked neatly, sending them crashing to the floor.

'You need to listen to me,' Nazia shouted as loudly as she could.

The Child in the Window

Hamza had never known Nazia to behave so defiantly. He'd rarely had to raise his voice to her or the twins and had never considered using physical strength to get what he wanted, but for a second, he was tempted to grasp Nazia by her shoulders and shake some sense into her. But, instead, he shouted, 'What is the matter with you? What are you doing?' He was thunderstruck.

'I want to go and visit my mother; she is dying. Haven't you heard a single word I've said to you?' Nazia had no reason to be afraid of her husband, but she had never seen him look so angry in all the nineteen years that they had lived together. From the expression and colour that suffused his face, she thought he just might hit her. However, she was determined to make him listen. She had entered willingly into the arranged marriage but living in England had opened her eyes. She didn't regret marrying Hamza, but she had gained an insight into the fact that there were different ways of choosing one's path. And she was prepared to fight for her freedom to choose hers now.

'I can't let you go; how will I take care of the shop? I can't do everything; it's impossible. I need you here.' He spoke quietly and held out his hands towards Nazia. 'It's not as though you don't speak to your parents every week. So why do you need to go all that way? You might never return.' Hamza shook his head, and his voice faltered as that possibility occurred to him.

Nazia snorted. 'Of course, I'll come back; what are you talking about? And…and you can get our daughter to come and help or even employ someone.' She reached out and inserted her hands into Hamza's calloused ones. 'You must understand; I need to go, or I will forever regret not saying goodbye correctly. I love my parents as you love yours; what if it were yours? Wouldn't you go?'

Hamza pushed his hair back from his forehead with a shaking hand but said nothing.

'Oh, you're impossible,' Nazia flung at him. She went behind the counter and watched Hamza as he picked up and restacked the tins. Then calmly turned the closed sign and lifted the latch on the door. That was when Nazia slapped her hand on the counter and disappeared from the room.

It was almost an hour later when Nazia returned to the front of the shop and waited until another customer left before speaking calmly to her husband. 'I'm sorry, Hamza, I truly am, but I think we should wait until later to discuss this further.' She picked up a duster from under the counter and began to run it over the countertop and items of stock that often needed attention as they collected dust from the entrance.

Hamza didn't reply but continued emptying boxes and stacking shelves. His mind had been working overtime while Nazia had been in the back, and he felt tired of arguing with her. They rarely had a cross word, and Hamza realised that it was because Nazia had always considered him entitled to respect and obedience and rarely expressed an opinion that she thought he wouldn't like. He had always known that she had felt herself to be plain featured and unappealing when he'd agreed to marry her, and he'd allowed her to feel grateful to him for doing so. At the time, he had been twenty-seven, and she was only sixteen, but he needed a wife and wanted someone who would help him with the shop that was in its infancy. The property had been rundown when he bought it, and he had no money left to employ shopfitters, so he'd done all the necessary work himself and Nazia's willingness to help had been all he wanted. Over the years, he came to appreciate her and thought that she was beautiful in many ways. However, he didn't recall telling her how much she meant to him in so many words.

The thought that she might choose to remain in Pakistan or that she might have an accident frightened him more than he could say, and he now realised that was why he was behaving so selfishly. He needed to put things right between them and intended to do so after the shop closed. But staying open, was as always, his primary concern. He'd devoted his life to making his business profitable and, to compete with the supermarket giants, he had to spend long hours ensuring he was there when people needed spur of the moment shopping.

Still deep in thought, Hamza went outside and checked over the boxes of fruit and vegetables displayed on the pavement. When he returned, he went to where Nazia was making notes in the stock book. He touched her face gently; he had always been a gentle lover and said quietly, 'I love you, and we will discuss your visit tonight. But, of course, you must go.' He felt touched by the radiant smile she gave him. A smile that remained on her lips for the rest of the day.

25

London *Saturday 28ᵗʰ July.*

Robert opened his eyes and watched as heavy raindrops smacked the window and sped down the trail left by its fellows. Miserable bloody weather, he thought but smiled; he certainly wasn't feeling miserable; he'd never felt so alive, so happy. He carefully eased himself up onto his elbow and gazed tenderly at the shape of the man who slept beside him.

Guy wasn't the easiest person to have as a bed companion. He looked peaceful now, but the way the pale blue top sheet wrapped haphazardly around his trim body belied the thought. Robert knew he tossed and turned restlessly, often pulling the covers from himself.

Robert's hand itched to reach out and run his fingers over Guy's body. He ached to feel the silky smoothness of skin that stretched taut over well-maintained muscles. However, he had learned on the first night that they became intimate not to startle his lover and now recalled every detail as he looked at this mysterious man he loved.

Robert remembered the excitement he'd felt when meeting Guy as arranged at Jerry's restaurant for the first time. All his senses had seemed heightened. The smell of cooking was overwhelming, and the napery felt rough to his fingertips. He knew he'd hardly been aware of anyone else in the room; he couldn't tear his eyes away from the fascinating man sitting opposite. They'd relished sirloin steak with all the trimmings, and then Guy had suggested they have coffee and perhaps something stronger at Robert's place. Robert had hoped that was how the evening would progress and, picking his phone from off the table, began to call for a taxi.

Guy had placed a restraining hand on his arm. 'You only live fifteen minutes away; why don't we walk some of this meal off?' he'd said.

Robert felt that there was something almost magical in the twenty or so minutes it had taken. They strolled side by side, saying very little to each other, but the way the slight breeze was playing games with Guy's neat hair left Robert wishing the time away. He couldn't wait to seduce or be seduced by this man who inadvertently, he was sure, affected his mind, breathing and heart rate.

When they entered the flat, Robert offered Guy a drink hoping that he would decline, and they could go into the bedroom where Robert had left a lamp burning and sprayed room freshener before he left. However, Guy said with a grin, 'I could do with a stiff one.' He laughed at Robert's startled expression.

Robert wondered if this man, who had scarcely been out of his mind since he'd first seen him, was just using him. He'd met men before who did that, hoping to gain some advantage. But, once they'd aroused his suspicions, Robert got rid of them too quickly to find out what their game was. He'd never wanted anyone enough to stand being messed about. He desperately hoped this wasn't the case with Guy. He thought only one way to find out and said coolly, 'Whisky do?'

Guy nodded and lounged back in his seat, still with a smile hovering about his lips that Robert wanted to kiss.

Robert went to a drink's cabinet in the corner of the room opposite the balcony and poured two glasses of amber liquid. He knocked half of his back in one swallow, loosened his tie, sat back in a chair and watched as Guy emptied his glass while surveying the assortment of books Robert had left stacked against one of the walls.

'Bathroom?' Guy said and yawned.

Robert indicated the door to a small hallway that led to both the bedrooms and bathroom. 'It's the furthest door,' he said and finished his drink, hoping that the evening wouldn't be a big disappointment. He'd had such high hopes that he'd finally met someone with whom he perhaps could form a long-term relationship. Robert had tried living with a couple of men before, but they hadn't worked out. He didn't want someone who had a nasty temper or a sponger, which they'd turned out to be.

The minutes ticked by, and Guy didn't return. Robert glanced at his watch. Then, after another five minutes, he went to the door and, feeling concerned, called along the hall. 'You alright, mate?' There was no reply.

Robert allowed another five to go by, then fearing he didn't know what, strode along the hall intending to knock and ask again. However, as he neared his bedroom, he could see the door had been pushed open. He looked in and saw discarded clothes strewn across the carpet. Guy was propped up in front of the pillows wearing only a small gold ingot on a strong chain around his neck. He was grinning.

'You took your time,' he said, and the grin became a belly laugh.

'Bastard!' Robert exclaimed and rapidly sent his clothes to join Guy's.

Later that morning, Robert woke to see the lilac painted walls were bathed in brilliant sunshine, and Guy was asleep on his side facing away from him. Robert felt elated as gradually the night's events became clear in his mind. The tenderness and passion that had carried them away had exceeded anything he'd imagined he'd feel. He remembered the joke that Guy had played on him and loved his sense of humour. On impulse, Robert stretched out an arm and tousled Guy's blond hair, wanting to wake him up. Seconds later, he regretted his action as he was pinned down, arm behind his back and Guy's left arm around his throat in a chokehold.

It only lasted for a couple of seconds before Guy groaned, 'Oh my God, I'm sorry,' released him, swung his legs out of bed and sat with his head in his hands.

Robert was stunned. He didn't know what to do. He'd hooked up with a couple of men over the years that liked rough sex, but they had made it clear what they wanted, and Robert had not indulged their kinkiness. This had been something different. Guy hadn't shown any tendency towards violence, and Robert felt such disappointment that he'd been so wrong about him. Robert's feet hit the floor without another thought, and he had taken himself off to the bathroom. When he returned, Guy was dressed and waiting for him in the sitting room. The tension in the air was tangible, and Robert said, 'I think you'd better go.'

'I can't,' Guy said miserably.

'Well, you'd better, or I'll have you removed.' Robert spoke firmly, but he felt like crying.

'You have to let me explain.' Guy scrutinized Robert's dejected face.

'There can be nothing that would excuse you attacking me like that. I want you to go and....' Robert choked back a sob that threatened to prevent him from speaking. 'I never want to see you again. Go and get your kicks elsewhere.'

Guy didn't move. 'I'm so sorry, Robert; I wouldn't hurt you for the world, and I can't explain my behaviour fully.' He sighed heavily. 'I can only say it's my training, and I should have warned you last night not to wake me out of deep sleep.'

'What do you mean? What sort of training?'

'I told you I work for the government, but I can't say any more than that.' He suddenly laughed, then stopped abruptly. 'You know the saying if I told you I'd have to kill you. Well, in my case, it's true. I hope you can believe I would never hurt you. I was startled. Believe it or not, you're the first man I've fallen asleep with in the last decade, and I'm so sorry I frightened you.' Guy never took his eyes from Robert's face while he spoke and the sincerity in his voice came across clearly. 'I hoped this could be more than a one-nighter,' he said quietly.

'So did I,' Robert had replied as he came to a decision. He had to trust Guy; it meant everything to him. 'Will you be able to tell me what you mean eventually?' he'd asked.

'Perhaps one day when we're old.' The twinkle that Robert loved was back in Guy's eyes. 'Let's try growing old together. What do you say?'

Robert groaned. 'That's the best plan I've heard in years, but I'll never wake you up again.'

'Not a good idea, but I promise I wouldn't hurt you. Do you think we could have breakfast? I'm starving,' Guy said.

Since that first night, Robert had flown to Las Vegas twice, but now he was considering leaving his current long-haul contract as he watched Guy sleeping. He missed him every second he was away despite phone calls.

Robert thought about Amanda and wondered how she would react if he brought Guy to meet her. He'd never admitted he was gay to anyone on the terrace but believed that Amanda, who knew him better than anyone else, probably suspected he was. He decided he wanted her to know for definite and planned to mention Guy the next time he went to Birmingham. It led him to wonder about Guy's history, and his thoughts meandered on while he patiently waited for his lover to come back to him.

26

3 Littlebrook Terrace Thursday 2nd August.

'Put the bloody kettle on; I'm parched and so glad to be home at last.' Rita flopped into a chair and put her feet up on the small, Scottie dog fabric-covered pouffe.

'Well, I've missed you, but I wasn't expecting you home until tomorrow night,' Lily said and went to do her friend's bidding.

Rita raised her voice. 'We weren't supposed to be home, but Andrew asked Steve if he'd mind because he wants to play in the match at the bowls club tomorrow evening. It's the Championship Challenge Shield, and someone has dropped out at the last minute. He had a phone call last night, and Steve asked me how I felt about it and to be quite honest, I was ready to come home. Anna's been a bloody nightmare at times.' Rita pulled a face as Lily came back into the sitting room carrying two mugs of steaming tea.

'Why, what's she done?' Lily asked.

'Oh, I can't be bothered to talk about her except to say she's kept up her moaning and been critical for the whole holiday. Nothing suited her. I'm sure she wasn't this bad last time. I heard Andrew tell her to be quiet a couple of times, and you know he is usually so patient with her.' Rita shrugged her shoulders as if casting off her mother-in-law. 'Anyway, I'd much rather hear what's been going on around here. What have I missed?'

'Not a lot; it's been pretty quiet. But you'll be pleased to know I've stopped smoking and Bethany's sticking with not eating chocolate.'

'Well done, both of you. Where's Beth, still in bed?'

'No, she's gone shopping for Amanda. She's a good girl, and I wish Ryan were half as responsible.' Lily sighed, making Rita laugh.

'He's a boy, for God's sake. He'll grow into it. Now come on, catch me up on the gossip,' Rita said.

'Well, Mrs Smith is working part-time at Hamza's and Manda's, minding Emma.'

'Oh, there's a surprise, how come?' Rita asked while tucking her feet up under her in the chair.

'Nazia's gone to Bangladesh because her mother's dying. No idea when she'll be back, Hamza told me. Not that I mind, she's never been very forthcoming, has she?'

Rita looked thoughtful. 'Mind you; I think she made herself liked well enough.'

'I suppose.' Lily put her mug down on the floor. 'Is Steve going to the club too? It's in Handsworth Wood, isn't it? I remember going past there last year. It looks like an oasis of green, easy on the eye.'

'It is. Why don't you come with us tomorrow? I've said I'll take Tilly, and we can watch. You'd enjoy it. There's a bostin clubhouse with a bar and everything. I've been to one of their social evenings when they played bingo and had a quiz.'

'Glorified marbles, isn't it?' Lily asked with a grin.

Rita smirked. 'I'm told there's more skill in it than that. What d'you say, will you come and bring Bethany. There are benches by the changing rooms that we can sit on.' She nodded encouragingly. 'Go on; I could do with the company. See if Greg wants to come?' Rita cajoled.

'Ok, you're on. I'll ask Greg, but he'll probably want to go to his club and meet his mates.'

Rita was curious about Greg's club, but Lily hadn't given her a straight answer when she'd inquired about it. She'd said with a peculiar shutdown look that it was a private club in town. She had no intention of asking again and perhaps making her friend feel uncomfortable, so she shrugged her shoulders and said, 'Now tell me more about Mrs Smith. What's she like?'

'Not a lot to say, really, but I'll tell you one thing, I think she's strange.' Lily nodded emphatically and picked up her drink.

'Hey, you can't leave it there. You must have a reason to say that,' Rita said.

Lily gulped tea and then spent the next few minutes recounting her visit from Mrs Smith, which had led to Amanda minding Emma.

'I thought you said it had been quiet while I was away.' Rita snorted.

Lily felt mean not telling Rita what she had learned about Maja, but she held her tongue. Trust meant a lot to her, and it had felt good when Maja had confided in her. She knew without a doubt that Maja could be relied on, and she'd made up her mind to share her concerns about Greg next time they had a chance to talk privately. But other than Greg's behaviour, she and Rita had shared hopes and fears and been one hundred per cent supportive of each other since they came to live next door. At least that's what Lily thought. She knew nothing of Rita's early abuse as she had said very little about her life before she met Steve. Lily assumed that Rita's life had been very much like her own. Relatively normal and uncomplicated. Lily's parents had both died when she was in her early twenties, and as Rita never mentioned hers, she believed they were no longer living and didn't want to rake up old sorrows. However, she wouldn't want Rita to think she kept secrets from her and felt relieved when Rita's phone played *Ride of the Valkyries.*

Lily grinned. 'I bet Steve thinks you've left home,' she said as Rita answered it.

'Alright, I'm coming now; keep your hair on,' Rita snapped her phone shut and stood up. 'I'd better get back; I know he wants to take some stuff over to his parents. Impatient bugger,' she said but smiled indulgently.

Lily grinned back at her friend; she knew how much Rita loved her husband.

As she neared the door, Rita turned and asked, 'When does Manda mind Emma? I thought I might take Tilly over to play. I want to see Amanda anyway; I've bought her some rock back.'

'Good idea, Mrs Smith is working this afternoon. She does Monday and Wednesday morning and Thursday and Friday afternoon. I think it's too much to expect Manda to mind Emma these days, but it's nothing to do with me. See you later,' Lily said as Rita pursed her lips, shrugged, waved a hand and shut the door behind her.

Rita phoned Amanda and asked if she was up for visitors. Amanda was pleased and invited them over. After Rita finished her conversation, she told Tilly, 'We can visit, but

Emma is very shy, and she's half your age, so it may take a little while before she becomes used to you. It might be ok if you treat her gently and talk quietly.' Rita surveyed her daughter's frowning face. 'Are you sure you want to do this, love?'

'Yes, but I hope she likes me,' Tilly said anxiously.

Rita laughed and hugged her daughter. 'Of course, she'll like you even if she is too timid to play. Come on; we'll soon find out.'

Amanda had left the door open for them, and they were greeted as usual by Henry's excited bark as Amanda called out to them to come in.

Rita bent to kiss Amanda's cheek, and Amanda pulled Tilly close. 'How was your holiday? I missed you, and so did Henry,' she said.

Tilly didn't even hear the question. She extricated herself from Amanda after hugging her, and her eyes searched the room for Emma, who was nowhere to be seen. 'Where's Emma?' she asked as her mother seated herself.

'I'm afraid she's hiding, aren't you, Emma?' Amanda paused then said, 'Why don't you come and say hello to Tilly? She's come to play with you. I told you she was coming, didn't I?'

Tilly began to giggle as Emma peeped from behind the chair where Amanda sat and gazed in wide-eyed wonder at the first little girl she'd ever known who was allowed to play with her. She'd only ever played with Harry when her mother had permitted it. Emma liked Bethany, who came to see them sometimes, but she was grown up in Emma's eyes, and she must not trust her. Emma had begun to trust Amanda, who was gentle and kind and never raised her voice to her. But she hadn't managed to say one word even to her. She was so frightened that she would say something she shouldn't, and her mother would know and punish her and Harry if she spoke.

Tilly held out her hand to Emma, and Amanda was delighted when her charge crawled out from her hiding place and, smiling, reached out until her fingertips touched Tilly's.

Praying that this would be the necessary breakthrough, Amanda and Rita watched as the two girls settled by Henry and began to ruffle his fur. Amanda had told Rita on the phone that Emma only ever spoke to her mother. After a few minutes, Tilly said to Emma, 'Are you shy? Mommy says you are, but I think we'll be friends, won't we?'

Emma smiled and nodded but put her finger to her lips and said, 'Shh.' Then handed a colouring book and some crayons to her new friend, and they both began to use them while sitting on the hearthrug.

Rita went to make a drink, and Amanda stroked Henry quietly, wondering what to make of the girls' interaction.

'It's ok; you can just talk when you want to. I won't mind, but I'll talk to you, is that ok?' Tilly said and smiled.

Emma looked a long minute at Tilly, smiled back at her new friend, and said, 'Yes.'

Rita came back into the sitting room with a tray. She winked conspiratorially at Amanda, who was beaming, hopeful that this was the beginning of Emma talking when her mother wasn't present.

27

8 Littlebrook Terrace Friday 3rd August

Penny opened her eyes and could see by the way light filtered through and above the cream vertical blinds that it was morning, but it felt too early to be awake. She lay still and gradually became aware that her sister Lucy's quiet crying had woken her. Although Lucy had told her that she'd strongly objected when forced to accommodate her baby sister when she was eleven, they had always shared a bedroom with rarely a cross word.

However, Penny had never heard Lucy cry except when she had fallen and bruised her backside while sliding down the hill at Barr Beacon in the snow. This sort of crying was different, and it frightened her. She eased herself up and rested her elbow on the sunshine yellow-spotted pillowcase. She held her breath, not knowing what to do. Was Lucy hurt? Something was wrong with her.

'Lucy,' Penny whispered. The crying ceased abruptly, and Lucy's quilt no longer moved. 'Lucy,' Penny said again, 'what's the matter? Are you in pain? Shall I get Mom?'

Lucy pulled her quilt away from her face and hissed, 'No, Christ's sake, mind your own business. I'm fine, go back to sleep.'

Penny hesitated. 'No, tell me. Something's wrong; you don't cry for nothing. Is it Philip? Have you split up?'

'Go to sleep, it's nothing,' Lucy said and swung her long legs out of bed, stood up and went to the bathroom.

Penny grumbled, 'Sisters.' Turned onto her side, faced the wall and tried to sleep, but her expectation that Lucy would return and still be upset kept her awake. Time passed, and when Lucy didn't return, Penny pulled on an old lightweight dressing gown and went to find her. She was in the conservatory slumped in an easy chair with her legs dangling over the arm, her shorts rucked up until they were barely seen under the strappy top she invariably wore to bed.

She wasn't at all pleased to be found. 'What are you doing here?' she said dully. 'You'll have Mom and Dad up if they heard you.'

'Well, they're snoring, so I'm staying where you are until you tell me what's wrong. I just might be able to help you know. I'm not just a little kid being nosey,' Penny said tersely.

Lucy wiped a hand across her dry eyes and surveyed Penny's sleepy face as though she'd never seen her before. Although they were sisters and got on very well, she thought they had little in common due to the age difference. She pushed her hair back from her high forehead and said, 'I know you'd like to help Penny, and I'm grateful, but there's nothing you can do.' She sighed heavily. Tears squeezed from under red-rimmed eyelids and trickled down her pale cheeks. 'There's nothing anyone can do.' Lucy's face crumpled as she burst out, 'I'm having Philip's baby, and he's dumped me.'

Penny jumped up and hugged her sister, then held her hand until new tears subsided. Then she said, 'You have to tell Mom, she'll know what to do.'

'I can't; I've ruined everything. I won't be able to get my degree now and then....' Lucy sobbed as if her heart would break.

Penny didn't know what she could do as Lucy curled into a ball and continued to make mewling noises. Neither heard the footsteps as Cathy clad in her flimsy nighty came into the room, took one look at Penny's pale face and frightened eyes and pulled Lucy onto the tiled floor where she folded her into her arms and held her eldest daughter until her sobs ceased.

'Put the kettle on Penny; there's a love,' she said.

Penny released the breath she'd been unaware of holding and felt relieved. She was still young enough to believe that her mother could cure all ills. When she returned with the tea tray, Lucy was still in her mother's embrace but no longer cried.

Cathy took the proffered mug. 'Thanks, love. Now, do you think you could tell me what's upset you, Lucy? I presume you've already told Penny?'

Lucy put her mug on the table. She took a deep breath. 'I'm pregnant, Mom. I'm sorry. I know how much you and Dad wanted me to finish Uni.'

Tears threatened again but were quickly stemmed as Cathy said firmly, 'You will finish, and you will get your degree, so stop crying now. You'll flood us all out the way you're carrying on. My nighty's soaked.' She stood unsteadily and sat in a chair, rubbing her legs to get the blood flowing again.

'I can't, Mom; I'm not having an abortion!' Lucy looked appalled at the thought.

'I wouldn't expect you to.' Cathy said. She ran her hands distractedly through her hair and scratched at her dry scalp.

'No, you can't kill a baby!' Penny exclaimed.

'Alright, Penny, calm down. That's not going to happen.' She turned to Lucy. 'What about Philip, does he know?'

'I hate him. I told him after I missed for the second time and did a test. He didn't want to know. He said he didn't want to be tied down and called me stupid.' Lucy looked at her toes and tugged distractedly at a hank of her hair. 'I suppose I am. I thought he loved me, but he doesn't,' she ended sadly.

'Well, good riddance, he's too fond of himself to make a good father. It's always the handsome ones….' Cathy sighed.

'What's Dad going to say? He'll be so disappointed in me, and I can't face him. Will you tell him, Mom?' Lucy got to her feet and headed for the door.

'I need to think, and he'll be down in a minute to go to work. Both of you go up, and I'll talk to him tonight. Do George and Lewis know?'

'No, and thanks, Mom. I'm really, really sorry,' Lucy said as she disappeared. Penny followed her.

Once they were back in their room, Penny said, 'I knew Mom would know what was best.'

Lucy smiled at her sister. 'I wish I had your faith; my life is finished.'

'Oh, don't be such a pessimist.' Penny grinned. 'I know you feel like that now, but a new baby to love. I'll be an

Auntie, and that's exciting. But I'm sorry about Philip. Do you still love him?'

'No, I bloody well don't, but it isn't the baby's fault, and I will love it even if I don't want to be a mom yet.' She kissed Penny's cheek. 'Thanks for being so sensible. You'll make a great auntie.'

'And you'll make a great mom, so stop being upset. Just think, Mom will be a grandma.' This thought seemed too challenging, and silence reigned as they heard their father's tread on the stairs.

Lucy's stomach churned as she wondered how her father would take the awful news. She was well aware that he'd worked long hours to provide for them and ensure they would have a good start. She flopped onto her bed and wondered how she could have been so careless as not to take her pill. She tried not to heed the tiny voice that asked if her omission had been deliberate. She had always loved playing with dolls. Had she wanted a real one of her own? Did she want to be a forensic scientist? Lucy shut her eyes and tried to understand her confused feelings. She didn't feel old enough to be a parent; her brain whirled until she suddenly fell asleep. Penny followed suit.

28

8 Littlebrook Terrace Friday 3rd August.

'Toast love,' Cathy pushed the rack close to David and kissed his cheek, 'do you want marmalade or jam?'

Her husband caught her hand as she left the breakfast bar and swung her around to face him. 'I'd just like a proper kiss to go with my toast, please.' Cathy obliged and giggled like a schoolgirl as she placed both jars before him, then sat opposite as he began to eat.

She bit into her slice of buttered toast and watched how David's Adam's apple bobbed each time he swallowed. She wondered why women didn't have one. Not that she wanted one; she considered their pronounced movement ugly. However, she thought that the rest of David's face, in fact, the whole of his lean body, was handsome. Cathy had always been more than a bit overweight and had never understood why David had fancied her. He called her his plump little duck, a tease she enjoyed.

David was blissfully unaware of his wife's gaze as he skimmed through yesterday's newspaper, and Cathy had no intention of talking to him about Lucy's pregnancy until he arrived home from work. She didn't want him mithering about one of the children while driving. Even after twenty-five years, they were very close, and Cathy found herself remembering how they had met.

She recalled how he had attracted her attention when he'd arrived in A&E at the Royal University Hospital in Liverpool, where she'd recently started work. He'd injured his hand when an insecure pallet had shed one of its crates while unloading at Seaforth docks. It wasn't a severe injury, but the cut needed stitches. Cathy had reassured him when she saw how the tall, serious-looking man's hand trembled at the sight of a doctor preparing a syringe. She'd stood between him and the preparation area and laid her hand on his arm. 'You won't feel a thing,' she whispered.

David had reached for her hand, something he often did even now and said, 'If I'm brave will you go on a date with me?'

Cathy had smiled and nodded, and on their first date at a local Indian restaurant, they had hardly noticed what they ate as they exchanged histories. Cathy had been reluctant to tell David she'd been brought up in an orphanage run by nuns in Tralee from the age of five. Her parents were killed in a farmyard accident, and her only grandmother had been in poor health and refused to take her. However, she hadn't found details until she was much older when one of the other girls tormented her about being unwanted by anyone. Cathy had felt unloved and found it difficult to let anyone get close. Food had been the one thing that she looked forward to each day. When she was a teenager, she'd gone on to study nursing at the hospital attached to the nunnery before coming to England to complete her training. But when David matter-of-factly told her about his parents, Joyce and Gilbert and how they had treated him, she'd felt able to share. She could see the lonely little boy as he told her how they had shown no affection or interest in anything he said or did. When he was in his teens, he'd lost his temper one day and accused them of not loving him. They had told him they'd never wanted him; he had been an accident that had spoilt their enjoyment and their plans. David had never forgiven them for their indifference and reserve towards himself. After his parents went abroad rather than attend his wedding to Cathy and then showed no interest in Lucy, he'd ceased to pay them even a cursory visit. Cathy had only met them once and thought they were more than a little pretentious.

However, David knew his mother was safe in a nursing home. But still, he somehow felt quite satisfied that his father, who didn't need nursing and was in a relatively nearby home, only occasionally managed to visit his wife. Aunt Eileen, his mother's sister also in her eighties, was not good with technology, and so although David was fond of her, they rarely spoke, and he remained aloof.

Sometimes Cathy knew that David was sad about his lack of family roots. On one occasion when he'd been falling asleep, he said he supposed he could find cousins or other Aunts and Uncles, but he didn't need them as long as he had her. Cathy was well aware that his only genuine concern was for her and their immediate family, who he loved fiercely. She knew David would be devastated to hear that his eldest daughter was considering allowing her pregnancy to prevent her from gaining a degree. So, as she waved David goodbye, she only said, 'I would rather you didn't work too late tonight love, I'm going to cook a special tea, so around six, eh?'

David smirked. 'Oh yes, and what's that in aid of, eh?'

Cathy smiled. 'Cheeky, just come home safe.'

After waving goodbye and blowing a kiss, Cathy poured herself another coffee and sat gazing into their pretty garden, her mind blank as she sipped. She shook her head; she needed to think before talking again to Lucy. There was so much she didn't know. How on earth were they going to cope with another baby in a three-bedroom house already at capacity? And would Lucy be able to continue her education whilst pregnant? Cathy's mind raced into the future as she tried to find solutions to all the new problems they would face.

To stop the rising heat in her chest that Cathy knew was the start of a panic attack, she opened the conservatory door and went into the garden. The perfumed heat slapped her. Everywhere was still; not a breeze stirred the petals on the roses, and their scent hung heavy in the early morning air. Cathy leaned forward and sniffed one of the peach blooms, her favourite. She continued down the crazy-paved path and sat on the swing they had bought when Lucy was small. She remembered David saying it would soon pull through the lawn because the anchoring pins weren't long enough. He had been proved wrong; it had never moved and was still firmly planted as Cathy pushed herself forward and then lifted her slippered feet from the scrubby patch of lawn that never had a chance to recover.

As she swung, Cathy's feeling of being overwhelmed gradually dissipated, she had David, and they had always managed their problems together. She felt lucky he would help to overcome this new problem. She wished Lucy hadn't become pregnant but remembered how she and David had been unwise when they'd first been together. The longer she sat feeling the hot air on her legs that hadn't yet become swollen as they usually did during a day, the more optimistic she became. This was their first grandchild, and once the initial difficulties were dealt with, she knew they would welcome this addition to their family.

'Hey Mom, you having fun?' Lewis called and disappeared.

Seeing her son, his hair still tousled from his bed, brought Cathy out of her reverie. She waited until the swing had reached its zenith and leapt into space, landing lightly on legs that wavered ever so slightly. On her walk back to the house, she decided to cook breakfast for her children and phone in sick to work. After all, this was a special day, and she never took a day off unless she was ill. She knew that because her legs would prevent it, she would never be able to go back to nursing, but now, as she thought about her work at the sweet factory, she wished she could.

When David arrived home at five-thirty that night, he expected a surprise of some sort. Cathy never asked him to come home early unless there was a reason. At first, his jaw dropped when they were all sitting eating around the dining table; even George had appeared without Ryan, and Cathy casually said as though it was an everyday occurrence, 'Lucy is having our grandchild.'

Cathy had forewarned Lewis and George, but David's fork dropped onto his plate with a clattering sound. 'What, what, now you mean?' He looked so startled and puzzled that his children all except Lucy laughed.

'Well, in about seven months,' Cathy said, and Lucy's cheeks glowed as she stared at her plate.

David scratched his forehead with his fingertips and licked his lips. 'Well, that is a surprise. I expect I should say congratulations.' He smiled at his daughter. 'You need to

149

tell me the details,' he said calmly and slicing into a sausage brought a chunk to his mouth.

'I'm sorry, Dad,' Lucy said, 'I've let you down.' Everyone held their breath.

David shook his head. 'No love, these things happen, and babies should always be a joy and wanted.'

Lucy got up, ran the short distance to her father, flung her arms around his neck, hugged him, and then burst into tears. Her father used his paper napkin to wipe them away.

George tutted loudly, and Cathy gave him a fierce look. 'You mind, you never get a surprise,' she said.

George's eyes opened wide and innocent. 'Who me?' he said and winked at Lewis.

'Enough,' David said, let's finish our dinner.' He looked at Lucy and then at Cathy. 'I think there's a lot to discuss but later, eh? I need to take this in.' He carried on eating, and everyone followed suit.

Cathy again watched his Adam's apple bob and thought how much she loved him for probably the millionth time.

29

***9** Littlebrook Terrace Monday 6th August 2012*

Helen stretched her arms above her head as her toes almost touched the baseboard of the antique-coloured pinewood bed and wondered what had woken her before the alarm went off. She glanced at the clock and swore; she could have had another ten minutes. Then the stench hit her, and she knew. She leapt out of bed, moved swiftly into the small room where Harry's cupboard was, undid the scarf from around the handles with fumbling fingers and yanked open the pinewood, narrow double doors.

'You little bastard, come out of there!' Helen hissed as she threw her dressing gown onto the floor and, grabbing Harry by his arm, yanked him onto it. He ended up by her bare feet and curled himself into a ball with his painfully thin arms protecting his head and his eyes closed.

Hearing her mother's raised voice, Emma ran into the room and held onto her mother's nightdress. 'Mommy, Mommy, he didn't mean it, I'll clean it up,' she cried and tried to insert herself between her mother and her twin brother.

Helen stretched out an arm and pushed Emma out of the way. 'You're as bad; get out of here before I lose my patience.'

Emma peeled herself off the bedroom wall and stumbled to the doorway where she remained standing. 'Don't hurt him, please, please, Mommy,' she begged.

'Hurt him; I'll bloody well kill the little bastard, trying to make me late for work. Don't you move,' she spat at Harry as she pushed past Emma and went to run water into the bath. As soon as it was two inches deep, she returned to the bedroom where both children hadn't moved.

Helen's face was flooded with angry colour as she dragged Harry on her dressing gown into the bathroom, stripped off his shorts and tee-shirt that were stuck to his tiny body, and dumped him into the water where he sat head bowed and shivering with fear.

'Stand up,' Helen ordered, and when he held on to the bath taps and stood shakily, she used a flannel to wash the shit from his hands and arms, backside and between his legs. 'Now get out and stand on the mat,' she said without looking at her son.

Harry gripped the taps harder and managed to climb over the side. He promptly slid down onto the mat; his strength completely used up.

'Oh, for God's sake,' Helen fumed as she threw his soiled clothing into the bathwater. She took a towel from a pile on a stool and began to dry Harry, who flinched every time she touched him. 'Hold onto the bath and stand still,' Helen said and looked up to see Emma hovering by the bathroom door. At that moment, she hated not only Harry but Emma as well. Helen pictured taking a pillow and smothering them while they slept. She remembered when she'd tried to do so once before and swept the thought aside. She couldn't do it, but she couldn't understand why Harry hadn't died. He should have died from lack of food and water, but he persisted in hanging on to life no matter what. 'You're just like your father,' she raged at Harry through clenched teeth, 'staying alive just to torment me and make my life difficult.' She threw the towel at Emma, 'Take it into your room and dress it. No time for breakfast, so blame it when you're hungry.'

Emma put an arm around Harry and half dragged him out of the bathroom into her bedroom, where she finished drying him and dressed him in clean shorts and a tee-shirt. They were the only clothes he had. Helen hadn't bought him socks and shoes or any warm clothing.

Harry continued to shake while Emma dressed him. 'It's alright, let's just stay quiet. I don't think she's going to hit us; she has to go to work.' Emma stroked her brother's back to try and soothe him. She could feel every bone in his spine and had counted his ribs before now. 'I'd better get dressed.' she kissed his cheek. 'It'll be ok,' she said and hugged him to her. He gently returned the hug.

Harry watched Emma and ceased shaking as she put on the clothes laid out the previous night. He loved her and knew she was his twin; she'd watched a programme on TV, explained it to him, and often said she loved him; he was special. However, Harry no longer spoke, but Emma didn't understand why and wished he did. She didn't know that the first and only time, he had said, 'Mommom,' in baby babble, Helen had smacked him hard across his face and said, 'Don't you ever call me that. I'm not your mother.' Emma had tried to get Harry to say Emma, but he hadn't even attempted it.

While the children were waiting to be told what to do, Helen took a bowl of hot soapy water, extracted the sleeping bag that Harry slept on and thrust it into a black bin bag and then washed the inside of the cupboard where his excrement covered hands had marked every surface he could reach. The only place he hadn't touched was the potty chair that shared his space which he was supposed to use and usually did.

Little bastard did this on purpose, Helen thought, trying not to breathe in through her nose. Even with some disinfectant in the water, the smell was appalling, and Helen gagged several times while she cleaned. She had twenty minutes to get to Hamza's by the time she'd slung Harry's clothing and her night attire into the washing machine and binned the sleeping bag. She quickly washed and dressed and, still seething, grabbed Harry, dragged him by his arm across the landing and thrust him into the still wet cupboard. 'I will kill you if you ever do that again,' she said coldly as she shut the doors together and tied the handles.

She turned to Emma. 'Come on; we need to go.'

'What about Harry's water?' Emma said and didn't move.

'He can bloody well go without; teach him a lesson. Now for Christ's sake, come on!'

Helen left the room, and Emma tapped on the cupboard door. 'I love you, Harry, see you later. Love you,' she whispered again and reluctantly followed her mother.

Harry lay down on the wet floor, and tears that he thought were all dried up trickled down his face onto the damp lino for a second. He could still smell his shit and gave a slight smile as he wiped his eyes and then his snotty nose on his wrist, then on his shorts. He didn't understand what being killed meant, but sometimes he wished that the woman, who hurt him and made him feel so bad, would carry out the threat she made frequently. But he knew Emma wanted him to stay with her, and perhaps being killed would take him away. He didn't want that to happen either. As he heard the front door shut, he felt his eyelids close, and he slept as he often did.

Before they left the house, Helen held Emma's hand. 'Now, not a word about this morning.' Her hand tightened its grip. 'Understand?'

'Yes, Mommy, I don't say anything. Will you give Harry some water when we get home, please?'

Although Emma didn't understand what she implied, Helen did. 'Of course, but he has to be punished, and so do you if you don't do what I say, my good girl. Harry isn't real; just remember that.'

'Yes, I will,' Emma said and sighed.

A couple of minutes later, she pushed open Amanda's door and bent to kiss her daughter goodbye, only to find Emma had already run gratefully inside, leaving her mother feeling irritated. Helen considered going in after her but instead hurried to the corner shop, where she was five minutes late. Hamza looked pointedly at his watch but said nothing as Helen hastily deposited her handbag just inside the stockroom, donned her overall and took her employer's place behind the counter.

30

The Corner Shop. *Tuesday 7th August 2012*

Hamza yawned. He had a headache but had shown his usual genial, cheerful face to the quaint lady who had popped in for a tin of cat food. He'd seen her many times before, and her purchase never varied. Neither did her attire. No matter the weather, she wore a straw hat over what was obviously a matted brown wig. The hat was adorned with plastic flowers around its brim and large enough to touch her small shoulders on both sides, where it met her faded green, chunky knitted cardigan. She wore a brown knee-length woollen skirt that had seen better days and thick beige tights that spilt over brown lace-ups. She was a Chatty Cathy and made him smile. He listened to her talk about her two Manx cats, who kept the mice from gnawing through boxes and eating her cereals. From what he could glean, it had happened once, but she behaved as though she had a plague of the little vermin as she called them.

Today he had listened patiently with one ear but was relieved when she eventually shuffled out, taking a faint smell of cats with her, and he was able to take a couple of pain killers. Two customers later, Hamza stood behind the counter and watched as the sky darkened dramatically and the heavens opened, pouring heavy rain which bounced off the paving slabs as if it were trying to return to the clouds which had produced the deluge. Thunder rumbled angrily, followed almost immediately by a flash of lightning which he saw reflected in the shop window of the dry cleaners opposite. For once, he didn't mind the freak storm, which he knew would keep customers away.

Hamza leaned his elbows on the counter and cupped his chin. Since Nazia had gone to Bangladesh, he'd been rushed off his feet, and Mrs Smith had undoubtedly not taken her place. He was finding her very off-putting. She rarely spoke to him or the customers if she could avoid doing so. He couldn't make up his mind if she wasn't a fast learner or if she was lazy. He'd spent so much time showing her the ropes that he found it quicker to do most jobs himself and leave her to just serve behind the counter. Not what he'd hoped for when he'd taken her on, and Hamza had considered finding someone else or asking Aleeza to help out again. But he knew Mrs Smith had a young daughter that Amanda was minding, and he couldn't bring himself to dismiss her.

Suddenly Hamza felt his spirits lift as one of his favourite people ran through the downpour with a raincoat over her head like a tent with its flaps open and burst into the shop. She held the door open, removed the wet, yellow waterproof, shook it vigorously outside, shut the door, and placed the coat over the back of a chair by the checkout.

Hamza beamed at Maja. 'You must be desperate to see me to brave the storm,' he teased.

'I was desperate to get away from Alek's temper. He's angry because our delivery of caster sugar hasn't arrived.'

Maja pulled a face which made Hamza laugh. 'I'd better buy some. Where about is it?' she said and smiled at the man who made her heart beat a little faster each time she saw him. She didn't understand the effect he had on her. He was friendly, good-looking, had a lovely smile, and always seemed pleased to see her, but these things didn't explain her guilt after each encounter. Or the number of times she pictured his face.

'How many bags do you need Maja, I'll get it for you?' Hamza said and came from behind the counter.

'Just two large, our delivery will be here tomorrow. It's just that Alek wants to bake tonight.'

Hamza watched Maja's generous mouth as she spoke. He had often felt disquiet about the number of times he'd imagined kissing her and running his hands along her arms to grip her hands in his. He invariably stopped his mind before it went further, but looking at her now with her long, blond hair mussed from where the coat had pulled across it, he longed to carry out his fantasy.

Trying to concentrate on the sugar, he brushed past her smelling her light perfume mixed with the rain and, picking up the bags, took them to the counter, where he packed them into a plastic carrier. Maja paid him, and as their hands touched, so did their eyes. Both quickly looked away. Then Hamza said something he'd never imagined before. 'I think you should stay and have a cup of coffee before braving the lightning again; I make good coffee.' He grinned but immediately regretted his foolishness, but to his surprise, Maja accepted.

Maja opened her mouth, the words no thank you on her lips, but what she said was, 'How thoughtful. Thank you, that would be lovely.'

158

Knowing the rain would keep people away, Hamza turned the sign to closed and dropped the latch. He invited Maja to follow him and led her to his living apartment, another first for him.

Maja had felt alarmed at her daring when she accepted Hamza's invitation, but she couldn't seem to stop herself. She wanted to get to know this man who was frequently in her thoughts. She followed him through the stockroom and genuinely admired the family photographs in gold frames covering one wall of their apartment. Hamza pointed out each family member, especially those who lived in and around Bangladesh. The pictures made her realise that Hamza and Nazia came from monied backgrounds. Both sets of parents lived in rural properties that looked well designed and maintained from the outside. Hamza spoke of them with pride.

Hamza gestured to a comfortable sofa and said, 'Won't you sit, Maja?' I'll make the coffee. Would you like a biscuit?'

Maja nodded. 'Yes please, then come and tell me more about yourself. I have just woken up to the fact that I know nothing about you in reality.'

'Oh, not a lot to tell, beautiful lady. Be comfortable; I will return.' Hamza disappeared into the small kitchen and found what he needed in the well-stocked cupboards, wondering what Nazia would say if she could see him and felt glad that she couldn't.

Maja leaned her head back against the red satin cushions and closed her eyes. She hadn't a clue why she had decided to have a drink with this man, but she reassured herself that it was all she had agreed to do, and she had no intention of letting their mutual attraction blossom. When Hamza returned, they talked for a while and drank the coffee from tiny cups. It tasted different to anything Maja was used to, but she enjoyed it, and Hamza told her how he made it. After the coffee had been drunk, even though Maja was determined not to be unfaithful to her husband, she found herself imagining becoming intimate with Hamza and felt her cheeks redden.

She knew he was thinking the same thing and said as she stood up and walked to the window, 'The rain has stopped, and I'd better get back. Alek will wonder what's taken me so long.'

'Thank you for keeping me company, beautiful lady. We must have coffee together again one day.' Hamza said as he too stood and led the way back into the shop. He opened the door, and Maja picked up her coat and left with the sugar. She didn't know whether to be glad or sorry that tea was all they had shared as she hurried through the puddles and went into the café.

Neither of them knew that someone else had been out in the rain, saw Hamza close the shop and take Maja past the counter. Pat Staples had needed bread and dashed to the shop for it under an umbrella. She'd returned home and told Eric she forgot what she went for and then tucked the secret, that only existed in her mind, away until she knew what she wanted to do with it.

31

8 *Littlebrook Terrace Wednesday 8th August 2012.*

'Lucy will have to find somewhere else to live, won't she, Ma? There's no room here for a baby,' George said out of the blue. He looked up and frowned, then continued to pack his rucksack, ready to go off for a couple of days biking with Ryan, who had a small tent.

Cathy handed him two pairs of shorts. 'No, she won't, and don't forget to change them,' she reminded him. 'And your socks.'

'Aww, Mom,' George tutted, 'I don't need reminding!'

'No, but you can be a dirty bugger sometimes. I do the washing, and I know things.' She laughed at her son's chagrined expression.

'Yes, ok, but where's the baby going to sleep? If it's a boy, a cot won't fit into our room,' George said and shoved the clean clothes into the overflowing bag.

'Don't be daft. The baby will sleep in with Lucy and Penny no matter what it is. Now come on, you'll have Ryan here soon, and I hope you've left room for some wash things. Are you planning on pitching the tent beside that stream again?'

'Dunno yet,' George said and rolled his eyes.

Cathy shrugged and left her son to it. As she went downstairs, the sound of her son's exasperation rang in her ears, making her smile.

The kitchen was deserted. David had gone to work, and Lewis had already been up, eaten, and was working on Robert's garden, ensuring he'd deadheaded and weeded so it would look perfect for when Robert arrived home. Robert had sent Cathy a message to say he'd be home at the weekend and would be bringing someone with him, so would she do some shopping.

As the sun beat down on his neck, Lewis dug the trowel into the dark, moist earth, speculating if Robert had a girlfriend and wondered what she would look like. Bet she'll be pretty, he thought and pictured a leggy blond that he'd seen in a magazine Lucy had left lying about the day before. Lucky devil, he thought and grinned to himself.

Cathy made herself a second cup of Nescafe, picked up her half-eaten piece of toast, which was now sagging in the middle and took a bite. She wasn't due at work until two o'clock but felt tempted to call in sick for the second time that week. The urge not to leave the house these days was becoming stronger. She felt secure in the home that she and David had struggled to buy and sometimes thought she wouldn't mind if she never saw its outside walls again.

Her indecision was giving her a headache. Should she risk getting sacked for lousy timekeeping or just stop being so silly and go to work? She didn't mind it when she was there, and it wasn't demanding, merely monotonous. Trying not to think, she meandered, toast in hand, into the conservatory and sat in the same chair from which she'd pulled Lucy when she was so upset.

The Child in the Window

The family had absorbed the news that a grandchild was on the way over the last four days, and Cathy had put it to the back of her mind. Now, as she cupped her hands around the blue, flowery patterned mug of coffee, feeling its warmth seep into her fingers, associated problems that needed to be dealt with weighed heavily. She agreed with David that children should be wanted and loved, and this one would be, but she knew it would be up to her to facilitate its place in the family.

Cathy tilted her head to one side and listened for sounds that would indicate Lucy and Penny making an appearance but could only hear George as he spoke to Ryan in the kitchen. Lazy bugs, she thought and decided to give them fifteen more minutes and call to them. She leaned back against the cushions and relaxed, deciding that she wouldn't skive off. They needed her income now more than ever. She looked up as George and Ryan joined her. Both handsome lads, she thought proudly as George came and kissed her cheek, followed by a smacker from Ryan on her other cheek.

'Ok, Mom, we're off now. Ryan says he'll phone you tomorrow but don't expect us to call every five minutes; the battery won't last.'

'I don't, and thanks, Ryan. I just need to know you haven't been captured by a Yeti in the woods.' When the laughter died down, Cathy continued. 'Seriously, take care and don't get separated, and don't trust strangers and---'

'Oh, Jeez, Mom, give over we'll be fine, see you on Friday for my birthday.' He grinned, and the lads followed each other into the garden where their bikes were ready and waiting.

Cathy watched as they began to wheel the laden vehicles past the shed towards the gate into the alley. Suddenly

George stopped and said something to Ryan, who held onto both bikes. He ran back to the window, pressing his nose against the glass until it became a caricature. Placing his hands around his head to shade his blue eyes, he peered in. George smiled at his mother's startled face and left lip imprints as he kissed the window. 'Love you,' he mouthed, then quickly turned and ran back to Ryan.

Cathy felt a slight pang of anxiety as she saw the gate close behind them, but she trusted them to be sensible and winged a brief plea to God, who she sometimes believed in, to keep them safe. Her mind turned to George's eighteenth birthday and the phone they had bought him as a surprise. She'd wanted to give it to him early, but David had disagreed. 'Better to wait until the family meal on Friday evening when everyone can see his face,' he'd said. When she thought about it, Cathy agreed. It wasn't often that any one of their children had been given such an expensive gift, and they knew George wouldn't have a clue that he would receive the present he had wished for many times. It would be brilliant for all of them to watch, she thought.

George knew they had booked a family table at The Old Joint Stock pub in town for his birthday treat, but Cathy felt they couldn't leave Ryan out, so he was included in the numbers. Lately, Cathy had begun to wonder if George and Ryan, who had been inseparable since they had been small boys, were gay and would always be together. No one in her family would mind, and no one would question either, so her thoughts stayed only with her.

Cathy felt her eyelids droop and allowed them to close, but seconds later, she heard herself give a loud snort which startled her back into reality. She reluctantly went to the bottom of the stairs and shouted, 'Lucy, Penny, get your bums down here, or there'll be no breakfast.'

The kitchen became a hive of activity not too many minutes later as the girls made their meal. 'Do you want some toast and a drink, Mom?' Lucy called to where Cathy remained seated in the conservatory.

'No thanks, love.' Then rapidly changing her mind, she called, 'Oh go on then and spread the butter right to the edges.'

Guiltily waiting for her second breakfast, Cathy recalled Saturday evening when the family had come together. It had been decided that Lucy would take a gap year and return to university after having the baby. She had agreed to find a job while her pregnancy allowed her to work. Cathy now found the thought of giving up her job and minding her grandchild while Lucy returned to obtain her degree, which would hopefully allow her to find a well-paid job, very appealing even if it meant them all having to go short for a while. She could wait, but meanwhile, she reached down the side of her chair and picked up her knitting bag.

At last, she thought and carefully extracted the bamboo pins sporting an inch of white ribbing, something worthwhile to get my fingers working. She smiled as she glanced at the pattern she'd found on Etsy. Her arms ached to hold her first grandchild. She wondered if it would be a boy or girl, and while her fingers flew over her stitches, her mind conjured possible names.

32

London *Friday 10th August 2012*

'Ooh, hang on, I have to pee.' Gilly gave a loud hiccup. She turned to Guy. 'Oops, sorry, pardon me, I've had too much wine.' Gilly giggled hysterically, crossed her legs, managed to stand and did a staggering run for the bathroom.

'You never apologise to me,' Robert called and laughed as he fetched both girls' coats from where they had spent the evening on the spare room bed.

'She never apologises to me either,' Steph said and grinned at Robert as he helped her on with her lightweight red, white and blue jacket. 'Come on, Gilly, hurry up the taxi's waiting; I'll make you pay more than half,' she called gaily.

Gilly returned moments later, still pulling her short skirt down and patting it in place. Guy stepped forward and helped her on with a similar jacket.

'Thank you, very nice man.' Gilly giggled, hiccupped again, then threw her arms around his neck and kissed his chin, which was as high as she could reach.

Guy laughed kindly. 'Thank you, very nice lady.' He strode to where Steph had just received a peck from Robert and kissed her gently on her cheek. 'Thank you for a lovely evening, very nice lady number two. Now come on, I'll escort you to your taxi.'

'We both will,' Robert said and held on to Gilly's elbow as they left the apartment.

When their friends were safely inside the taxi, Steph called, 'Our turn to cook for you next time.' She blew a kiss, and both men returned it as the cab drew away.

Guy linked arms with Robert and entered the foyer. He released him and said, 'Come on, I'll race you up the stairs and took off.'

By the time they reached the apartment, Robert was out of breath, but Guy looked like he'd been for a stroll.

'Alright, show off. I know you're fitter than me, and as you are, I think you should do the clearing up.'

'Oh, no, I cooked; we'll both clear up.'

Laughing, they entered the apartment. Robert locked the door and said, 'You know Guy, I've never been so happy. Thank you.'

Guy turned and took a step towards him. 'Me neither, we fit, don't we?' They kissed.

'We do, and thank you for how you were with Steph and Gilly. They have been such wonderful friends ever since I met them at a party six years ago.'

'Doesn't surprise me; they're sweet and also entertaining. I could stand seeing a lot of them.' He grinned. 'Mind you; I love it when we stay in on our own too.' He gave Robert a lascivious leer and nodded towards the bedroom.

'No, you sex maniac. We need to clear all this away.' He indicated several glasses and a couple of empty wine bottles.

'You bring the things in, and I'll load the dishwasher.' Robert said, pushing Guy gently towards the coffee table.

Guy laughed. 'Proper houseproud, aren't we?' he teased.

Robert grinned. You haven't forgotten I'm going to Birmingham tomorrow, have you? I can't face this lot in the morning.'

'No, I haven't.' Guy picked up the wine bottles. 'I'm going to miss you. It's bad enough when we have to work, but I shall be twiddling my thumbs when we could have been together.' He took the bottles into the kitchen, and Robert fluffed the turquoise cushions that matched the ultra-modern sofa.

Guy returned and picked up the glasses between his long slim fingers. Robert looked up and gazed tenderly at this man he knew he loved as he'd never loved anyone before. 'Well, come with me then,' he said, expecting Guy to refuse.

Guy followed him into the kitchen and watched as Robert scraped plates into the bin and then filled the washer. 'I thought you were still in the closet in Birmingham. Have you ever taken anyone home with you before?'

Robert felt as though the air between them had somehow become electrified as he slowly shook his head. 'No, I never wanted to. I haven't cared enough about anyone to want to share my turf with them.' He stood still, his breathing shallow, a dishwasher tablet held tightly in his curled hand.

'Don't you mind what your friends and neighbours would say? You must have kept your proclivity a secret,' Guy said.

Robert shrugged. 'No one who knows and cares about me will say anything. I've never lied about my personal life, but I've never had to.' Robert filled the kettle from the hot water tap as Guy spooned drinking chocolate into two squat mugs.

'Oh.'

'Now you mention it,' Robert scratched the stubble that was putting in an appearance on his chin, 'I suppose it is peculiar. I don't think even Amanda; I've told you she's like my grandmother, has ever asked me when I'm going to get married.' He paused then said, 'Oh, wait a minute, Hamza, the bloke who runs the corner shop, did ask once when I was going to settle down, but he was just passing the time of day. Anyway, I don't care what anyone thinks or says. I would like you to come and see where I was born and keep me company. I hate being apart from you now.' He poured hot water into the mugs, stirred vigorously, and they took them through to the sitting room.

'I know it's dark, but let's sit out; it's warm enough,' Guy said.

When they settled on the balcony watching life-size ants in the street below, Guy said, 'Alright, I'll come with you, but you aren't planning to return until next Wednesday. I don't know if I'll be able to stay that long, but I'll try.'

'That's great,' Robert grinned and sipped the cocoa, mirroring Guy. 'Are you ever going to be able to tell me what you do, Guy?' he asked in a solemn voice.

'Probably not, it's classified, and it wouldn't be in your best interests. I care about you too much to put you in danger.'

Robert reached across the gap between the two chairs and placed his free hand on Guy's knee. He looked towards the high building opposite. 'You know I love you, don't you, Guy?'

Guy smiled. 'I love you too,' he said sincerely, 'we're lucky at our ages to have found each other.' He squeezed Robert's hand. 'Now come on, drink up and let's get some sleep.'

'Sleep?' Robert laughed as he stood up.

'Yes, sleep. We have a long drive in the morning, and we have to go to my place and pick up some more clothes first.'

Robert had been to the small flat where Guy lived and wondered as he undressed if it was time to suggest moving in together. On the two occasions when he had shared, it had been at the other person's request, and as time had moved on, he realised they had been running away from something, not to something. Guy was different. They had only been together for just over a month, but he knew he was the one. Once the thought was in his head, Robert couldn't budge it; he mulled it over and over. Then just before they slept, he said, 'Do you think it's daft keeping two places going when you tend to stay here even when I'm working? What about moving in with me?'

Guy was silent for at least a minute, then he said. 'I've never shared my space with anyone permanently and always had a bolt hole, so to speak. Would it work?'

'I think, in fact, I have no doubt it would. Say yes and make me happier than I am this minute.'

'Yes, now go to sleep. Plenty of time to talk about it tomorrow.' He turned away, then turned back to face Robert, smiled lazily and said again, 'I love you, and I have never told anyone that before.' He pulled the top sheet up over his exposed shoulder, closed his eyes and slept almost instantaneously.

Robert felt elated. He watched Guy as his muscles relaxed when sleep claimed him. It took him much longer before he allowed his eyes to close.

33

***10** Littlebrook Terrace Saturday 11th August.*

'I say, great garden you've got here,' Guy said as they approached Robert's house from the alleyway.

'Thanks, but I can't take the credit. It's mainly down to Lewis next door, and I pay him to look after all three of the gardens on the terrace.' Robert laughed ruefully. 'He's supposed to be helped by his older brother, George, but I'm sure his input is negligible. He's due to start Uni next month, and he's more than a little preoccupied with getting as much sleep as possible.'

Robert unlocked the door and inhaled deeply through his nose as they entered the conservatory. Thanks, Cathy, he thought as the aroma of lavender polish and air spray gave credence to her thoughtfulness. He'd asked her to shop, but he knew she would also ensure the house was aired and clean. A memory of the time he returned home after a month in London and had forgotten to empty the bins before he left prodded him. He sometimes had a laugh with Cathy about the awful stench that greeted him on that occasion. Since then, Cathy had never let him down. If he sent her a text, she made sure he would be comfortable.

The Child in the Window

After dropping his suitcase on the floor in the hallway, Robert went into the kitchen, and Guy followed suit. They were both parched, and Robert immediately filled the kettle. He turned to Guy. 'Look, I'm not showing you around; make yourself at home and go where you please. If you take your case upstairs,' he laughed, 'will you please take mine an' all?'

'An' all, an' all.' Guy choked with laughter. 'I see, back in Brum and speaking Brummy talk, eh?'

'Shut it,' Robert said, joining in his person's teasing.

Guy transported both cases while Robert made coffee and toast, which they took into the sitting room.

Guy gazed around before he sat. 'Bit different to the apartment, he pictured the glass and stainless steel in London, but cosy. A family home. Bet you haven't changed a thing since your parents passed, have you?'

'Nothing, I just haven't been able to force myself to. I've thought about selling up and moving to London, but no go. Perhaps now I might, but I worry about Amanda.' Robert frowned.

Guy looked thoughtful. 'Well, let's face it, there's no need to sell up, is there? From what you've told me, you'd still want to return here frequently while Amanda's alive, wouldn't you? And the properties give you a good income, don't they?'

'Mmm, yes they do, and you're right about Amanda,' Robert's brow furrowed even further, 'but I'd always want to be in London while you're there.'

'And I wouldn't want it any other way, but neither of us can be in London every day, can we?' Guy didn't wait for an answer. 'And it's only two and a half hours to get here, and at least we'll have somewhere to stay.'

'You mean you'll always come with me?' Robert's face lit up. Had he heard right?

Guy sighed. 'Haven't you cottoned on yet? You aren't the only one who wants to spend all our free time together. Twenty-four seven wouldn't be long enough. Mind you; it's only because you're good in bed.' He laughed briefly. 'Actually, I'm tired of being lonely.' He laughed uproariously at the incredulous expression on Robert's face. A delighted smile had replaced his frown, lifting his often-serious countenance. Guy's laughter died away as he said, 'You do realise though that I could be summoned back to work at a moment's notice, and I'd have to go. I'd have no option; I'd be fetched to wherever I was needed.' Guy looked more solemn than Robert had ever seen him except when he'd apologized after their first night together.

Robert studied his lovers face. 'Sure you can't tell me what you do?'

'Fraid not, love.' He shrugged and held out his hand's palms up. 'Let's just get on with our lives and take our happiness while we can, eh?'

Robert could feel a lump forming in his throat, a precursor to crying. Guy picked up the signals, reached across and slapped Robert's arm, just enough to make him smile instead. He then gestured around the sitting room. 'How about we come here every chance we get for a while, and I help you to modernise a bit?'

Robert nodded and took a deep breath.

'I'd also like to get to know the wonderful woman who competes with me for your attention.' He raised his eyebrows. 'Are we visiting her today? She knows you're here, doesn't she?'

Robert cleared his throat. 'She knows you're here too, and so does Cathy next door. They'll be curious as to who you are.' He looked puzzled. 'Strange, I don't know how to introduce you,' he laughed, 'I've never done it before. Boyfriend sounds childish, doesn't it? And lover a bit coarse.'

Guy laughed.

'Come on, help me out here,' Robert said and felt his cheeks redden.

Guy laughed even louder, stood up and took Robert in his arms. 'Don't sweat the small stuff. Partner sounds just fine because that's what I am at the moment. You are my partner, and I am yours. Now, how about we….'

Robert felt overwhelmed. Hearing Guy offer things that he'd wanted for a very long time made him feel like doing something impractical and crazy right at that moment. Images of a spaceship or a balloon ride over the Grand Canyon flitted in and out of his mind. He shook his head and stepped away from the person he never wanted to be more than a few feet apart from for the rest of his life. 'I love you, and I'm going to phone Manda and tell her I'm bringing you with me. I want her to know and love you too,' he said, interrupting Guy mid-sentence.

'Go ahead; I really want to meet her.'

Half an hour later, they walked in to find Amanda in her chair, waiting to see her favourite person in the world and the man he wanted her to meet. Henry growled a warning to the stranger, but it quickly subsided as he greeted Robert excitedly. Robert stroked him, ruffled up his soft fur vigorously, knowing Henry loved it, and then said firmly, 'Go and lie down.' Henry retired to the side of Amanda's chair, keeping a watchful eye on Guy.

'Hello, my darling,' Amanda said as Robert bent to kiss her cheek.

He took her face between his hands and studied it intently. 'You look well,' he said as they hugged.

'And who's this handsome man you've brought to see me? We like to see new people don't we, Henry?' Henry's tail thumped several times on the floor.

Guy stepped forward and took Amanda's thin hand in his strong, tanned one. 'I've heard a lot about you, and it's lovely to meet you at last.'

'Well.' She cocked her head and gave Robert a quizzical look, 'I've heard nothing about you, so you'd better sit down because I have a feeling we are going to see more of each other.'

Guy sat, then Robert perched by his side on the arm of the chair and said, 'This is Guy, Manda, and yes, you'll be seeing more of him. I hope you'll grow to love each other as much as I love the both of you.' He opened his mouth as if to speak again but snapped it shut as Emma suddenly appeared from where she'd been hiding behind Amanda's seat, making both the men give an involuntary start.

Guy recovered quickly. 'Hello there, little girl; where did you come from?'

'This is Emma, Mrs Smith's little girl who I mind weekly when her mommy's at work. And today, her mommy has gone shopping. She'll be back soon, but we're in no hurry, are we, Emma?' Amanda said as Emma crouched beside Henry with her arm draped protectively over his back. 'Do you think you could say hello to these two very nice men? I used to mind Robert too when he was a little boy.'

The Child in the Window

Emma peered at Robert from behind a handful of Henry's fur. 'Hello, I love Amanda and Henry. Do you love Amanda and Henry?'

'Yes, I do,' Robert said.

'And I'm sure I will, too,' Guy said.

Emma shot back into her hiding place as a knock came at Amanda's front door.

'Oh dear, is it a bad time for us to be here, Manda?' Robert said.

'No, it'll be Helen, Emma's mother, she won't stay. Will you let her in, Robert?'

'Hey, it's your Mommy,' Guy called softly to Emma.

Robert returned with Helen. 'I'm just about to make a drink, Helen, would you like one? We've just met your beautiful daughter.'

'No, thank you,' Helen said stiffly. 'Come on out, Emma, I want to get home; I've got a lot to do.'

Emma obediently came to her mother's side and stood waiting to leave. 'Thank you for looking after her again, Mrs Pierce. I'll bring her back on Monday if that's ok?' She glanced at Robert and Guy, her expression a puzzled frown, but she didn't ask who they were, and no introductions were made.

'Of course,' Amanda said and gave a slight smile. 'Bye, bye Emma, see you on Monday.' Henry whined and heaved himself up to lick Emma's hand. Emma did nothing. Merely walked out with her mother. Robert watched from the doorstep as Helen hurried home with her seemingly reluctant daughter, trying to keep up. Funny she didn't even say hello to Guy or me, Robert thought, then he realised that she wouldn't have known him. They'd never met; even so, her behaviour was a little strange, bordering on rude, in his opinion, but he also wondered why he hadn't introduced himself.

Robert returned just as Guy spoke. 'My word, she seems a little standoffish. Is she always like that?' Guy asked Amanda.'

'I'm afraid she is, but let's talk about you and Robert.' Both men laughed.

'I thought we'd surprise you,' Robert said with a twinkle.

'Hmm, that's what you think; this is no surprise at all, is it Henry? Why don't you make that drink and then tell me all about it?' Amanda beamed at them both.

34

10 *Littlebrook Terrace Sunday 12th August 2012*

Being careful not to wake Guy, Robert slid out of bed and went to the bathroom. When he returned, Guy hadn't moved. Rather than risk disturbing him, Robert settled in the faded, chintz-covered easy chair next to the bed and became deep in thought.

His mind flitted about; so many things had happened in such a short space of time. He thought about how happy he was to be with the mystery man who occasionally gave tiny snores. He found it difficult to believe they had met just over a month ago and now had committed to spending the rest of their lives together. Even in his most outlandish dreams, Robert hadn't expected to fall so deeply in love with anyone and have that love returned.

He looked at the mound of bedclothes where a tuft of blond hair protruded above the green and white striped duvet. Robert desperately wanted Guy to wake just to see his face, which invariably wore a smile when their eyes touched. He tried concentrating hard, willing this to happen, but he grinned and gave up after a few moments.

His thoughts turned to Amanda and the little girl that she minded. He'd been surprised initially and concerned that the task would be too much for her. However, after hearing Amanda say that she needed to help Emma and why she felt she should, he decided to keep an eye on the situation and help where he could. Amanda took pains to explain that Emma was a well behaved, obedient child who seemed more than shy. She had gone on to say that it had taken two weeks before Emma uttered one word other than to her mother, and even now, rarely spoke. Robert had thought that Amanda seemed upset and asked why she thought that was. Amanda thought for a second, then told Robert that Emma seemed to be afraid and had asked her not to tell her mother that she had said anything.

'For all the years I was a teacher, Amanda added, I was seldom so concerned about a child as I am about Emma. My instincts tell me that something is wrong, but I can't quite put my finger on it.'

Robert knew that Amanda wouldn't exaggerate and now also felt concerned. He knew nothing about the woman he'd let number nine to and, thinking that perhaps he needed to delve a little, decided to see what he could find on his laptop.

He shifted position and crossed his long legs at his knees as he remembered how the rest of that afternoon had fled while he taught his teacher how to use her new phone. She'd quickly proved her mind could still learn new things, something she'd been doubtful about, and Robert felt proud of her. His meandering thoughts were interrupted as Guy turned over, farted inelegantly and woke himself up. His hand reached over and swept across where Robert slept; finding only emptiness, Guy sat up and looked around the room.

'Morning, lazy bones,' Robert said and grinned.

Guy smiled roguishly and patted the crumpled sheet. 'Come back to bed, pleeese.'

'Not a chance. I'm going to shower, and then we have to introduce you to Cathy and enjoy our day. I'd like to take us all out to lunch at the Crown; they do a carvery on a Sunday. What d'you think?'

Guy flung the duvet aside, stretched and sat on the side of the bed. 'Sounds like a plan. I'll race you to the shower,' he said. He moved quickly, making the gold-coloured ingot shape, that he never took off, bounce low down on his chest

Robert didn't move, merely admired Guy's lean, muscled body as he loped provocatively past and then followed him.

It was an hour later before breakfast was on the menu, and Robert invited Cathy, David and their brood to lunch, making it clear it was his treat. He could hear Cathy as she relayed the invitation to David. And felt even more warmth towards the family he'd always lived next door to when David enthusiastically replied that, of course, he wanted to come and he'd work later in the afternoon. Robert hoped that revealing his sexuality and introducing Guy to them all wouldn't have any adverse outcome. He wasn't expecting any from these people he'd known and loved seemingly forever. He'd never heard any of them utter a bigoted idea, but he supposed it had been a long while since he'd spent time with the younger ones. Nevertheless, they were David and Cathy's children and hopefully, their parents' views of the world had been passed down.

Amanda was waiting dressed in a blue and white summery suit and had put on eyeshadow and lipstick when he called around for her. She rarely went out and was feeling almost breathless with excitement. 'Now you be good and don't make any noise; I'll be back soon,' she said to Henry. Robert held onto her arm and pulled the back door shut, hearing the clunk as it locked.

'You are good to me, Robert,' she said as he helped her to the alley where he'd parked the car close to her back gate.

'Rubbish, it's no more than I should be. You are very precious, Manda, and you look lovely,' he said and assisted her into the front seat. Guy was sitting in the back and leaned forward to help Amanda with her seat belt. As it clicked into place, she patted his hand gratefully. He kissed his fingertips and touched them to her lined cheek.

The pub was a fifteen-minute drive from the city and nestled among a beautiful rural landscape in Staffordshire. Green hills gave way to densely wooded areas, and Robert fleetingly thought he would like to live somewhere close by and wake each morning to such a view.

When they arrived at the black and white pub, it was to find Cathy's family had beaten them to it and were seated in the outside waiting area drinking in the hills that seemed to shimmer variegated greens and yellows in the bright sunshine.

Robert was pleased that his request for a table as near the serving area as possible had been accommodated. Once Amanda was seated comfortably on the bench seat behind a country-style wooden table, the middle-aged waitress, who reminded Cathy of the TV character Mrs Overall, arrived slowly and took their order.

'Shall I get yours for you, Manda?' Robert asked.

'Yes, please, but don't overdo it, Robert love.'

'Will you get mine, and I'll stay with Manda,' Penny said to her mom, who nodded.

The Child in the Window

When everyone had their food and began to eat, the waitress brought their drinks, spilling a considerable amount into the tray. Cathy grinned and refused to tell anyone why. Everyone began to eat, and Cathy raised her eyebrows at how much food both George and Lewis had piled onto their plates. 'You've gone a bit wild, haven't you, lads? Don't I feed you enough at home?' The boys looked a trifle sheepish but tucked into their meal, which was swimming in thick dark gravy.

Moments later, Cathy winked at Robert and said, 'Are you going to introduce us to this handsome young man then Robert?'

Robert smiled. 'Of course.' He reached across the table and deliberately stole a small roast potato from Guy's plate, popped it in his mouth, chewed and said, 'This is Guy Meredith, my partner.'

Guy laughed at the expression on George and Lewis's faces as they stared at him. Both had stopped eating and gawped with their mouths open. He couldn't tell whether Roberts's actions or his words surprised them.

George's face had taken on the colour of the rare slice of beef on his plate as he turned to Robert. 'You mean you're gay?' he sputtered.

'Hey, calm down,' David said and smiled at his eldest son, 'it's not exactly news, is it?'

Cathy laughed. 'Anything you want to tell us, my son?'

George's face was now scarlet as he shook his head and shoved Lewis, who had sniggered, almost making him fall from his seat.

'Watch it,' Lewis growled, his voice had only recently broken, and its timbre wasn't too steady.

'Enough!' David leaned forward and looked at the boys with a frown on his usually benign face.

Cathy turned to Guy. 'Well, welcome to our world Guy, I must say you're a lovely addition.'

Guy grinned cheekily at her and blew her a kiss. 'Now, let's get on with our meal, shall we?' he said without any trace of embarrassment.

After a few moments of silence broken by chewing sounds, the group chatter turned to generalities. Robert was inwardly mocking himself for thinking that he had managed to keep his lifestyle private until now. He wondered how many others of his friends and neighbours had always considered him gay and thought it was possibly or perhaps probably most of them.

His thoughts were interrupted as David said, 'When are you going back to London?'

'Wednesday, I have to work next weekend.' Robert said and smiled at Guy.

'What about you Guy, what line of work are you in?' David asked.

Robert immediately piped up, 'Guy works for the government but can't say which department, so don't ask.'

'Oo-er sounds funny. Is it spying?' Lucy said, her eyes twinkling.

Guy twinkled right back at her. 'Well, if it is, I couldn't say, could I?' He winked.

'Is it like James Bond?' Lewis asked, his eyes wide.

'Ok, enough already. Tell me how you're doing with the gardening? Guy thought mine looked great, and I told him you do it,' Robert said.

Easily distracted to talk about his favourite subject Lewis gave them a gardening lesson. Suddenly, Lucy yawned and said, 'Has Mom told you I'm having a baby, Robert?'

'Well, congratulations. Does anyone else have any more surprises?' Everyone laughed. 'Ok, tell me about this baby, and keep me in mind as a Godparent,' Robert said as the waitress cleared away the plates.

'Me too,' Guy said with a smile, 'but I'd like ice cream right now.' He looked around the table. 'Anyone else?'

35

8 Littlebrook Terrace Sunday 12th August 2012

'Can I go to see Bethany, Mom?' Penny asked the minute they returned from lunch at The Crown.

Cathy hesitated. 'We...ll, yes, I suppose but only for an hour mind. You promised to help me with the ironing. I don't know where it comes from, but there's a mountain again, and I can't stand long enough to do it all, you know.' Cathy collapsed onto the sofa and tucked her legs up, with a heartfelt sigh.

'Can't Lucy help? Why's she disappeared to the bathroom again? She went just before we left the pub.' Penny frowned.

'I told her to have a lie-down; her back's aching again. Anyway, you're much better at ironing than she is.'

'Oh, whoopee do. I almost wish you hadn't taught me.' Penny laughed as her mother pulled a hurt face, 'no, I don't mean that. I'll be back soon. I just want to tell Bethany something.'

'You can tell Lily too while you're at it,' Cathy called after her daughter's disappearing form.

Penny put her head back around the door frame. 'What do you mean? How d'you know what I want to tell Bethany?' What can I tell Lily too?'

Cathy laughed. 'I'm your mother, and I know you can't wait to tell Bethany about your meal and Robert.'

'Oh, Mom!' Penny's cheeks glowed, and she rolled her eyes as she disappeared again, shutting the door quietly behind her.

She hurried across the pavement, knowing she would be first for once having something interesting to relate to her friend. Usually, George managed to tell Ryan any news, good or bad, before she had a chance to shine, but not this time. After seeing Amanda safely home, Robert and Guy invited George and Lewis round as Robert had said during lunch that he had a present for George's birthday that he'd missed. When Robert first began his flying career, he had bought a silver model of Concorde that George had coveted since he was six years old. Robert considered that George was now old enough to look after it and felt he could part with it. Penny didn't exactly want the plane, but sometimes she felt as though she wasn't as important as her older siblings, and this was one of those times.

As soon as she and Bethany were alone in Bethany's bedroom, Penny could contain herself no longer. 'You'll never guess what,' she said excitedly.

Bethany carefully replaced the red pencil that she'd been using to colour a rose petal in her book into its space in the plastic sleeve and faced her friend expectantly. 'What? What? You look fit to burst,' she said. Penny's excitement was infectious.

'It's Robert,' Penny blurted out, 'he's gay, and his boyfriend is old but very good looking and very sexy.' As the words left her mouth, Penny felt her elation go with them. She was confused and wanted to amaze Bethany, but perhaps it was a secret she should have kept to herself.

'Oh, really, have you met him then?' Bethany said wide-eyed.

Penny wanted to claw back what she'd just told Bethany until suddenly she remembered her mother saying that she should tell Lily too. She proceeded to relate everything that had happened at their momentous lunch.

When Penny finished talking, having enjoyed all the oohing and aahing that her friend interjected, she was gratified to know she'd achieved her aim when Bethany said, 'Come on, let's tell Mom before Ryan does.'

The girls raced downstairs and went to find Lily, who was reading a Stephen King book in the garden hammock, enjoying the only sunshine for a couple of days. In her haste to tell her tale, Bethany tripped as she stepped from the conservatory onto the decking and skinned her knees exposed below her short shorts. 'Fucking hell,' she exclaimed as she surveyed the abrasions giving her more of her mother's attention than she required.

'Bethany, mind your language!' Lily reprimanded her. 'Are you alright?'

'Sorry, Mom, yes I am, but I wanted to tell you about Robert.'

Penny hung back a little behind Bethany just out of Lily's line of vision. 'Is it something Penny's told you? Where is she?' Lily said.

Penny stepped forward. 'Yes, Lily, I told her about our lunch.'

'Yes, and about Robert being gay,' Bethany said as she gently dabbed at her knees with a somewhat grubby tissue Lily had been using as a bookmark.

'Oh, for goodness sake, go in and wash those cuts and put some Germolene on them. I don't want you getting tetanus,' Lily said.

Bethany felt disappointed at her mother's lack of reaction to her news and stepped back into the conservatory. Penny started to follow Bethany, but Lily said, 'No, stay here, Penny and tell me what you've said to Bethany about Robert. Come and sit here.' She patted the end of the hammock, and Penny obediently but cautiously sat where Lily said.

'If you put your feet on the other side of mine, we can swing a bit,' Lily instructed. Penny did so, and then Lily said, 'Ok, what's all this about Robert being gay?'

With Rosy cheeks, Penny repeated what she'd told Bethany, but she was nonplussed when Lily merely said, 'Nice looking then is he; this man called Guy?' and proceeded to move her hand on the grass, making the hammock swing gently.

'Yes, and he speaks nicely, and he's funny and kind. I think they love each other.' Penny said simply, 'Do you think they'll get married?'

'Well, if he's as nice as you say, then perhaps they may be able to one day, but it would be illegal right now. I suppose they could have a Civil Ceremony, which is very similar. Let's wait and see. I would love to see Robert settled down happily, and I think everyone who knows him will be happy for him.' She stopped swinging and picked up her book. 'Now go and find my daughter and see if she's stopped bleeding. Oh, and will you pass me my phone from the table; I want to ring Rita.'

Lily took the phone and began to press buttons as Penny re-entered the house.

'You busy? Good, pop round. I want to talk to you about something. I'd come round to you, but I'm not fit to be seen.' Lily listened, then, 'No, leave her with Steven, it's not for her ears.'

36

***10** Littlebrook Terrace Sunday 12th August 2012*

Robert chewed his bottom lip as George proudly carried his present home. He wasn't anxious; he knew George would cherish the model of Concord as much as he had; nevertheless, he felt a slight sense of loss.

'You old softy. Why did you part with it? I bet George wasn't expecting you to give it to him.' Guy smiled sympathetically, although he had little empathy with the need for possessions. The rule in his house was to share and show you care. He'd been given the usual birthday and Christmas gifts from his parents and close relatives, but his two younger brothers had made short work of them. Being the eldest, he had no option but to go along with it. The boys had subsequently destroyed a Canon digital camera, which he loved, and other small gifts. But the final straw which led to his lack of materialism was when Ryland, who was eight, had taken his yellow Chopper out against his wishes and returned home without it. It was never found. Guy now owned very little of value and liked it that way. However, his bank balance was more than healthy, and he'd come to terms with his losses, both animate and inanimate.

'Oh, I know, but I have moved on. I think George will get more pleasure from that plane than I ever did.' Robert flopped into a chair. 'Nice afternoon?'

'Enjoyable. They're an entertaining bunch, your friends, and I could love Amanda.' Guy smiled. 'Didn't seem to faze anyone very much introducing me as your partner, did it? How d'you feel now you don't have to hide anything from them?'

'Made me wonder if Mom and Dad knew. I wish I'd been able to talk with them about it.' Robert sighed. 'I never could, though. Sad.'

After a long minute, Guy said, 'I know it's fanciful, but I sometimes feel their ghosts are here, especially by their picture in the hallway. Perhaps they did know and would be glad you're happy here with me. It's not a spooky feeling, though; I feel welcomed.'

Robert's jaw dropped. 'I feel them too, and it's one reason why I can't sell up. You understand?'

'Mmm, I think so. Do you think they would mind if we modernised?' Guy said.

'No, I think it's a great idea, and they were both so kind. Let's do it. We'll make a list.' Robert fetched a pen and writing pad, yellowed around its edges, from a sideboard drawer. 'Don't think this has seen the light of day since I was at University,' he said and grinned.

'Ok, but I'm going to make a drink and a sandwich first. I don't want to go out again to eat. Would you like coffee, tea or a beer?' Guy asked as he did a type of handspring out of the chair, landing lightly on his feet, making Robert laugh.

'Show off,' Robert said and blew Guy a kiss. 'Coffee and a cheese and ham sandwich sound good. Then an early night? I want to show you around town tomorrow and introduce you to Hurst Street.' Robert winked.

Guy did a mini cartwheel as he left the room. Robert chased after him to help, but the meal took longer as a consequence.

After they'd eaten, the rest of the evening flew by as they discussed in detail how they would like the kitchen to look, agreeing on most of the major alterations.

'What about the bathroom?' Guy said and looked at his watch. 'How on earth did it get to be nine o'clock? I want a shower before bed; come and join me?'

'Ok, I'll deal with these.' Robert carried the crockery into the kitchen and then climbed the stairs.

It was an hour later, as Robert said he'd like to get rid of the bath and have a walk-in shower, that Guy fell asleep. Robert smiled indulgently and shortly afterwards followed suit. Thinking how little he knew about this person sharing his bed.

'Oh, my God, what's the matter?!' Robert exclaimed as he woke to Guy's hand shaking him none too gently.

'I have to phone,' Guy said as he perched on the side of the bed, picked up his mobile and punched in two numbers, listened for a moment and then said, 'Right, fifteen minutes. I'll be there.' He snapped the phone shut and headed for the bathroom. 'Where's Pendray Park?' He called to a speechless Robert as he emptied his bladder.

No longer groggy with sleep, Robert swung his feet out of bed. 'Five minutes along Singerbrook Road; why?' He answered, then watched, feeling ineffectual as Guy hurriedly pulled on yesterday's clothes.

'I need to get there quickly. Will you show me?'

'Now?' Robert said as he stepped into his boxers and went to relieve himself following Guy's example.

'Yes, I'm sorry, but I don't have much time. I told you this could happen.' Guy said as Robert dressed.

'What about your clothes and toiletries?' Robert said.

Guy checked the pocket of his suit jacket, pulled out his passport and some papers, then stuffed them back inside. 'I don't have time. I'll see you back in London. Will you bring my things with you?'

'Of course. Come on; it'll be quicker if we walk.' Robert said as he followed Guy into the night and shivered as the cool air hit him. 'Is that all you can tell me? Why the park?'

'They're picking me up there and will have everything I need, as always.' Guy chuckled. 'Even a toothbrush.'

After five minutes of brisk walking along deserted roads lit only by an occasional streetlight, Robert led the way into the car park expecting to see a waiting car, but there was no sign of one.

'Ok, where's your lift then? I thought they said fifteen minutes?' Robert peered round as though expecting a car to appear from the nearby wooded area.

'This is the car park. Where's the football pitch?' Guy gave Robert a quizzical look which he could only just see.

Robert gestured. 'Over there behind the line of trees.'

Guy sped off in the right direction, and Robert quickly caught up with him, wondering if it was possible that he was being hooked up in a joke. 'How did you know to make a phone call?' Robert asked in a suspicious voice.

Guy stopped and faced Robert. He showed him the ingot shape that he pulled up from between his nipples and said, 'This, it vibrates strongly, and I always respond when it goes off, even from a deep sleep.'

The Child in the Window

'This isn't a joke then?' Robert held onto Guy's hand.

Guy shook his head. 'No, I wouldn't do that to you. I've told you I love you, and believe me, if I didn't have to go, I wouldn't.' He drew Robert into an embrace and kissed him passionately as an area near the middle of the football pitch became lit from above. Moments later, they heard the whoosh of propeller blades and smelled kerosine as a small black helicopter landed several feet from where they stood. Robert screwed his eyes shut and then opened them after thinking for a second that he might be dreaming. The all too familiar smell was still assaulting his nostrils. This was no dream.

Guy squeezed the top of Robert's arm. 'I have to go, look after yourself. I love you. See you soon.'

'I love you too. Stay safe and come back to me.' Robert said quickly as Guy took off at a run across the yellowing, parched grass area and was greeted by a man in a suit who stepped down from the aircraft. No sooner had they boarded, the door closed, and the helicopter took off, banking sharply as it rose.

Robert looked carefully to see if he could spot a distinguishing decal or writing, but there was nothing to interrupt the shiny black expanse. He turned away, spirits flagging and began to walk home, wondering who he had fallen for and whether he would ever see him again. The thought brought a panicky feeling into his chest and a lump to his throat. He couldn't bear the thought of losing him.

37

The Corner Shop, *Thursday 16th August 2012*

Hamza stood in front of the bevelled mirror over the white sink in his bathroom. He snipped the last couple of hairs from his beard that he'd just patiently trimmed, patted his face dry and picked a couple of strands of lint from his bushy eyebrows.

He usually only glanced at his face, but today was different. It was his forty-sixth birthday, and he was feeling old. He knew it was foolish, but he felt sorry for himself as neither his wife nor his children were there to help him celebrate. He shrugged his broad shoulders, turned away from his miserable image, picked up his laundry, and hurried to get on with mundane tasks, remembering it was stock check and ordering day.

Two coffees later, his usually positive character asserted itself, and he hummed a tune he'd heard the previous evening on the radio, which he kept behind the shop counter. It had stuck in his brain, and he continued to hum it on and off all day. He booted up his computer and, birthday or not, knowing the shop opened in about an hour, got busy with ordering stock.

The Child in the Window

A picture of his uncle Omar, his mother's brother, entered his mind as he checked the stock lists. Omar had loaned him the money to come to Britain and open the shop, and today would see the last repayment transferred into his uncle's account. The thought brought Hamza to count his many blessings and cease to be concerned about his appearance or things he could not affect, like missing his loved ones. He remembered that Aleeza and her husband had phoned to say they would be visiting at the weekend. The twins' birthday was the next week, and she wanted them to celebrate with a meal at a posh restaurant on Broad Street. Hamza had agreed to shut the shop early. He knew that Aleeza missed her twin and had phoned and told Ramis that he would pay for his flight home for a few days, but he'd declined. Hamza wished his son to learn more of his heritage before he insisted he come home, and his parents wanted him to stay longer, so Hamza complied with their wishes. However, perhaps in another few months, he should return as he needed to learn the business that he would inherit.

Hamza had no thought that Ramis might have other ideas. He'd worked long hours to ensure his son's future, and Ramis knew his father's plans for him. All will be well was Hamza's final, personal thought as he put everything aside to concentrate on business matters.

The day was busy, and it was nine-forty in the evening when Hamza had a chance to open a tin of curry and boil some rice. Not a meal he was looking forward to, but it was quick, and he was hungry. He ate at a small table with an intricately carved pattern chiselled into the brass top, which could be removed and used as a rather large tray.

As soon as the hungry lion in his belly ceased to roar, he opened his birthday cards and family letters. He was gratified and touched that many of his customers had sent greetings to him. He opened each one and read carefully, but by the time he began to read Nazia's letter, he felt sad and put it to read later in bed.

He moved the table aside, stretched his long legs out in front of him, picked up the TV remote and looked for something to entertain and take his mind off himself. He caught the tail end of John Bishop's *Britain* then began seeing but not watching the BBC news. He heard a tapping sound, turned the volume down with the remote and cocked his head to one side, unsure if the noise was on the screen or the shop door. It came again. He turned the TV off and looked out of the window, then smiled as he could see Maja, who had stepped away from the shop and was looking up. She waved and held a round plastic container up so he could see.

He waved back, and his heartbeat revved as he gave a thumbs-up signal and hurried downstairs and through the shop. As he opened the door, Maja stepped forward and quietly sang happy birthday to him. 'I brought you a birthday cake I baked especially for you,' she said and smiled lazily.

'Come in, come in, and thank you. I was just thinking of going to bed,' Hamza said and then laughed nervously. 'By myself, I didn't mean….' He brushed a hand through his thick dark hair and then through his beard. 'Please forgive me; that was awkward,' he said as Maja laughed and stepped across the threshold. Since the first coffee that Hamza made for her, they had shared a little time talking about their lives, but Hamza had forgotten he'd mentioned his birthday and was amazed that Maja, who he now had deep feelings for, should remember in this way.

The Child in the Window

Maja's smile was painted on when she said, 'I had intended to bring this to you earlier, but my sister phoned and wanted to chat. She doesn't do that very often. I hope you don't mind.'

'No, it is delightful that you should do this for me, lovely lady. I hope you will share some with coffee I will make for us. But where is Alek? Did he not wish to come?'

Still smiling, Maja made a slight movement towards the door. 'Thank you, but I'd better go, it's late. I should've waited until the morning, but Alek is in Manchester until tomorrow. He has a business contact there. I suppose I wanted to talk to you,' she ended slowly.

'Maja, please stay. It is good we are friends. Now come up, and we shall have a small piece of this cake you have been kind to make for me. I needed cheering up, and you have made my heart lighter. No one wants to spend their birthday alone.' Hamza gently took the cake from Maja's warm hands and walked upstairs.

Maja followed, feeling that she shouldn't but wanting nothing more than to be here with this man who attracted her so strongly and was never far from her thoughts. Knowing it to be wrong and dangerous, Maja couldn't bring herself to be sensible and return home. Ever since Alek had told her his plans to meet up with John in Manchester, she'd known what she intended to do. She hadn't wanted Alek to go, and they'd argued about it. But as ever, Alek had insisted that the man John wanted him to meet was honest and trustworthy. Maja didn't believe it, she knew John was crooked and felt sure whoever he was friends with would also be nefarious, but in the end, she said, 'Oh, get on with it! Yes, I can manage on my own, and I'll get Lucy to come and help in the café.'

Maja had managed and appreciated having Lucy to talk with, but she had deliberately baked the cake for Hamza and waited until she knew he'd closed the shop before knocking on his door.

Maja felt that the last few hours spent in Hamza's strong arms had been inevitable as he kissed her for the last time before letting her out to cross the pavement, then turned away and hurried back to bed.

Damn it; she railed against fate. Are there always going to be consequences when I follow my heart? She heard the shop door close behind her as a taxi drew up on the corner by her cafe and disgorged its passenger. A very tall woman walked with her head down, the few short steps to where Maja stood, key in hand. She stopped next door at Lily and Greg's house. Maja couldn't believe her eyes as she recognised Greg despite the female clothing. 'Greg?' She burst out her mouth agog.

Greg didn't look at her as he said in his deep voice, 'Let's keep all this to ourselves, Maja, eh?' He inserted his key and went inside.

Maja's breath became shallow as she realised Greg had seen her come creeping from Hamza's door at two in the morning. She eventually went to bed and tried to sleep, but it was impossible. Would Greg let on where she'd been, she wondered, and what was he doing dressed as a woman? She also wondered if Lily knew but decided that wild horses would not drag the fact that she'd seen him from her mouth. She hoped Greg would do the same. As she eventually drifted off at five after setting the alarm for seven o'clock, she relived her time with Hamza and considered it had been worth getting caught. She just hoped that Alek would never need to know.

38

The Sunshine Café *Monday 20th August 2012.*

'What have you done to the bloody weather?' Rita called as first Lily, and then Cathy burst into the café amidst the clatter of the bell and fierce shaking of wet umbrellas.

'Oh, I know, I'm fed up with it. It's been miserable all week. Summer, what there was of it, has come and gone in a hurry,' Lily said.

'If I'd known it would be like this, I'd never have taken this week as holiday.' Cathy pulled a disgruntled face.

'Zeta's the same; she's on holiday this week, and look at it.' Lily glanced out of the window. She might join us this morning. I told her we wanted to make plans. Shame Nazia's away.' Everyone nodded.

Maja finished serving a couple who were caretakers at the nearby Catholic school in Fentic. They regularly breakfasted at the café before heading into Birmingham town centre to shop each week during school holidays. Maja had told Lily before that they were good tippers; not like most of you English, she'd added and laughed.

However, Lily had taken the joke seriously and always told Maja to keep the change when she paid cash; but she never had.

Cathy eyed the Perspex covers on the counter. 'Is it too early to eat chocolate cake?' she said to no one in particular.

'Certainly not,' Lily chortled.

'No, why would you think that? Anytime is cake time.' Rita grinned.

'There's not much chocolate cake left, but Alek baked lemon drizzle and Victoria sponge last night if anyone's interested?' Maja said.

'Lemon drizzle it is then,' Cathy said.

'Just toast, two rounds and butter for me.' Lily picked up her apricot-coloured Radley handbag from where she'd placed it on the floor next to her.

Maja raised her brows at Rita. 'Toast for me with butter and marmalade, please, Maja.'

'Usual pots of tea?' Maja asked. Rita and Lily nodded. 'What about you, Cathy?'

'Same please,' Cathy replied and glanced out of the obscured window at the dull day to see Zeta as she hurried in her stilettos that matched her shiny red handbag and umbrella, a contrast to the snug-fitting low-cut black and white dress and jacket that looked classy.

Similar thoughts went racing through all the friend's minds. Everyone liked Zeta and envied both her figure and zest for life.

Maja pushed another table to where the group were seated and could feel her face redden as she wondered if Greg had told Lily about their meeting in the early hours. She had been fretting ever since and was so scared in case Alek ever got to hear of her betrayal. She had a good idea that Lily would disapprove and wasn't a hundred per cent sure that she would be supportive. Pushing her guilt to the back of her mind, she asked Zeta what she could get for her.

Zeta declined anything except black coffee. 'Oh, aren't you good? No wonder you've such a great figure,' Rita said admiringly

Zeta grinned. 'Well, I can't eat cake and drink alcohol, and I know which one I'd rather spend my calories on. You're all married, but I'm not yet,' she said, making everyone chuckle.

As Maja pulled up a chair, Alek's head peeped around the kitchen arch. 'Hey, you lovely lot, just keep it clean now, mind.'

'Go back to your place.' Maja stuck her tongue out at her husband, and he obliged. Everyone enjoyed the look on his face, and even he laughed. Although Alek was usually solemn, he could be fun at times, and most people who knew him understood his ways.

After the toast and cake had disappeared, there was a lull in the conversation, which was broken when Lily said, 'Ok, first we need to decide where we're going. I suggest Paxton Manor.' She looked around expectantly.

'Hmm,' Rita pushed her still wet blond hair off her forehead, 'what about Alton Towers?'

'Or Dudley Zoo?' Cathy chipped in. 'Penny loves animals, and it's so close.'

'The Safari Park at Bewdley isn't too far; we could hire a minibus. I've been there. It was great until the car became too hot and we couldn't even open a window, and the air con didn't work,' Zeta volunteered.

Lily held a hand up, and everyone became quiet. 'All good suggestions. We need to vote to see which one gets the most hands. Everyone nodded in agreement. Lily went through the list, and it turned out that Paxton Manor was their favourite.

Zeta looked bemused. 'I've never been anywhere except the Safari Park, so what's at Paxton Manor?'

'It's an amusement park near Stoke on Trent, and there are all sorts of fairground attractions and a small zoo there. I think you'd enjoy it and I know the girls will love it as their birthday treat. It's nice their birthdays are only one day apart. Do you think they were destined to be friends?' Lily speculated and made crazy eyes as she crossed and uncrossed them several times, making everyone titter.

'It'll be my birthday treat too,' Zeta chimed in, her face animated as she clapped her hands together.

'Yours is on the first, a week after Bethany and Penny, so which day shall we go for?' Lily asked.

'I can celebrate mine early. Let's go out on one of the girl's birthdays. Perhaps Saturday twenty-fifth?' Zeta said.

Lily looked at everyone in turn. 'Is that decided then?' Rita, Cathy, and Zeta nodded enthusiastically.

Maja stood and collected the used plates. 'I wish I could come with you. It sounds like you'll have a great day, but Saturdays are too busy to leave Alek. More tea, anyone?'

'No thanks,' they all chorused, and Maja cleared the tables and went through to the kitchen.

Rita looked thoughtful. 'I'm just sorry for poor little Emma; she never seems to have fun. I think that mother of hers is a miserable bugger. Emma loves it when Tilly goes to Amanda's. And she sometimes speaks now.' Rita frowned.

After a moment of silence, Lily looked around. 'Why don't we ask Helen if we can take Emma with us?'

'We could, but I wouldn't want to do the asking,' Cathy said, 'she always walks past me with her nose in the air, never speaks. I've given up trying to talk to her.'

'I'll do it!' Zeta exclaimed, 'I'll say it's my birthday treat. Emma's such a sweet little thing, and Helen can only say yes or no. It's worth a try.'

'Ok, I'll get Greg onto seeing about hiring a bus. He'll get a good rate. That'll be….' She counted on her fingers everyone that would be going. We'd better hire a twelve-seater to be on the safe side. She paused, and everyone stayed quiet as it was apparent she was thinking. 'If you all let me know what you'll be bringing for the picnic, I can see if there are gaps or too much of one thing. Ok?'

'Do you want to know right now because I need to think?' Cathy said.

'No, but by tomorrow, eh? Write it down so I won't get muddled,' Lily said. Everyone agreed, and a short time later, the group went their way, rejoicing that the rain had stopped and happy that it was Zeta rather than themselves who would talk with Helen. She had become everyone's least liked person. Not that anyone went out of their way to be unkind. They just didn't have an opportunity to be kind. Helen held everyone at arm's length.

39

7 Littlebrook Terrace Tuesday 21ˢᵗ August 2012

'For goodness sake, what is it about that woman? She's making you all pussyfoot around her as if you're scared she'll curse you or something.' Claude tamped down the tobacco he'd just filled his pipe with and then washed his hands at the kitchen sink.

'It's not that. It's just that we feel so sorry for Emma. I'm not scared of Helen, although I think some others might be.'

Claude turned to look at his daughter while he dried his hand on a piece of kitchen towel. 'But why? She looks cared for and is well behaved. Not every parent indulges their children, and Helen has to work, don't forget. I think it's sad she lost her husband so tragically. It must have meant a big upheaval for her. Her husband sounded quite controlling from what she told Lily; he did everything and never allowed her to work. She's probably never got over it.' Claude said and sat down at the table.

'You don't see or hear everything. Amanda has only just got Emma to say a few words. She wouldn't talk unless her mother was with her and…and she seemed frightened when she asked Amanda not to tell her mother that she'd spoken.

What's that if not a sign that somethings wrong?' Zeta waved her hands in front of her to emphasise her question.

'I don't know. Children can behave erratically; they're not all the same. They have very vivid imaginations at times.'

'What do you mean exactly?' Zeta raised her well-shaped eyebrows and looked intently at her father. She respected his opinion but sometimes didn't get his drift at all.

'We...ll, take you, for example, you went through a phase when you were, three nearly four, imagining that there were snakes in your bed hiding under the blankets just waiting to bite you if your feet should touch one.' Claude smiled affectionately.

Zeta laughed incredulously. 'I didn't.'

'Oh, yes you did. Your mother or I had to pull back the covers and show you every night before you would get into bed.' Claude chuckled. 'It used to worry your mother, but you grew out of it.'

'Hmm, perhaps you're right, and we're reading too much into Emma's behaviour.' Zeta began to clear the table. 'What time's your flight tomorrow?'

'Not until three, so I'll get a train from New Street in the morning.' He looked hard at Zeta. 'You'll be alright, won't you? I'll only be gone until Monday. I just need to sort out a few things at the museum and see a couple of people. Sure you don't want to come with me?' Claude said, and clicking his lighter for the second time, introduced the tall flame to the sweet-smelling tobacco he invariably smoked.

'No, I'm fine here. Make sure you take that present for Aunty Lou, though and tell her I'll see her at Christmas, won't you?' Zeta said.

'Of course. Now, why don't you nip round to Helen's and put your mind at rest? I'm sure she'll want Emma to go with you all.' He looked thoughtful. 'Perhaps you should have invited her to go too?'

'Oh, my God, no! That would make me very popular, I don't think. No one can stand her. You're the only one I've ever heard say anything positive about her. Don't fancy her, do you?' Zeta gave a throaty chuckle.

Claude grinned. 'Might do,' he said, then answered her chuckle with a deep one of his own.

'Oh, my God, no! I don't want her as a stepmother!' Zeta exclaimed.

Claude shook his head. 'Don't even think such a thing. Do you suppose I could replace my wonderful wife with anyone, let alone a miserable woman like Helen?' He picked up his newspaper and placed his spectacles on the end of his tip-tilted nose. 'Now let me read this and do what you have to do.'

'No, I know you wouldn't. I'll just get dressed, and I'll go round. Can't say I'm looking forward to seeing Mrs Misery.'

'*Harumph*,' Claude muttered but didn't look up as Zeta left him to his paper and went upstairs to shower.

When she returned to the kitchen, she looked as though she was off out on a date. Her hair was sleek and shiny, makeup carefully applied, and she had on a figure-hugging, mid-thigh length, sage green, linen dress.

Claude turned from watching Lewis weeding the edges of the concrete path as his daughter entered. 'Dressed for battle, are you?' he said and smiled.

'Well, you know me, I feel confident if I think I look good. Not overdone, is it?' Zeta asked anxiously.

209

'You look lovely, my darling. Go get her.' He grinned.

'I'm going,' Zeta said. A few minutes later, Claude heard her knock at Helen's door as he went upstairs to pack a suitcase.

'Oh, it's you. I was expecting a parcel,' Helen said as she opened the door.

'Yes, it's me, sorry I'm not a parcel. I'd like to talk. May I come in?' Zeta took a step forward, expecting Helen to say yes.

Instead, Helen frowned. 'No, I'm sorry, I'm busy and don't invite people into my home. I like my privacy.' She began to chew at her lip. 'What did you want to talk about?'

Trying her best to stay calm, Zeta said, 'Well, it's Bethany, Penny's and my birthday soon, so we decided to go on an outing to Paxton Manor Park on the outskirts of Stoke on Trent. Rita's daughter Tilly will be going too, and she loves to go over to Amanda's and play with Emma and—'

'So?' Helen interrupted, lips compressed into a thin line.

'So, we wondered if you would like Emma to come with us. It'll be a fun day out, and I'm sure she'd enjoy it. I'd look after her myself; you wouldn't have to worry.' Zeta finished and could feel herself becoming more annoyed with every word as Helen's expression didn't alter.

Suddenly it did. Helen's face contorted with fury. She stepped up to Zeta, placed one hand on her shoulder and pushed her away from the door. Zeta tottered on her high heeled mules and only just managed to stay upright. She looked at Helen in amazement. 'What, do you think—'

'Get away, you bitch, not content with everything you have, you want my daughter. Well, you can't have her.' Helen screeched. Spital sprayed from her snarling mouth and hit Zeta's chest above the tight-fitting bodice of her dress.

Zeta was dumbfounded. 'I didn't mean permanently, I just thought—'

Helen sneered as she interrupted Zeta's explanation. 'You can't fool me, coming round here flashing your tits and arse and pretending to do good. I suppose you can't have children, so you'll make my Emma love you and want to live with you! Well, it's not going to happen. I kept her, and you won't get away with it. And as for your lecherous father, tell him he's wasting his time waving to me over the garden fence. I'll tell the police he's making a nuisance of himself.'

'Go ahead; you're crazy. You should see a doctor. I feel sorry for Emma having you as her mother,' Zeta said calmly and turned to go home.

Suddenly Zeta was on the pavement with her legs in the air, unsure of how she'd got there at first. After a moment, she realised that Helen had tugged at her ponytail, pulling her over onto her back. Zeta heard Helen's front door bang shut as she got to her feet. She was shaken and unsure what to do. Her first instinct was to retaliate, but as her head cleared, she knew it would do no good. She felt sure that Helen was deranged. She needed help, and Zeta thought she should ask Lily what to do about the assault. Claude had heard the commotion; he appeared and helped Zeta into the house.

'Sit down. Are you alright, my love?' What did she do?'

Zeta began to relate what had happened as Cathy knocked, came in, and asked the same question. Zeta gave them a potted version of the awful confrontation.

'I'm going round there,' Claude said and moved towards the door.

'No, please don't, Dad. I'm not hurt, and she is mad, I'm sure of it. God knows what she'd do or say. Leave it, please.'

'Well, I'm going to get in touch with Robert. He'll soon have her out,' Cathy said. 'We've never had problems like this before.'

'No, think of Emma. What will happen to her? At least Amanda can keep an eye on her while she's here.' Zeta reached around to the back of her head and touched her scalp with gentle fingertips. She flinched and gasped, 'That's sore.' She got unsteadily to her feet. 'You know, she's unstable and needs help. That's what we should be trying to do. Perhaps get someone else to talk to her.' Zeta gently shook her head.

'I'll have a word with Lily; she always knows what to do. Come on,' she beckoned to Zeta, 'I'll make a pot of tea,' Cathy said.

Claude pulled his phone from his pocket and cancelled his flight. 'I'll go some other time. Everything can wait.' Zeta hugged him fiercely and followed Cathy, who she felt like hugging too, into the kitchen.

40

9 Littlebrook Terrace Tuesday 21st August 2012

After Helen slammed the door, she leaned back against it. Her body rigid, fists clenched, she shook from head to toe. Don't scream, don't scream over and over in her mind as she bit down on her wrist and drew blood. She tore two tiny pieces of skin from her already scarred flesh but felt nothing. Minutes passed as in a dream while she listened for either the police or Claude to bang on her door. She heard Cathy's voice but didn't understand what she said; fear robbed her of rational thought.

Eventually, her heartbeat steadied; she lurched into her kitchen, swigged the remainder of the previous night's wine, then stared blankly at the bottle held loosely in her bloodied hand.

The bang at the kitchen window caused her to allow the white wine bottle to slip from her fingers. It bounced without breaking on the tiles, then rolled under the table hitting chair legs as it spun around. Helen's eyes focused on the window where a large bird had left an imprint of its outspread wings and solid body.

'Mommy, are you alright?' Emma's slight form clad in her nightdress with a printed sleepy face on its front was framed in the doorway. Her eyes were two wary orbs.

'I thought I told you to stay in your room?' Helen said dully.

'Yes, but I thought you were hurt; you were making strange noises.'

Helen said nothing, merely stared hard at her daughter.

Emma looked frightened. 'Sorry, I'll go back.' She turned and ran.

Helen's nose wrinkled, and she lifted her arm and sniffed her armpit. A children's nursery rhyme had replaced the urge to scream. Half a pound of two penny rice, half a pound of treacle, that's the way the money goes...repeated. She put her head into her hands and wept. Please stop, oh please, she begged her brain. I need to think. The song abruptly ceased, only to be replaced by Del Shannon's "Runaway".

'Yes, that's it. I have to go from here. I don't fit in, and they want to take Emma away from me,' she said aloud. You can't run away from yourself, a small voice said spitefully and laughed merrily. Helen placed a hand over her ears and shook her head several times back and forth, hard. It seemed to get results as all the voices disappeared. She stood, went to the window and stared out, not seeing the beauty, only the faded sun-scorched grass of the narrow patch of lawn.

As time passed, Helen alternated between angry thoughts that she must move on and despair, thinking she would never find anywhere private enough to feel safe. There will always be someone wanting to interfere in my life, she thought; even though Tony was dead, his legacy lived on through his children. Helen wished, once again, that she'd dared to smother them both when they were born. She would have been able to build a life where she was safe and away from the prying eyes of people that wanted to hurt her.

While trying to fathom a way out of her dilemma, Helen paced the kitchen. Back and forth from the door to the window like a caged tiger. She wanted Harry to die and sometimes Emma too, but he just wouldn't, even though she only fed him enough to stop him from howling. He's not going to die unless I physically kill him, and I need to do it while he's small and weak enough for me to handle, she thought. But not yet, a voice warned. The police might still come if Zeta has reported you.

Helen shook her head again and, as she passed the kitchen table, noticed a bowl of soggy cornflakes and a piece of toast with a knife covered in marmalade leaning against it. She remembered she'd been making breakfast when Zeta had called around. The sight made her stomach grumble, and as it did so, she heard a tapping sound from upstairs which became louder and more insistent. Helen knew it was Harry; Emma wouldn't dare make a noise like that. He was becoming bolder.

The tapping ceased, and Helen crossed the hallway and called to Emma. 'Come down and get your breakfast, my good girl.'

Emma appeared at the top of the stairs. 'What about Harry? He's hungry, Mommy, and he's crying.'

Helen gritted her teeth. 'Well, you come down, and I'll take something up to him,' she said.

Emma slowly descended, and Helen returned to the kitchen. Emma followed and stood by the door. Then as Helen's back was towards her, she seemed to gain courage and sat at the table. She pulled the cereal dish forward and had a spoonful halfway to her mouth when Helen placed a

215

fresh bowl of cornflakes in front of her and poured on some skimmed milk.

'You eat that, and I'll take this,' she picked up the bowl with the mushy mess to that thing upstairs.'

Emma's mouth opened, she wanted to say Harry's name, but her courage failed as her mother turned away and left the room. Emma began to eat. She was more hungry than frightened at that moment. She loved Harry and couldn't understand why their mother hated him and pretended he wasn't real. She felt an incredible sadness as she spooned her breakfast carefully into her mouth. She wanted to cry but had learned when tiny that tears were dealt with harshly by their mother. She pictured Amanda and Henry and wished that Amanda was their mother. She was kind, and Emma had come to love her and Henry, who smelled warm and felt so soft. Emma thought that Harry would love Amanda too if only she could get him to her. At that moment, Emma realised she wasn't just frightened of her mother; she didn't love her. She wasn't sure what hate felt like but thought the cold feeling inside her chest meant she hated her.

Suddenly Emma dropped her spoon, and it clattered into her half-empty dish. She'd been startled by a scream and a bang. Now she could hear slapping sounds from Harry's cupboard. She remained where she sat; paralysed with fear. Had her mother found bits of food Emma had been smuggling to Harry every chance she had? Emma knew she'd punish her if she had seen anything, and Harry would become hungrier than ever. She reached across the table and, with her brave heart thudding painfully, took a slice of bread from the open packet and hid it under the side of her knickers. She was sure that whatever had happened to cause the scream meant that Harry wouldn't have breakfast.

Emma couldn't know that when Helen had opened the cupboard doors, Harry had launched himself at her and sunk his teeth into her calf, drawing blood. It had taken all Helen's strength to prise him off her leg and push him back into the cupboard, where she slapped him repeatedly in a panic, not caring how much noise they made or if the neighbours could hear. Helen had shut the doors and sat on the floor, both Harry and herself now exhausted. Despite her neglect, Harry had become stronger, and she knew she would not be able to contain him in this way for much longer. She would have to kill him and soon. Helen sat for a long while hearing Harry whimper, but she felt no sympathy or remorse for how she treated him. Her hatred seemed to strengthen with every beat of her heart. She was the victim, not him, her twisted mind told her. Thanks to nosey neighbours, she thought she should move as far away from here as possible, but she couldn't contemplate transporting Harry yet again.

Eventually, Helen thought if she apologized to Zeta and allowed Emma to go to the birthday outing, it would give her time to make plans. She believed Emma loved her and wouldn't talk to anyone about what happened at home, so she felt that would be the best way to move forward. She had to work; her money had almost dwindled to nothing, and her job at Hamza's, much as she disliked working for him, kept her going. Having made a decision for the immediate future, Helen stood, looked at her blood where it had soaked into the carpet, and went into the bathroom to tend to the jagged hole in her leg.

After bandaging the wound and having no doubt that Zeta would forgive her, Helen ordered Emma to stay in the sitting room and went next door. As Zeta opened the door, she took a step away from this woman, who she considered was mad with a capital M, not knowing what to expect.

Helen forced a smile and spoke quickly. 'I just wanted to come and apologise for my awful behaviour this morning. I hope I didn't hurt you.'

Zeta said nothing, just stared at Helen.

'You see, I'm on some medication that makes my sleep patterns erratic, and I wasn't thinking straight at all when you spoke to me about Emma.' Helen looked contrite.

Zeta's mouth fell open. This was the last thing she had expected following on from the assault. Claude had tried all morning to persuade her to get the police involved, but Zeta had refused because of Emma. Now she said calmly, 'I will find it difficult to forget what you did, Helen. I was upset and angry; you're lucky I haven't taken it further.'

Helen put on a glum expression. 'I know, I am so sorry. I don't expect you to understand, but I've been through a tough time in my life, and I am frightened that someone will try to take my daughter from me. I find it difficult to talk to anyone. Please forgive me, and of course, Emma can come with you. I know you'll look after her.'

Zeta was almost speechless at Helen's about-face and barely knew how to respond but said after a moment, 'Well, let's forget it. I'm glad Emma can come, and I'm sorry you've had such a hard time. I will always listen if you want to talk.' Zeta then stepped towards Helen and said grimly, 'But if ever you lay a hand on me again, I will involve the police and social services, make no mistake about it.'

'Thank you,' Helen said and promptly returned home, congratulating herself for the way she'd handled everything. She had hated apologising to the Canadian bitch as she thought of her, but it would give her some much needed time.

Zeta's only thought was of Emma's wellbeing as she told Claude what had happened and begged him to replan his trip. Helen's apology had only convinced Zeta that she was deranged, but she wasn't frightened by her. However, she intended to talk with Amanda as soon as she could.

41

Paxton Manor Park *Saturday 25th August 2012*

After Zeta and Cathy related Helen's behaviour to Lily and Rita, they decided that no one person should collect Emma for the birthday trip. Therefore, at eight o'clock on Saturday morning, Cathy with Penny and Lewis knocked on Zeta's door. While the children went through Zeta's house and into the alley, Zeta and Cathy went next door.

Zeta was feeling somewhat nauseous as she waited for Helen to appear. She hadn't completely recovered from Helen's behaviour the previous Tuesday.

They could hear Helen walking to open the door, and Cathy could feel how tense Zeta was. She gave her a big grin. 'It's alright; she won't take two of us on,' she whispered. Zeta smiled gratefully.

'Good morning, Helen,' Cathy said pleasantly, 'is Emma ready?'

Helen looked from Cathy to Zeta and back to Cathy; her face lacked expression. 'Yes,' she muttered, then turned away and clip-clopped in worn blue fluffy mules into the depths of her house. Her flimsy floral dressing gown billowed behind her as she went. Minutes later, she returned with Emma, who looked tearful.

'Ah, there you are.' Zeta smiled widely at Emma as Helen placed her hand behind Emma's back and encouraged her to move forward.

Emma hesitantly placed her hand in Zeta's outstretched one and smiled. The smile rapidly disappeared as her mother said, 'Now be my good girl and remember what I've told you.'

'Yes, Mommy, I will,' Emma said and gave Zeta's hand the tiniest of squeezes.

Without looking at Helen, Zeta felt it and said, 'I'll look after her, please don't worry.' She stepped next door with Emma, and Cathy followed.

'Are you ok, Emma?' Cathy asked as they trooped through into the garden, where they waited while Zeta picked up some bags of food and locked the door.

Emma nodded. 'Yes, thank you. Can we hurry up?' She tugged at Cathy's hand.

Cathy chuckled. 'Are you excited then?' she asked.

'Mommy might change her mind in a minute if she sees we are still here.' Emma shuddered.

'It's ok, she won't.' Cathy tried to reassure Emma but began to walk towards the back gate as quickly as possible.

'She said she might if she sees me in the alley,' Emma said and began to cry silently as they neared the gate.

Cathy took her through into the alley and, kneeling on the grassy verge, took Emma's shaking form into her arms and rocked her. 'It's ok, it's ok, look here's Zeta now, and there's the van. Everyone's waiting for us.' Cathy got stiffly to her feet and dried Emma's eyes. 'It's ok, no more crying, we just have to laugh on birthday outings.'

Emma smiled, looked sideways at the back gate of number nine, and led Cathy towards the van where Steve lifted her into the child seat next to Tilly and ensured she was secure.

The van fairly buzzed with excited chatter. Tilly reached across and held onto Emma's hand as Greg started the engine and pulled out onto Singerbrook Road. He tooted the horn as they passed the front of the café, and Maja waved madly. She had supplied many goodies for the trip, and everyone felt sad that she had to work. Lily waved and mouthed Wednesday, but she didn't know if Maja saw her. They had arranged to spend the day with Rita in town and were looking forward to having a good chinwag.

When Greg filtered onto the M6, Lily turned to her husband and said, 'Now ok?'

'Yes, but I'm not singing.'

'I know,' Lily replied, turned around in her seat and said, 'Ok folks, let's sing Happy Birthday to Penny, Bethany and Zeta. Not too loud, though; we don't want to drive Greg off the road. The noise in the van was deafening, but it left everyone, including Greg laughing.

Zeta sat across the aisle from Tilly and Emma and watched Emma's face as the singing bounced off the van's walls. Her mouth was a wide O matching her enormous, rounded eyes. She didn't know the words and had apparently never been in a group that sang. Zeta felt an urge to cuddle and protect her, and a fresh wave of anger towards Helen washed over her. As the song faded, Zeta looked out of the window, but it was some time before she became aware of the cars and lorries zooming past. Her mind was occupied with speculation about Emma's life.

'Hey Zeta,' Rita shook her arm, 'come back to us. I've asked you the same thing twice now; you never even heard me, did you?'

'No, sorry.' Zeta smiled. 'What was it? I was miles away.'

'I said, any chance you can join us on Wednesday? We're planning afternoon tea at Marco Pierre White's.'

'Afraid not, I'm back at work then. Shame, I'd have loved to go with you,' Zeta said.

'Another time, eh?' Lily called from her seat in front.

Suddenly, some of the travellers heard a sharp intake of breath as Greg swerved to avoid a box partially blocking the inside lane.

'It's alright; it's alright, everyone. Let's get on with enjoying our day out; we'll be there soon,' Greg called without taking his eyes from the busy motorway.

Later after Lily and Steve helped to sort wristbands, the party split up to go on different rides and arranged to meet back at the picnic area for lunch. Zeta, who had always thought she didn't have a maternal bone in her body, looked after Emma as if she were her own child. After sitting on the bench seat of a car that went around in a circle for the second time and enjoying her charge's delight, Zeta settled on the grass in the sunshine, gave Emma a carton of juice to drink and then took her to the toilet. Eventually, they caught up with Rita, Steve and Tilly and spent time in the small zoo with them.

Again, Zeta felt annoyance with Helen burning in her chest as she watched Emma. It was plain that she had never experienced most, if not all, of the things that many children do. She was enthralled and kept asking questions about each of the animals. Although Emma was obedient, when it was

223

lunchtime, Zeta had to persuade her to leave the creatures she was fascinated by, promising to bring her back again.

Emma said very little except please and thank you, but every once in a while, she pulled at Zeta's hand and said sadly, 'I wish Harry could have been here.' or 'I wish Harry could see this.'

When they had eaten and were clearing up, Zeta said to Emma, 'Who is Harry, Emma?' Emma looked frightened and clamped her lips tightly together. 'It's ok, you can tell me, I won't laugh. I used to have an imaginary friend when I was young lots of children do.'

Emma stared up into Zeta's eyes. 'Mommy said he's not real, but I think he is.' She looked guilty. 'You won't tell her I said that, will you?'

'No, love, I won't tell her, but you can tell me anything. Perhaps you could show me, Harry, sometime?'

Emma shook her head, making her curls dance. 'No, I couldn't do that; he has to stay in the cupboard.'

She looked so worried that Zeta said, 'Come on, Tilly's calling you. Let's run and catch up.' She picked Emma up, as Steven and Greg gathered the bags of food to take back to the van, and ran, bouncing Emma and making her laugh as they joined the others.

At four o'clock, as they set out on the return journey, the level of noisy chatter was twice that of the outward ride, but both Emma and Tilly fell asleep and stayed that way until Greg pulled into the alley.

Zeta looked around this group of happy people who were unloading the van and knew they had become not just neighbours but firm friends. She looked at Bethany, and Penny then raised her voice and said, 'Thanks for sharing;

it's been a lovely way to celebrate my birthday. Bet you feel the same, don't you?'

'Yes, they chorused enthusiastically and made everyone smile indulgently.

'We've had a great time, and we must do it again,' Lily said before they parted company.

Cathy, Lewis and Penny stayed in front of Zeta's house while Zeta knocked and brought Helen to her door. Zeta kissed Emma's cheek and said, 'Thank you for being such a good little girl Emma.'

Emma said politely, 'Thank you for taking me.' She let go of Zeta's hand and walked past Helen into the house.

'Thank you. I hope she was good. Do I owe you any money for her meals?' Helen asked, and when Zeta confirmed Emma had been good, and nothing was owing, she turned without another word and went inside.

Zeta looked at Cathy, who smiled and shrugged then said, 'I must get back and see if George and Ryan have returned. We're going to the pub later if you'd like to join us.'

'I just might do that, but enjoy the rest of your birthday, Penny,' Zeta said and waved as they crossed the pavement and went indoors.

42

Birmingham City Centre *Wednesday 29th August 2012*

'Good morning, Manda. Are you sure this is ok?' Rita said, knowing precisely what Amanda's reply would be.

'No problem at all,' Amanda said as she gave Tilly a welcome pat on her head.

Tilly's eyes went beyond Amanda as she said, 'Hello, Manda. Is it ok if I find Emma and Henry?' She barely heard Amanda give permission. She ran and sought out her friend, who always hid behind Amanda's chair whenever anyone came to the door.

Rita pulled a rueful face, but Amanda laughed. 'Don't worry, I'm used to children's ways, and I love having them here. I just wish I could get about easier and interact more with them. Anyway, they're fine, so go and enjoy yourself.'

'Thanks, Manda; I don't know what we would all do without you. I hope I can follow your example when I start in the classroom next week.'

'You'll soon get used to it, but it can be a bit hectic. I miss it. Now go on, and I'll see you later. Helen's only working until one, but I'll keep Tilly as long as you wish, so don't hurry.'

Rita repeated her thanks and turned to see Lily waving to them. She touched Amanda's hand gratefully and went to join her friend while Amanda pushed her trolly along her hallway feeling just a tad sad that she couldn't go with them. She used to love the town.

Lily and Rita walked around the corner and went into the café that looked so familiar to them. 'Won't be a minute,' Maja said and disappeared into the kitchen.

Lily smiled as Lucy came from behind the counter dressed in an overall that was slightly tight across her hips. 'You holding the fort, are you Lucy?' Rita said and cocked an eyebrow in her direction.

'Oh yes, I love servicing customers.' She laughed. 'Perhaps I shouldn't go back to Uni.'

Lily didn't know if Lucy realised what she'd said but chose to ignore the double entendre. 'Hmm, it'd break your parents' hearts,' Lily said.

'Oh, I'm only joking. I know what I want to do, and it isn't waitressing.' She chuckled again.

Maja showed her face. 'She's looking forward to being a mom, though, aren't you, Lucy?'

Lucy patted her bump, and her face was now serious. 'Yes, yes, I am.' She scowled. 'Not looking forward to giving birth, though.'

From where she sat at a table in the corner, a woman wearing a wide-brimmed, green hat that would have been suitable for a wedding piped up, 'You'll soon forget it, love. I've had five; the memory goes.' She half-turned to face the dark-haired man who had just finished his drink. 'All grown up now, aren't they love, but I'd do it all again,' she said wistfully. Then she grinned. 'Mind you; it's more enjoyable to conceive than get the blighters out.'

Everyone chuckled half-heartedly, and Lily Maja and Rita left to wait for the bus into town. When they were seated, Rita said, 'What time have you booked afternoon tea for?'

Lily chewed her lip, scraping off most of the pink lipstick she habitually wore. 'I thought we'd have it early. So, two o'clock. That, ok?'

Maja and Rita nodded. 'Just the thought of it makes me feel hungry,' Lily said. 'I've put on pounds since packing in smoking.'

'Probably on the soles of your feet, you look no different to me,' Rita grinned.

'Oh, you,' Lily patted her midriff. 'Here, I mean.'

'Perhaps a little,' Maja said, 'but it will balance out again.'

The time slipped by, and after trailing around town, up Colmore Row and down New Street window shopping and buying nothing except a couple of hand towels, the friends headed to The Mailbox. Neither Maja nor Lily had been there, and they were impressed with the modern interior. As they stepped from the lift and walked into the restaurant, they were greeted by a pleasant waitress and shown to a table overlooking the city.

'Wow!' Lily exclaimed. 'Just look at that view.' She walked near to the panoramic window and stood gazing out, fascinated.

'Come and sit down; you can do the scenic thing when we've ordered,' Rita said firmly.

Lily sat down and apologized to the waitress who had lingered by the table.

'That's alright. We get this reaction a lot.' She smiled. 'Now, what would you ladies like this afternoon?'

Maja asked for coffee and the other's tea. 'It's lovely to be here and know that I don't have to prepare or wash up anything,' Maja said quietly as the waitress headed for the kitchen.

'Yes, it must be, you don't get much time away from the café, do you?' Lily said sympathetically, then looked around at the few occupied tables. 'Not many here, is there? I hope the food's good. It had better be; this place is so hyped.'

'Well, wait and see. I'm going to enjoy myself anyway,' Maja said. Rita nodded.

Just then, two cake stands arrived loaded with sandwiches and small cakes. The aroma of sweetness from the cakes was immediately apparent. 'Well, it looks good,' Lily said and inhaled deeply as soon as the waitress left.

Rita poured tea through a strainer, added milk and took a triangular, smoked salmon sandwich from the display and bit into it. Silence reigned for a few minutes, and then they talked about the new developments around town and what was planned for New Street Station. Steve and his father kept Rita up to date, and she seemed to think it would be impressive and a massive improvement. Cathy believed the planners should stop messing about, as she called it, and it soon became apparent that not everyone felt the same, and Lily quickly changed the subject.

After enjoying her sandwiches, Rita tried one of the small Macrons and said, 'Nice, but I could buy these. They aren't made here.'

'I don't know about you two, but it's not what I expected; I think we could make better afternoon teas than this for half the price,' Maja chipped in.

'Ah, but you wouldn't have this view. Anyway,' Lily grinned mischievously, 'I thought you were just going to enjoy it.' They all laughed, and Maja wrinkled her nose and put out her tongue.

'Well, it is just a bit less than I expected,' Rita said as her phone began to vibrate. She took it from her jacket pocket and glanced at it. 'Sorry, but I'd better answer; it's Steve.' Lily nodded and pointed something out to Maja, who looked out of the window. They tried not to listen as Rita said, 'Hello love…oh, my God. What? Where? Where are you now? Right, I'll get a taxi. It'll be alright, love, try not to write him off, eh?' Rita stood up and pulled her jacket off the back of her chair, where she had insisted it remain when they arrived. She held it in one hand and picked up her handbag. Her pallid face said it all as she looked at her friends. 'I've got to go. Steve's dad has had a heart attack, and he's just been taken by ambulance to the A&E at the Q E hospital.'

Maja stared at Rita with her mouth open. While Lily said, 'Go on then, got the number?'

'Yes.' Rita punched numbers into her phone and arranged to be picked up. 'See you later; please finish your meal.'

'Let us know how….' Lily's words trailed off as Rita hurried towards the lifts.

'Should we go?' Maja looked worried.

'No, what would be the point. We can't do anything to help, and we may as well stay here and finish our meal. I wanted to talk to you about Greg anyway, and I know I can trust you to keep a secret. Greg told me you had seen him when he came home that Thursday night nearly two weeks ago, and I feel sure you haven't told anyone, have you?'

Maja felt her cheeks flame. Oh my God, she thought. He promised not to say he'd seen me. Those weren't the words he used, said a small voice and Maja knew it was right. He'd not promised. Maja was sure that Lily would strongly disapprove if she knew she'd slept with Hamza. 'No, I haven't,' she said emphatically, 'it's none of my business, and it certainly isn't anyone else's either. What did he say exactly?'

'Only that you had seen him dressed in his special clothes when you left Hamzas. I must admit I'm curious as to why you were at Hamza's shop in the middle of the night.'

Maja forced herself to laugh. 'It's silly, really. It was Hamzas birthday, and I baked him a cake. I've told you about my daughter; well, she rang, something she hardly ever does, and she wanted to tell me what was upsetting her, so we were on the phone until quite late. I should have left the cake until the next morning as Alek was away in Manchester, but I wanted Hamza to know someone cared. It was late when I got there, and he made coffee, and we ate some cake, then we talked, and the time just went by. Before I knew it, it was two o'clock. If ever Alek finds out, he would be so angry. You won't tell him, will you?' Maja was out of breath when she finished speaking and quickly drank some water.

'No, of course, I won't. I suppose you didn't expect to bump into my husband, did you?' Lily smiled ruefully.

'No, I didn't; I hoped no one would see me. Had Greg been to a fancy dress party?' Maja didn't think that was the case, but Lily could have pretended if she wished.

'No, he likes to dress up. Has done for years, and I don't mind, but we have kept it secret even from the kids. He has always taken his special clothes to his club and changed there, but after the night when you saw him daring to come home dressed as a woman, he wants it out in the open.

231

We've argued about it when the kids have been asleep, but I've given in. If that's what makes him happy, we will tell Ryan and Bethany together next weekend. It's up to Greg then what he does. I can only imagine what people around here will think and say. Anyway, I wanted to thank you for not ratting us out.'

'We've become good friends, Lily, and I wouldn't do that. I hope it will turn out alright. It will be a big thing for your children, though, won't it?'

'Yes, but I can't shield them forever, and he will still be the same Dad they have always known, so.' Lily shrugged. 'I'm more worried about Steve's Dad at the moment, and I hope he makes it.' She suddenly grinned. 'I'm going to eat this last slice of cheesecake and order more coffee. Would you like some?'

43

London *Friday 31st August 2012*

Robert grabbed his bag from his grey metal locker and headed for the exit.

'Hey, where's the fire? Not coming for a drink?' His friend and co-pilot, Richard, said as he slipped his feet into worn Nike trainers and placed his shiny black lace-ups into his locker situated opposite Robert's.

'No, sorry, not this time, there's someone I have to meet. Catch you next time. I'll buy you one.' Robert waved a hand and strode out into the busy terminal. He stood for a second, looking around this place which brought a feeling of ownership and excitement into his midriff. Until recently, Robert had lingered and breathed in the atmosphere taking in the buzz and light that reflected off shiny surfaces giving an illusion of freedom. Now he couldn't wait to get out and felt confined by the mass of people milling about. He boarded the shuttle and minutes later arrived at what had always been the love of his life until recently, his car.

He got in and put his foot down. He hadn't seen or heard from Guy since he had waved as the helicopter whirled him away to Lord knows where and Robert had been on tenterhooks during his latest flight to Los Angeles. He knew his unusually short temper had made his colleagues raise their eyebrows, but they had shrugged it off. He'd never confided anything to any one of them about his private life.

He thought of nothing else but Guy as he drove to the flat. Would he be there, or wouldn't he? Not knowing where this man who had become his whole life was or what he was doing was torture. On Wednesday the sixteenth, Robert had returned to London from Birmingham hoping to find that Guy had come back to the flat, but there was no sign he had been there and no message either.

For the first time since he had become a pilot, Robert had been tempted to plead sickness and remain in London. However, he hadn't succumbed and flew to Los Angeles on the following Friday as arranged. When he returned, and there was still nothing from his lover, rather than stay in the flat obsessing about his whereabouts, Robert opted to fly an extra shift enabling him to tot up his hours and take an extended break.

After Robert garaged his car, he strode into the lift and pressed the button for his floor, feeling his heart pounding in anticipation.

The key turned quickly in the locked door, and Robert stood still listening for any slight sound that would indicate Guy was there. He dropped his bag onto the hall floor. 'Hello,' he called, knowing it was futile. He searched all the rooms looking for signs that Guy had at least been there at some point while he had been away, but again there was nothing. Not knowing what or even how to feel, Robert poured himself two fingers of Talisker, added ice to the glass, and took it onto the balcony, where he sat and looked out without seeing the people below.

The Child in the Window

The whisky hit the back of his throat, making him cough and bringing unwelcome tears to his eyes. They continued for longer than the cough warranted. After a few minutes, he dashed them away and shut his eyes. Will I ever see him again, he wondered, feeling lost? He couldn't even ask anyone about Guy. He'd never questioned him closely about his friends or family.

By the time his glass was empty, Robert had decided to return that night to Jerry's, where he'd first seen the man that now meant everything to him.

He refilled his glass and phoned the one person he could bear to speak with at that moment. He had to talk to someone, or he thought he'd go completely mad.

'Hello, love, you're back safe and sound again.' She blew him a kiss. 'Have you caught up with my other person yet? Is he there with you?' Amanda sounded worried.

Robert's breath caught in his throat, making it difficult for him to reply. 'No... n... no, Manda, I'm afraid not. As far as I can tell, he hasn't been here, and God alone knows what's happened to him.'

'You know, love, Guy, didn't strike me as someone who would mess you about. If he's not been there, he's not able to at the moment. You need to have faith and be patient.'

Robert sighed. 'Oh, I know, Manda. I never thought he wasn't genuine, even though he couldn't tell me what work he does. I've never told you, but I've lived with two other men for periods, and they were impossible. Guy isn't like them, I'm sure of it.' He coughed. 'Anyway, tell me about you. Are you coping, and what about Emma? Have you minded her this week?'

'I'm fine, and so is Henry, aren't you?' Henry wagged his tail, and Amanda told Robert he was saying hello. 'You know I love having Emma here; she makes me feel useful, a part of the world again. She is such a bright child, but deep down, she's sad.' Amanda sighed then continued. 'At least she talks to me now, but if I ask her about her mother or their life at home, she clams up. There's something wrong, and I know there is.'

'What do you mean? Do you think Helen is abusing her?' Robert felt anger replacing his concern about Guy.

'No, not in the way I think you mean. Well, I don't think so. I've been able to check for bruises a couple of times but found nothing untoward. I dare not say anything to Helen in case she stops Emma from coming here.' Amanda sighed again. 'Emma still never speaks to me when her mother's present.'

'Strange. Would it help if I had a word and tried to find out more? Surely Helen loves her? She's such a sweet little thing.'

'Oh, I think she does in her own way, but I don't think it's a good way.'

No sooner had Amanda finished her sentence than Robert heard a key in the flat door. 'I'll ring you later,' he said, flung the phone onto the sofa and rushed into the hall in time to see Guy stumble over his suitcase.

Guy grinned lazily. 'You're an untidy bugger,' he said and kicked the door shut as he gazed at Robert, who was red in the face as relief washed over him.

'Welcome home,' Robert said, feeling as though he'd become fifteen again full of uncertainty about himself.

Guy hadn't stopped smiling. He walked determinedly to where Robert stood in the lounge doorway, pushed him against the wall and kissed him hard. They headed for the bedroom, shedding clothes as they went.

'Hope you brought my gear back with you? I haven't even got a toothbrush,' Guy said as he emerged wrapped in a towel from the shower.

'Don't be daft, of course, I did, and I did your washing and ironing before putting everything away. Haven't you looked? Daft question, of course not.'

'Thanks. Now before you start with the questions, I can tell you nothing. You just have to trust me. I will not put you in danger. But something I did forget,' Guy reached into his jacket pocket and withdrew a slip of paper which he handed to Robert. 'If, or should I say, when, it happens again, and I am out of touch for a while, you may ring this number and just say I'm looking for two nine five. They will not tell you anything other than I am safe. I have never done this for anyone else, so they will know who you are but don't bother asking questions. You'll get no answers.'

Robert gazed in amazement at Guy. 'Thank you. I wish I'd had this before; I've been out of my mind with worry.' He rubbed at his wet hair with the towel from around his waist and pulled on his boxers.

'I know, I'm sorry, but no one has ever got close enough to me to worry before, and until you; that's how I liked it.' Guy reached into the chest of drawers and waved a pair of boxers at Robert. 'Thanks for these.'

Robert laughed. 'My pleasure,' he said and leered at Guy.

'Dirty bugger. Now, what are we doing about going to Birmingham? I don't suppose you've been there since I left, have you? I feel like getting stuck into working on our place.'

'If that's what you want to do? I've got two weeks before I fly again. How long for you or don't you know?'

Guy looked serious. 'I shouldn't be called on for a while now, so let's see what happens. I may well have at least two weeks.'

Robert beamed as he pulled on a tee-shirt sporting a Nike logo. 'Let's go then and see Manda and pull my house apart. I can't wait.'

44

3 Littlebrook Terrace Saturday 1ˢᵗ September 2012

Lily watched her son Ryan and her almost son George put their dishes into the sink and move towards the sitting room before saying, 'Hey, come back. I need to talk.'

Ryan let go of the doorframe, rolled his eyes to the ceiling and swung himself into a dining chair. George remained standing, blinking his eyes. He resembles an owl, not properly awake yet, Lily thought.

'What!?' Ryan said with an exasperated sigh.

'Your dad will be down in a minute, and I want you to stay here and,' she looked at George, 'you to go home.'

Ryan's mouth twisted in disbelief. 'Why, what have we done? I've taken the bins out like you said.'

Lily bit her lip to stop herself from smiling. 'It's nothing you've done or haven't done. Your dad wants to talk to you and Bethany, and she'll be back from Hamza's in a minute.'

Ryan tutted. 'Oh God, what now?' He pushed the opposite chair from under the table with his foot.

'Stop that! No one's stopping you going to the football.' I think you'd better go now, George, before your mate gets told off. He'll see you later.'

George's eyes were now wide with astonishment. He didn't remember Lily ever sending him home before. 'Have I done something to upset you, Mrs Bedford?' He ran his hands through his mop of dark hair.

'No love.' Lily smiled. 'Not that I know of anyway. Anything you want to get off your chest?'

George looked as though he was thinking hard. 'I've done nothin'. See you later, Ryan.' He almost ran to get away from a situation that smacked of trouble in whatever shape.

'Christ's sake, Mom. What d'you have to do that for? George will be worried now in case.' He shook his head. 'Oh, I dunno why, but I'm worried now. What's going on?'

Lily looked hard at her son, who she saw infrequently. Ever since he and George met in junior school, they had been inseparable. It was probably only the second time she had told George to go home without Ryan. The memory of the previous occasion made her lips twitch. It had been the state of the kitchen. When the boys were twelve, she'd returned home from a meeting of her reading group to find the kitchen covered in flour and their version of cupcakes smoking in the oven while they were watching TV. Her slight smile disappeared as she thought again of the possible consequences of their escapade. They had been foolish many times, but being grounded for three days had the desired effect. Nothing so dangerous had been attempted again. However, she had taught them both to cook and could now trust them with making a full evening meal.

Her mind let go of the past as she said, 'Have patience. It's nothing you nor George have done, and we just need to talk, that's all.'

'Well, tell me now, please.' Ryan said.

'It's up to your dad to tell you, not me.' Lily looked fed up and blew her nose on a piece of kitchen roll.

'You're getting divorced, aren't you?' Ryan accused, his eyes blazing.

Bethany had just walked into the room in time to hear the tail end of Ryan's outburst. She placed a brown seeded loaf and a box of eggs onto the counter. 'Who's getting divorced?' she said nonchalantly.

'Mom and Dad are,' Ryan said and stood up, knocking his chair over in the process.

'Sit down now! We are not getting a divorce. Now for God's sake, shut up and find something to do while you're waiting,' Lily growled. No one moved, and the kitchen clock ticked loudly in the silence. A moment later, they heard Greg as he came downstairs and went into the sitting room.

'Come on,' Lily said to Bethany and Ryan, and they all trooped to where Greg had settled in his favourite chair.

They sat like birds on a wire gazing at him expectantly. After a few seconds, Ryan burst out, 'Well, what have you got to tell us that is worth upsetting George for?'

'Why is George upset?' Greg said with a frown.

'I sent him home so you could talk to your children,' Lily said quietly, 'now will you please get this over with before I have to put up with any more hassle?'

Greg surveyed his children. He tasted bile, so he coughed and swallowed. Then he said, 'I hope you'll understand that I'm still the same person who has loved you from before you were born.'

Ryan opened his mouth to speak, but Lily put her hand in front of his face and hit him with a stern look. 'Let your dad finish. Go on, Greg.'

Greg cleared his throat. 'The club…my club that I've never talked about,' he coughed again, 'it's a man's club.'

'Oh, for Christ's sake, don't tell us you're gay!' exclaimed Ryan.

'No, I'm not gay, but I'd still be the same person you've known all your lives if I were. My club is for men who like to dress in women's clothing, and I'm one of those men.'

'You mean like a drag queen?' Ryan's eyes looked towards the ceiling, the window, and the floor. He felt as though his dad had hit him with the cricket bat he kept on the wall in his room.

'Yes, a drag queen, that's exactly what I mean. It's an entertainment thing. I like to dress up in outrageous women's clothes and have done so for years. At my club, we all dress up. We have contests sometimes, and we have fun.' When Greg finished speaking, he had two spots of high colour on his cheeks.

Ryan looked at Lily. 'You knew about this?'

'Yes, I've always known. It makes your father happy, and that makes me happy.' Lily said clearly.

Bethany crossed the small space and sat on the arm of her father's chair. 'I knew Daddy. I've seen some of your clothes and your face in the mirror when you and Mom tried different cosmetics. You thought I was asleep, but I wasn't.' She grinned, 'I love you. You look beautiful with make-up on.' She kissed Greg's cheek.

'But why? And why tell us now?' Ryan asked, tapping his foot and scowling. 'I don't understand.' His foot became still, and his face crumpled. He coughed a few times to hide his distress, determined not to cry.

Greg shrugged and said, 'I'm sorry I have to share this with you. I'm sure it's making you uncomfortable, but I've

242

been seen coming home as a woman, and I didn't want you to find out from anyone else.'

'On a brighter note,' Lily interjected, 'now it's in the open your dad is taking part in a charity show at the Little Theater in The Green. I'm going, and you might like to come too after thinking about it. Let us know.'

'Is it still a secret, or can I tell my friends?' Bethany asked.

'You may tell whoever you like. We're fed up of secrets.' Lily said. 'Now I'm going to make a drink. Anyone?'

'Can I go now?' Ryan said.

Greg nodded.

45

6 Littlebrook Terrace Monday 3rd September 2012

'I thought you'd got over that nonsense.' Eric's lips narrowed, and his teeth clenched, bringing a network of fine lines towards his chin.

'Got over it when you can't wait to get to the pub most nights, and those you don't, you just sit and never say a dicky bird to me.'

Eric gave a heartfelt sigh. 'I need to mix with other people, Pat. I've told you that. You do too, but you're too miserable to see it.' He put down the nail clippers he'd been using to trim his filbert shaped nails for the second time that month. He always cut them short and gave a passing thought as to why they grew so much quicker as he aged. He felt sure there was a biological reason for it. He would have liked to share his thought with Pat, but she no longer seemed interested in anything except the odd TV programme. And what you are doing, his conscience told him. Pat sat staring out into the Terrace. She'd insisted they fit vertical blinds a year ago and knew just how to angle them so she could see without being seen.

Eric picked up his book *To Fly Without Wings* by Keith Scott Mumby and carried on reading. After a few sentences, his mind began to wander. He pictured Zeta wearing one of her low-cut dresses. He could almost feel the warmth and smell the perfume of her breasts as he leaned forward to kiss them.

Pat pulled him sharply out of his daydream as she said, 'You haven't turned a page in the last ten minutes. Thinking of the Canadian trollop, or have you found someone else to drool over?'

'No, I was thinking how much I'd like to shut you up permanently if you must know.'

Silence reigned except for the sound of Eric's pages as he turned them deliberately. Suddenly Pat spoke aggressively. 'And why do you keep changing the kitchen cupboards around? Tell me that.'

'What? I don't know what you mean.' Eric took off his reading glasses and placed them on his book on the side table.

'You do. Oh, yes you do. Last week it was the saucepans and plates you swapped, and yesterday you put all the tins where I keep the cereals. I've had to change everything back again today. I don't know why you bloody well interfere.' Pat glared at Eric, who wasn't guilty of changing either cupboard. He barely knew where anything went and certainly couldn't be bothered to mess about in the kitchen.

'Don't be daft, Pat. Why would I do such a thing?'

Pat got up and began to pace. Her printed cotton skirt flapped around her legs as she walked. 'I know why. You're trying to drive me mental, so you can have that trollop living here.'

'What trollop?' Eric was aghast to hear such thoughts expressed by his wife.

'You know, the Canadian one or is it the Polish one? They're both as bad.' Pat ran her hands along the top of the fireplace and dislodged a small figure of a penguin and its chick, which she liked. It smashed on the tiled hearth. 'Now see what you've made me do!' Pat exclaimed and bent to pick up the pieces. Futilely attempting to hold them together, she suddenly threw them towards the bin. Most didn't find their target, but Pat didn't notice. Her eyes narrowed as she looked at Eric. 'I know what you're thinking and what craftiness goes on,' she said.

'Now, what are you on about?' Pat shook her head. 'It can't be anything to do with me because I've done nothing to upset you.' Eric stood up and took a step towards his wife.

'Maybe not, but it's more than I can say about the Polish trollop and Hamza. I saw them cosying up in the shop while Nazia is away.'

Grateful that Pat had moved away from himself and Zeta, Eric wondered if it was true but said, 'Do you have any idea of the trouble you'd cause saying things like that? You're not right about me, and I don't suppose you saw anything other than Hamza being chatty to a customer. You need to keep your nasty mouth to yourself.'

Pat put her head into her hands and clutched her forehead.

'Is your headache still bad?' Eric placed an arm around Pat's shoulders. 'Why not take some tablets and go upstairs. Try to sleep it away. I'll bring you some lunch up later.'

Pat removed her hands and looked Eric in his eyes. 'Ok.' All traces of aggression and spite had disappeared.

'Do you need me to help you?' Eric tightened his arm around Pat and stroked her back sympathetically.

Pat shrugged him off. 'No, keep your hands to yourself. I can manage. I've got a headache, not a broken leg.' She swallowed the paracetamol that Eric pressed from a new box on the table and swigged water from the bottle he handed her. 'Thank you,' she said and made her way to the room she had occupied alone since the end of July.

Eric stood at the bottom of the stairs and watched until she was out of sight. He had no idea what had happened to put such a gulf between them, and neither had questioned why they now slept in separate rooms. After their argument, he'd been more amused than anything else to find she had left their bed when he returned home. But he had been shocked when Pat had said nothing but continued the arrangement closing the spare room door, firmly shutting him out. After a couple of days, he had felt annoyed but thought she would stop being silly. However, after a week, he relished having the bed to himself and enjoyed revisiting his schooldays form of sexual release with the image of Zeta never far from his mind's eye.

Now he shrugged his shoulders and returned to the kitchen where he made a hot chocolate drink while trying to put his finger on when Pat's behaviour had first become a cause for concern. He concluded that he'd noticed some small character changes while away on their last holiday. The frequent headaches, false accusations, forgetfulness and Pat's wild mood swings worried him. The more he thought about it, the more he could pinpoint significant cracks developing in their relationship. Eric sipped the hot, comforting drink and wondered if there might be a physical reason for all the changes Pat was exhibiting. Before he went to bed, Eric had decided that he should try to get Pat to seek medical help. He thought she might have a hormone imbalance or even a brain tumour. The way she was with himself at the moment made the thought of trying to convince her to see a doctor intimidating, but he knew he would have to face it and the sooner, the better.

46

3 Littlebrook Terrace Tuesday 4th September 2012

'Got everything?' Lily said, a frown tumbling her tousled hair onto her forehead.

'Yes, stop fussing.' Ryan gave her a look.

'Your bus pass? Lunch?'

'Yes, Mom, now give me a break, I'm not a little kid, and here's George,' Ryan said as his friend passed the window and tapped the door.

'Morning George, you excited?' Lily asked with a smile.

'Oh Mom!' Ryan sounded exasperated.

'Alright, love; hope you have a, well you know. You too, George.'

Ryan smiled. 'I do, and we will.' His smile broadened. 'It's gonna be great. See you later.'

Lily stood on her doorstep and watched the lads as they rounded the corner into Singerbrook Road. Both young men were nearly six feet tall, and Lily felt proud. Her son, going to university. He was going to have a good life; she just knew it.

Lily shut the door as Bethany came downstairs. 'Has the selfish pig gone?' she said without feeling.

'If you mean your brother, yes, but why the selfish pig?'

'Well, he is. He deliberately woke me by dragging the duvet onto the floor, and he knew I didn't have to be up as early as him.'

Lily chuckled. 'Never mind, come and have some breakfast. I've done your sandwiches. Mind you eat them and remember how well you've done by not eating chocolate. Don't be tempted now you're back with all your mates.'

'I won't, Mom. I don't really miss it, and I love being slimmer. You don't be tempted either. Your morning cough's gone, and you don't stink of fags anymore.'

Lily smiled. 'I've almost stopped thinking about cancer sticks now. I'll not start smoking again.'

'Good. I bet you feel better now everyone knows about Dad, don't you?' I didn't think we'd see so many of our neighbours at the charity do. Is everything a nine days wonder, do you think?'

'Mmm,' Lily bit into her toast and licked marmalade off her fingers. 'I suppose there's always something else to gossip about. Look how quickly the novelty of Robert and Guy became commonplace. I tell you what, though, your dad doing the sketch with the vacuum cleaner as though he was Freddie was hilarious. I didn't know he had such a good singing voice.' She laughed and sipped from her cup of coffee. 'Is Penny calling for you?'

'Yes, she'll be here in a minute. Dad was funny. I was proud of him.' Bethany drew circles with her finger in the drop of milk spilt from her cereal bowl. She frowned and waved her spoon towards the adjoining wall. 'Rita wasn't happy though, was she? Has she got over it?'

Lily sighed. 'Yes, we're alright. I've just spotted her walking past with Tilly in tow. I suppose I could have confided in her, but,' she shrugged, 'well….' she trailed off. 'Anyway, you'd best get a move on. Y'know you could offer to let Tilly walk with you to school, save Rita the bother.'

'Don't be daft, Mom. Rita starts work today. She's got to go there anyway.'

'Oh, yes, I forgot.' Lily kissed Bethany on her cheek. 'Have a super-duper day, love. Don't forget your lunch; I'd best get ready for work. See you later, don't forget you're making tea.'

'I won't, now stop fussing.' Bethany picked up her school bag and left as Lily climbed the stairs while thinking about Rita. She had been upset that Lily hadn't told her about Greg's dressing up, and Lily felt bad about it. They hadn't fallen out exactly, but Rita had certainly acted a little cool towards her. It worried Lily, especially as Rita had her in-laws staying with them. She had a lot on her plate with Steve's dad recovering from his heart attack and his mother carrying on as though she was the invalid, not her husband. While she dressed, Lily tried to think of something she could do to make it up to her friend but came up with nothing. She put it to the back of her mind and, glancing at her watch, picked up her pace and followed her children out of the house shortly after.

As she hurried along Singerbrook Road, Lily wondered if Greg would agree to ask Rita and Steve to come for a Chinese meal and break the ice a little. But as Lily went into Aldi and her supervisor assigned her tasks for that day, everything else left her mind. She was on the tills, and that allowed no time for thought.

251

Greg agreed as soon as Lily suggested an evening out. Unsurprisingly Rita and Steve jumped at the chance to have some fun and leave his parents to mind Tilly for the evening. They chose to go to a place they'd enjoyed previously, and Greg volunteered to be designated driver allowing Steve and Rita to have a relaxing drink. Their local Buffet Island restaurant served first-class food and a wide variety of dishes. Eventually, their immediate hunger assuaged, they were able to have a break and chat. It wasn't long before the subject of diversity was thrown into the conversation, and Robert and Guy were discussed positively. Then Rita looked at Greg and said, 'Mind you, I was surprised. I must be thick as two short planks. I never gave Robert's sexuality a thought; no more did I imagine you dressing up and being a drag queen.' She looked at Lily. 'You might have told me, you know. I felt hurt hearing it from some old biddy in Hamza's.'

'I know, and I'm sorry. I didn't like talking about it because I couldn't bear the thought of anyone judging my husband. I didn't mind him dressing up, but I felt sure not everyone would be so tolerant as they have been.' Lily's lips quivered slightly as she said, 'I am really sorry, Rita, forgive me?'

'Nothing to forgive. I know what that feels like. I never talk about my family or my God-awful childhood, and I don't want to be judged either. I love you pair, and perhaps when we're alone, Lily, I'll tell you what it was like. Now let's forget it and get on with our meal. I'm going for seafood this time.' Rita stood up, and Lily walked around the table, leaving the men looking slightly bemused, and tucked her arm in Rita's as they assaulted the buffet again.

The Child in the Window

Back at the table with all four plates piled up with prawn curry and chips, the talk turned to Steve's parents. 'I think Andrew is looking better than he has in ages. Does he feel better, Steve?' Lily put down her fork and began to chew.

'Oh, I should say so. He's talking about going back to work soon. He's bored, and Mom's constant moaning is getting him down. I don't know why she has to go on so. There's very little the matter with her, but she craves attention all the time. It drives me mad, let alone Dad, and I'm not with her twenty-four-seven.'

'I thank goodness I'm at work now; otherwise, I know we'd argue. If Anna wasn't Steve's mother, well, I don't know what I'd do. Probably gag her,' Rita said, and everyone laughed.

The rest of the evening passed pleasantly, and the following Monday, Rita was glad she didn't work when Lily met her as usual at the café. Over breakfast, Rita told both Lily and Maja many of her life's shocking details, which she'd kept hidden. Lily was appalled to realise that what she'd assumed about her friend was so far from the truth and told Rita she admired her strength. Before they left the café, Lily felt the bonds of friendship tighten and promised herself not to assume anything about anyone again. Rita went home feeling a cloud had left her now she'd finally admitted to someone the reality of her teenage years.

As she watched the two women who she'd become close to walking past the window on their way home, Maja felt sad that she had done something so foolish that she would never be able to share it with anyone. Since that night, she had been into Hamza's shop, when necessary, but they hadn't discussed the night of his birthday, and neither wished it to be repeated.

47

10 Littlebrook Terrace. Monday 10th September 2012

Robert filled the electric kettle from the bath taps and plugged it into the socket by the bed.

'Like camping, isn't it?' Guy sat up and ruffled his hair, making it stand on end.

'Mmm yeh, too bloody much like it.' Robert laughed as he spooned coffee into the mugs.

'Yes, but just think how much we've achieved in just over a week.'

'Oh, yes, we've no kitchen and no sitting room or dining room. We're doing great.' Robert grinned, poured water onto the coffee granules, added milk, stirred and chucked the wet spoon onto the tray where it clattered and lay upside down.

'Ah, but so far, it has cost us nothing except the price of a skip and Lewis's money towards his guitar, which you'd probably have given to him sooner or later.' Guy sipped his hot drink and cussed as the mug touched his bare chest.

'Well, he deserves it. He's a good lad, works hard. His input has allowed us to get on with the heavy work. And we wouldn't have got half so much in the skip if he hadn't broken the furniture up. Most of it wasn't fit for the charity shops, and we'd have had to take it to the tip.' Robert sat and surveyed his partner. 'I'd never have done this without you. You're like a force of nature when you start, but I'm glad we're letting professionals fit the kitchen.'

'Me too. I could have done it, but it would take too long. We can start decorating the sitting room tomorrow now we've finished the dining room.'

'Yes, ok, but let's go to the café for breakfast now, so come on and get up. I'm going to phone Manda and see if she would like us to buy her and Emma some bacon and egg sandwiches, and we could take ours and eat with them. I'd like to see Emma again. She fascinates me with how she talks, so young and yet so old in the head. I'd have loved a little daughter like her or maybe two or even three.' Robert smiled at his flight of fancy.

Guy looked thoughtful. 'Me too. I'd love to belong to a big family. Mind you; I suppose I did in a way.'

'What do you mean? Each time I've asked you about family, you've made it clear you didn't have anyone.'

'Well, I haven't.' Guy blinked a few times rapidly and swigged his last mouthful of coffee.

Robert held his hand up. 'Oh no, not this time. Tell me properly. What about your parents?'

Guy spoke slowly. 'When I was ten,' he swallowed hard, 'my parents and two younger brothers were all killed in a housefire.'

'Oh my God.' Robert climbed onto the bed and took Guy in his arms. 'Why didn't you tell me?'

Guy chewed his bottom lip. 'I never talk about it, and I hardly ever think about it either. It was a long time ago.' He paused. 'I lived with my Grandma Tucker until I was eighteen, and then she died, and I was on my own.' Guy spoke matter-of-factly and didn't sound even a tad sorry for himself, but Robert could hear the sadness and held him close.

After a few minutes, Robert asked, 'What did you do then?'

Guy grinned. 'If you want my life story, I shall need another cuppa.' He held out his empty mug.

While Robert made another drink, Guy continued to speak. 'I was one of the lucky people. I didn't even think of drugs or alcohol or getting in with a bad crowd. I had money; you see. My parents came from wealthy backgrounds, and I inherited both sides' accumulated cash and property.'

'Yes, and?' Robert handed Guy his coffee and sat back down in the bedside chair.

Guy laughed. 'You want more?'

'I want to know everything you can tell me.'

'Well, it's quite simple. I sold Grandma's house, rented my apartment in London, found a martial arts school and trained five days each week.' He sipped at his drink and continued. 'When I was twenty, I joined the army and went wherever I was sent. I loved the life, and when I was twenty-five, I was approached by,' Guy raised his brows and held his hands up towards the ceiling, 'I don't know to this day, who it was, but I found out that the government wanted to complete my training.'

Robert let his breath out, unaware he'd been holding it. 'Go on,' he said.

'I'm afraid I've reached a point where I cannot. You knew I would.' Guy gave a rueful smile. 'You know everything now. Is it enough?'

Robert smiled. 'Of course, it's enough. Knowing you love me would be enough, but I'm glad you've told me what you can. And I'm sorry you have no family left. Perhaps we should see about making one of our own.'

Guy's eyes opened wide. 'Seriously, you'd do that for me?'

'I'd do it for both of us. I think we'd make great Dads.'

Guy chuckled. 'So do I. Let's get ready and go and see our two favourite girls.'

Robert leapt to his feet, picked his phone up from the bedside table and phoned Amanda, then Maja to give her his order. Half an hour later, Emma threw herself into Robert's outstretched arms and kissed his cheek enthusiastically. Then did the same to Guy. When they'd all finished eating breakfast and Henry had stopped sulking after being admonished by Amanda for begging, Amanda gazed around the sitting room at this group of people she loved with all her heart. She wished her life could always be like it was that minute but knew that the men had to return to London at the end of the following weekend.

'Hey Manda, come back to us.' Robert laughed as Amanda jumped. He knew without being told what she'd been thinking and said, 'We could hold off on the painting if you'd like to come out with us in the car for a change.'

'I'd love to, but I can't. Helen is only working until twelve today, and I don't think she would allow Emma to be missing when she arrives.'

'Never mind, I'll ask her if she would mind Emma coming out with us when she's working tomorrow afternoon. We can hire a scooter for you again and perhaps go to the zoo.'

'Mm, that would be nice. Not sure if Helen will agree, though. Didn't you hear how she behaved with Zeta over the birthday trip?

'Yes. Not good but little pitchers and all that.' Guy looked at Emma, who was stroking her beloved dog. 'Would you like to do some colouring in the book with your new pencils today, or shall we do some more of the jigsaw puzzle?'

Emma looked thoughtful, then scratched her nose as she said, 'I'd like it if you'd learn me how to tie my trainers. Mommy does the knots, and I want to do them. I'm a big girl now.'

'You need to ask them to teach you so you can learn Emma, not learn you,' Amanda automatically corrected her.

Guy rolled his eyes until Emma laughed. 'Yes, you are a big girl; are you nearly three?'

'No, I'm nearly four, and so is Harry,' Emma protested. 'Will you show me?'

'Don't tease her.' Amanda chipped in.

'Of course, we will, but it takes lots of practice. It's not easy for small fingers,' Robert said.

'I will practice,' Emma said fervently.

'Ok, I'll make you something to practice with tomorrow, but meanwhile, let's use your trainer.'

The next hour flew by as Emma persevered until she was almost crying with frustration.

'Hey,' Guy put an arm around her shoulders, 'you've done really well. We said it's not an easy thing to learn. We'll stop now, and let's put this back on before your mom gets here. We'll practice some more tomorrow.'

'Please don't ask Mommy if we can go out tomorrow, Robert; I want to practice knots.'

Robert looked at Amanda, who nodded. 'Alright, that's what we'll do. Now come and give us a hug before you have to go home.'

Emma smiled. 'I love you and Guy and Manda.'

Henry's tail thumped on the floor. Emma laughed. 'And you, Henry.' Suddenly her face crumpled as a knock sounded at Amanda's door. 'Don't tell Mommy I'm learning knots, will you?' she asked them as she hid behind Amanda's chair. 'And don't tell her I love you, please.'

'We won't, don't worry, love,' Amanda said and raised her eyes to the ceiling.

48

8 Littlebrook Terrace, Monday 17th September 2012

'It's awfully quiet now they've gone. Mind you, Robert's asked me to let the fitters in tomorrow, so the banging will start again.' Cathy applied chapstick to her dry lips. 'I shouldn't moan; it's lovely to think they're doing the place up to spend more time here. I miss Robert when he's in London.'

'Guy's a good un too, and I just love his mysterious life. Sometimes I try to imagine what he does that would warrant a helicopter to fetch him, but I can't,' Lucy said.

'He's probably an assassin.' Cathy gave a belly laugh. 'Can you imagine that? He's so kind and gentle.'

'No, I can't.' Lucy smirked.

'I was at Amanda's on Friday, and you should have seen how he was with Emma. He'd make a lovely Dad.'

'I know, it's a shame. But so would Robert.' Lucy glanced at the kitchen clock, a black cat with a swinging tail, 'Hey, come on, you've only fifteen minutes, get a move on.'

'Oh, I know; I wish I could put a door in the wall; I wouldn't have to walk around then. Neither would you.' Cathy finished tying her hair into a ponytail. 'Are you looking forward to your first shift?' Shame the supervisor couldn't have put us on the same one today. Miserable bugger.' Cathy picked up her handbag and pecked Lucy's cheek.

'Yes, I am, but I'm a bit worried about standing for so many hours,' Lucy said and sighed.

'You'll be alright; it's only for a couple of months. They'll stop you at seven; I think—safety issue. Anyway, I'll see you later.'

'Bye, Mom.' Lucy poured the dregs of the teapot into her mug and sipped the cold tea. She was looking forward to earning, but the thought of doing repetitious tasks appalled her. She stared at the washing up in the sink. The men in this house do bugger all, she thought resentfully but knew she only meant her brother, George.

Lucy drained her cup and began to run hot water into the bowl, ready to do a chore she hated. She held her hand under the hot flow for a moment and placed it on top of her shorts. The heat had the desired effect; she felt a sliding sensation as her baby responded to the change in temperature. It brought a smile to her face. 'I'll be a good Mom to you and make up for your father's lack of love,' she said aloud.

When the kitchen was tidy ready for the next onslaught, she went into the sitting room and stood looking out into the terrace. A fine drizzle was falling, making her shiver. As she turned away to get dressed, she glimpsed Emma in the window opposite and waved. A few minutes later, still clad in her worn pj's, she hurried to answer a tentative knock at the front door.

The cold air hit her, making her aware of the wet handprint. She shivered while her brain tried to make sense of the figure in a dark suit peering at her from under his black umbrella. The man spoke. 'Hello Lucy, may I come in?'

'Go away; I don't want to talk to you.' Lucy shut the door and backed away along the hall.

Philip waited a full minute, hoping that Lucy would change her mind and let him in. He then knocked again and bent down. 'I'm going nowhere until we talk, Lucy,' he called through the letterbox.

The door opened, and Lucy stood staring at the man who had hurt her. 'What?' she eventually said.

'Let me come in, you're not dressed for this weather, and I'm getting cold too.' Philip smiled at her showing his even white teeth in the attractive mouth she had kissed so ardently.

Lucy turned and walked into the sitting room, leaving Philip to shut the door and follow her. He was right; it was too cold to talk in pj's on the step. She was aware that she must look a mess, and her heart was beating far too quickly for comfort.

Leaving his brolly in the hall, Philip began to follow Lucy when she darted past him. 'Sit down; I'm going to get dressed.'

Philip watched her go and then went to look out of the window into the back garden where most of the annuals were giving in to their need to die down. Lewis had already emptied some of the pots and stacked them ready for next year.

Minutes later, Lucy was back dressed in denim jeans and a tee-shirt depicting Mickey Mouse. 'Ok, what do you want? I thought we'd said all that was necessary.' She unconsciously placed a protective hand on her belly.

'I want you, Lucy. I've been so stupid, and I'm sorry,' Philip said miserably.

Lucy gave a bitter, sarcastic laugh. 'You can't do this. You said I was stupid to think you loved me; well, I'm not stupid enough to let you mess me about. You'd better go.' She turned away and began to fluff the cushions from the sofa and replaced them in their spot. But Philip never moved. She continued with her back towards him, 'I said go, I'm not interested. I start a job this afternoon, and I can manage perfectly well without you.'

'I know you're angry and disappointed with me, Lucy, but I've had time to think.' Lucy straightened up and gave the last cushion a hard slap, then chucked it into place. She felt near to tears as she faced the man she still loved. All she really wanted to do was believe he loved her and touch his face, which always creased so readily into laughter lines.

Lucy breathed a deep sigh as she said, 'How can I ever believe you, and how could I trust you not to let our baby down. You're not a bloody child; you're twenty-eight; you can't really expect me to fall into your arms just because you've had time to think.'

Philip took a step towards her, but Lucy backed away and held her hands out to ward him off. 'Please, Lucy, forgive me; I'm so sorry I put you through this. I love you so much. I wanted to chase after you and beg your forgiveness almost as soon as you left. I was a coward. After seeing how my parents split up, I didn't think I could ever love anyone enough to marry and risk being hurt the way my father was. It destroyed him.'

Tears trickled down Lucy's cheeks, and she took a step nearer to Philip, whose eyes were overflowing onto his pale face and running into the side of his mouth.

'Please forgive me, Luc'; I want you to marry me, and we can bring our baby up together.' He went down onto his knees and held out a ring box he'd taken from his jacket pocket; he'd seen it was the thing to do on a film. 'Please, will you be my wife, Lucy? I love you more than you'll ever know. I've not been able to concentrate on anything since we split up.'

Lucy hesitated long enough to bring a sob from Philip, then she said, 'Yes, I love you, you know I do. But if you ever hurt me again, I will leave you.' By the set of her face, Philip knew she was more resilient than he deserved and that she meant what she said.

He stood up and slipped the diamond and sapphire ring onto her finger, then they clung together and kissed. Time passed until Lucy remembered she had to start work. 'You'd better go. I'm working until eight. Will you come back then? Mom and Dad aren't going to understand; we need to talk to them.'

'I will, but you don't need to go to work; I earn enough to keep us comfortably, and the flat belongs to me. We can live there until we need a bigger place.'

'Don't jump the gun. I'm the one who needs space to think now. We can talk later tonight, and I'm going to start work. I don't want to be late on my first day there, and Mom would be furious after she put a word in for me.'

'Ok, love, I'll be back after eight.' Philip found it hard to let go, but Lucy eventually untangled herself and, smiling, pushed him out of the door.

By the time Philip returned, Lucy had heard all the reasons she shouldn't trust him, and Cathy and David had come around to accepting that a wedding needed planning.

The Child in the Window

As Lucy was dropping off to sleep, she remembered seeing Emma in the window opposite but dismissed it as a trick of the light distorted by the rain. She knew that Emma was minded by Amanda each Monday morning, and she had glimpsed Helen bringing her daughter home just before Philip left.

49

9 Littlebrook Terrace, Monday 17th September 2012

No sooner than they had crossed the threshold than Emma said, 'Quick, mommy, I need the toilet.'

'Go on then.' Helen let go of her daughter's hand and went into the kitchen to make lunch.

Harry sat on the floor by his cupboard, staring at patterns of sunlight that had replaced the rain shortly before Emma came into the room. The light stretched across the pale carpet in rainbow lines, and Harry was fascinated by its brilliance.

'Quick, come on before Mommy sees I've let you out,' Emma whispered. She took Harry's hand and half dragged him back inside his hiding place, and he lay down on his new sleeping bag. 'Now be quiet, and I'll try and let you out again tomorrow.' Emma shut the doors without making a sound and tied the silky grey tie, which she knew had been her father's favourite, back through the handles. It was the first time she'd dared to untie her mother's knots and open the doors, although she'd untied and tied them several times while Harry and their mother slept, and Helen hadn't noticed. All the time, her stomach was churning as she listened for her mother's footsteps. 'Be good,' Emma whispered to her brother and sped to the bathroom, where she stood over the bowl and retched.

'Emma, lunch is ready. What's taking you so long? Do you need me to come up?' Helen called impatiently.

'No, Mommy, my tummy's a bit upset. I'm coming now,' Emma called. She felt so frightened she didn't know if she'd be brave enough to let Harry out again and wasn't sure if she would be able to eat anything. She took a deep breath and headed downstairs, knowing her mother would shortly appear to see what was keeping her as she was rarely allowed to spend much time on her own.

'Are you alright, my good girl?' Helen asked as Emma sat at the table and began to nibble at half a banana, then put it down and took a bite from a cheese spread sandwich.

Helen finished her meal and cleared the table except for Emma's orange juice and her plate. While Helen stacked the morning dirty dishes in the washer along with her own plate and mug, Emma took another small bite of her sandwich and pushed the remainder down her white sock. She finished the banana and said, 'May I get down, Mommy? I need another wee.'

'Of course, but don't be long. I need to use the bathroom, and then we're going for a ride in the car. You'd like that, wouldn't you?'

'Yes, but what about Harry?'

'It'll be fine. Hurry up before you wet yourself.' Helen spoke sharply, and Emma ran from the room. She hid the part sandwich in the bottom of her wardrobe and went to pee as fast as she could.

Half an hour later, they walked down the garden to the alley and got into the car that had scarcely been used since

Helen drove from Devon. 'Where are we going, Mommy?' To the seaside?' Emma asked.

'I've told you never to mention the seaside and anyway that's too far, but we'll try to find some nice, quiet countryside. I think out towards the River Severn would be good, and we can get some fresh air. You'd like that, wouldn't you?'

'Yes, Mommy. Is it for…, will we be gone a long time?' Emma was scared, this behaviour was different, and her mother sounded somehow funny.

'For God's sake, stop worrying about your… the thing, he's not real, and you just imagine it.' Helen's head began to pound above her eyes. She fumbled in her handbag on the passenger seat and put on sunglasses. 'Now look what you've done. My damned head's going to explode,' Helen said weakly and then while keeping her eyes on the road, she scrabbled about for some paracetamol that she couldn't find. She pulled into the side of the road by a newsagent shop and a hairdressing salon, found the tablets and swigged water from the bottle she kept in the car. It was warm and fusty tasting, but she needed it.

Emma observed her mother, half hoping that her head would explode as she often said it felt like it. She wondered if it exploded, would it make a mess in the car, or would it just stop her being wicked like the witch in Hansel and Gretel?

As Helen pulled back into the traffic and continued to drive, she wished again that she'd dared to kill Harry at birth. It would have been so much easier to have disposed of a tiny body. She berated herself for being a coward as now she had the much bigger problem. But first, she had to find somewhere quiet to allow his body to disappear into the fast-flowing river. She'd thought of little else since Harry had bitten her and had spent some time on the internet trying to find somewhere suitable. The woods and forests surrounding the Severn banks by Bewdley had seemed to be ideal according to the maps, but she needed to identify the right spot.

On and on, Helen drove, occasionally stopping at what she thought might be a good spot only to dismiss it for one reason or another. Eventually, as she approached Arley, she found what she'd been looking for. The river was close to the road, and trees grew on either side of the narrow pathway. No houses were nearby, and Helen hadn't seen another car for the last half mile.

Helen's spirits lifted, and she spoke to her daughter at last. Emma had remained silent for the journey, and Helen had almost forgotten she was in the back seat. 'Well, that was good, wasn't it? Shall we head back now?'

'Yes, thank you, Mommy.'

'There's my good girl. Why don't you shut your eyes and try to doze for a while? I'll put some nice music on.' Helen tuned the radio to Smooth and, committing her exact location to memory, did a U-turn and hummed along to Abba's *Dancing Queen.*

The traffic was heavy, and it was five-fifteen by the time they reached home. As they walked in the front door, they could hear Harry scratching weakly at the inside of his cupboard. Helen went upstairs, and as soon as he heard someone enter the room, Harry began banging with all the force he could muster. Even though they were far enough from their nosey neighbours, Helen couldn't risk it. She untied the tie and stood looking down at the son she hated and intended to dispose of as soon as she could. Helen's eyes narrowed; she had to control him; she needed more money before carrying out her plan to start another new life with only her daughter. 'Do you want to come and play with Emma?' she asked. Harry nodded, picked up his empty water bottle and held it out to the woman he knew was his mother. Helen took it. 'Well, be quiet, and I'll allow you to come out for half an hour and go into Emma's room with her. If you make one more noise, it will be the last time. Understand?'

Harry nodded and stepped out of the cupboard. He'd been eating every scrap that Emma had smuggled to him and doing the simple exercises she'd taught him. Although he was frail, he no longer had to crawl. He walked slowly past Helen and went to Emma's room, where he sat on the floor by her bed.

Seconds later, Emma joined him joyfully carrying his replenished bottle of water. He drank greedily, and Emma quickly unearthed her half-eaten sandwich from the wardrobe, and Harry wolfed it down. Emma refilled his bottle from the bathroom and put it by his side. She fetched her pack of cards from a drawer in her dressing table and said, we'd better pretend to play, or Mommy will get cross. But I'll rub your legs for you. Just nod if you think two cards are the same, ok?' Emma split the pack in two and put a few cards face up between them. 'Stretch your legs out. I've seen this on TV.' Harry always did exactly what his Emma said; he knew how much she loved him and the risks she took for him. He was as intelligent as she was. She massaged his legs until they heard Helen's footsteps on the stairs. By the time she came into the room, Harry had pretended to point to two matching cards, and Emma said, 'Snap.'

Helen carried a bowl with a Weetabix and a small amount of milk into the room and set it down by Emma. 'Feed It, then put it away. Then come down for your tea, and I'll be up to do the tie.'

'Yes, Mommy,' Emma said, and Harry's eyes smouldered with hatred as he watched his mother leave the room.

50

6 Littlebrook Terrace, Friday 21st September 2012

'I tell you what, love, why don't you get yourself ready, and I'll take you out for a carvery, eh?' Eric spoke gently. He'd been trying to get through to his wife all day but had no joy.

Pat had been acting strangely since she came downstairs in her matching nightdress and gown that he'd bought for her the previous year. Bubblegum pink they were; something to brighten you up, he'd said when she opened her present. Pat had enjoyed wearing them for a couple of weeks, even behaving provocatively on one occasion. Now Eric didn't think they'd seen the inside of a washing machine for some time, and he wasn't sure how often her personal hygiene needs were taken care of either. He had caught a whiff of an unpleasant smell at least twice recently and had encouraged her to take a shower diplomatically, but each time, she'd accused him of saying she stank and become belligerent. Following both these arguments, Eric had left the house and found she had complied with his suggestion on his return.

However, today Pat's behaviour changed. After she had eaten the toast and damson jam which she'd asked him for, she'd fetched her winter coat, and a hand-knitted woollen scarf from her wardrobe put them on and sat by the window, craning her neck to watch passers-by where the terrace met Singerbrook Road.

After about an hour, Eric had asked her if she'd like a cup of tea, and she'd nodded. When she finished drinking, Pat handed him the empty mug and continued to gaze out the window.

By two o'clock, Eric was in a state. He had tried a few times to elicit a response from Pat, but she ignored him. He had no idea what was going on with her or how to intercede. In desperation, he phoned their doctor's, and the receptionist said that she should come to the surgery on Monday at ten in the morning as long as she wasn't harming herself or others. He didn't know how he would get her there but let the solution wait, hoping she'd snap out of whatever was happening to her.

Shortly after the phone call, Eric had warmed tomato soup for her and placed it on the table, but he couldn't persuade her to take off her coat although the house was warm. She ate the soup without a word, and then as soon as it was finished, Pat returned to her chair.

Eric was at his wit's end, and when he asked her if she'd go out with him for the second time, she eyed him balefully and said, 'Fuck off!'

Eric's patience took a hit. 'I don't know what you're playing at, but I'm not staying in the same room as you. I've booked an appointment for you at the doctors on Monday, and if you don't go, then I'll tell him how you are behaving,' he said, expecting some response from his wife. She never moved. 'Ok, I'm going. I'll see you later. Try and have a wash or a shower; you stink!'

273

Eric grabbed his jacket from the hall and made his way to The White Swan. His brain was on overdrive as he sought reasons Pat was behaving in such a strange way. He was no doctor and didn't know anyone else who had been through the same type of thing. However, he knew he was wasting his time.

As he sat with his pint of Carling, the idea that Pat might have a brain tumour entered his head, and his heart sank as he contemplated their future. He needed to talk to someone and was pleased when Cathy and David walked in, and Cathy joined him while David went to the bar.

Cathy greeted Eric cheerfully and sat down opposite, looking towards her husband.

'You're early, aren't you? David doesn't usually finish work until eight.'

'Well, we wanted to talk, and sometimes it's like Bedlam in ours. George and Ryan are supposed to be completing an essay but prefer to watch footie replays. Lucy won't stop talking about her wedding and Penny's sulking because we still can't afford to buy her a phone. Seems all her mates have one. There's only Lewis doesn't drive us up the wall at the moment.' She laughed. 'How come you're here this early anyway?'

'Oh, I dunno. I'm just fed up and worried sick, seeing as you ask.' Eric picked up his glass and took a swig.

'Hey, this isn't like you.' Cathy leaned across the table and touched Eric's face gently. 'Do you want to talk about it?'

'I wouldn't know where to start,' Eric said as David placed a half of cider in front of Cathy and took a pull on his pint of Carlsberg before putting the glass on the table, shrugging out of his coat and sitting down.

'Start what?' David asked Eric.

'Eric's worried, and we need to listen if he wants to talk,' Cathy said, giving her husband a shut up now look.

'Tell us what's up, mate?' David said and picked up his glass.

Eric coughed. 'It's Pat. She's going through a bad time, and I'm finding it hard to cope. That's all.'

'Never mind, that's all. That's a lot. Does she need to see a doctor?' Cathy said sympathetically.

'I've booked an appointment for her to see a doctor on Monday, but I'm not sure I can get her to go.' Eric's shoulders slumped.

'Get it off your chest, man. What's been happening?' David said.

Cathy nodded wisely. 'You'll feel better. Come on; we're not liable to gossip.'

Eric smiled inwardly; he knew that Cathy sometimes gossiped with Pat, but he was desperate to talk and couldn't resist detailing Pat's behaviour and mood changes.

'Oh, dear, sound like she may be having a breakdown. If she doesn't go to see the doctor, you need to insist he comes to her. I haven't seen her for a couple of weeks now I think of it,' Cathy said.

'Is she safe like? In the house on her own? Shouldn't you be getting back to her?' David asked gently.

Eric stood up, drained his glass and said, 'You're right; I'd better be off. See you soon.'

'Chin up, let us know if we can help,' Cathy said, hoping they wouldn't be called on. Pat was not one of her favourite people, and a Pat that was acting peculiarly sounded very off-putting.

As Eric left the pub, David said, 'Poor bugger, sounds like trouble.'

'Hm, she's always had her funny, to say the least, ways, but it sounds as though she's in a bad way. Makes our problems look good, really.' For a few minutes, both Cathy and David stared blankly at the exit thinking about Eric's plight but soon began to enjoy being together with problems they could sort out as a team.

When Eric arrived home, he found Pat's coat and scarf lying on the floor by the chair he'd left her sitting in. After seeing no sign of her downstairs, he peeped into her bedroom, and she was there, snoring gently, still in the same nightdress and gown.

Eric shut the door quietly, went downstairs, made himself a cold chicken and tomato sandwich, which he ate while watching a quiz show on TV, then went to bed where he read for ten minutes and then slept.

It was two in the morning when a loud banging on his door dragged him from a dream about Indian elephants picking leaves from low branches. In a panic, Eric leapt out of bed, went to the window and looked out. Donning his slippers and dressing gown, he rushed outside. He was horrified to see his neighbours gathered around Pat, who stood in the middle of the terrace yelling at the top of her voice.

Pat was shouting, 'I've won the lottery, a million pound, and I want to share it with you.' She looked demented.

'She's knocked us all up, everyone on the terrace. You haven't won, have you?' David looked appalled.

'No, we fucking well haven't. God, I don't know what to do.' Eric stepped towards Pat. 'Come on, love; it's late.

These people need to sleep, and so do you,' he said cautiously.

'Get away from me,' Pat screamed at him. You always spoil things, and I want to dance; let me dance.' Pat began to whirl around, waving her arms in the air.

'I've called 999, and they're alerting the police and sending an ambulance; Pat needs more help than you can give her right now,' Cathy said to Eric. 'It's taken us a while to rouse you, and I hope I've done the right thing.'

Eric clutched his forehead, and Cathy put an arm around his shoulders while Pat continued to twirl to the sound of music only she could hear. Seconds later, the sound of sirens ceased as a police car, followed by an ambulance, turned into the terrace and stopped in front of the apprehensive group.

51

4 Littlebrook Terrace Monday 24th September 2012

Amanda watched as Helen walked past her window and heard the small bang as Emma pushed her front door shut. She ran into the sitting room seconds later and hugged and kissed Amanda, then Henry.

'Good morning, my little treasure,' Amanda said when she could get her breath back. 'Are you pleased to see us then? Because we're pleased to see you aren't we, Henry?'

Henry made chuffing noises, licked Emma's hands, and aimed a lick at her face, but Emma jerked her head back and giggled. 'I never want to leave you and Henry, I love you both, but Harry needs me,' she said, finishing on a sad note.

Amanda chose to ignore Emma's dip into sadness and said, 'Did Mommy go straight to work?'

'Mmm, Mommy said I'm a big girl now and don't need molcolding. May I have porridge again, please?'

'Yes, love, I've got it ready for you. Would you like banana cut up in it today?'

'Mmm, please.'

'Well, take your coat off and put it on the chair. I won't mollycoddle you either, and I'll go and warm it through. Do you want some Henry?' Amanda said, and Emma laughed as Henry thumped his tail on the floor.

Amanda stood and, holding her walker, went into the kitchen where she prepared the meal that had become a ritual even if Emma arrived in the afternoon. She always seemed to be hungry. But as with most things, Emma had asked Amanda not to tell Helen that she ate anything. Initially, Amanda had asked why, but all Emma would say was her mommy wouldn't like it.

Amanda cut up a banana and wheeled the two bowls into the sitting room, where Emma was already seated at the small table with Henry lying at her side. Amanda placed one dish in front of Emma. 'Now blow on it, don't burn your mouth, and here you are, Henry.' Amanda bent stiffly and placed Henry's bowl on the floor, where he made short work of his favourite human food.

'Thank you, Manda,' Emma said after cooling it down and eating a couple of spoonfuls. 'It's lovely, isn't it, Henry?'

'You're welcome, love.' Amanda sat down in her chair and watched Emma as Henry nosed his empty bowl. 'Anything to tell me today, Emma?' It was a question Amanda asked her each day in the hope of gaining some insight into her home life. Usually, Emma merely shook her head, making her curls dance.

Today Amanda was surprised when Emma said flatly, 'Yes, I have. It's my birthday, erm this week and Harry's.'

'Oh, that's lovely; which day is it, do you know?'

Emma turned to look at Amanda. Porridge dripped from her spoon as she bit her lip thoughtfully. I think it's Friday.' She carried on eating.

Amanda looked at her phone. 'That will be the twenty-eighth, does that sound right?'

'Mmm, yes I think so.'

'Will you be ten?' Amanda teased.

'No-o, four,' Emma said indignantly, then giggled.

'You'll be here on your birthday then, and so will Robert and Guy; they're coming home on Thursday. Shall we have a party with cake and balloons?'

Emma's lip began to judder, and she put her spoon down. 'Mommy doesn't like parties, and she said she will take me to Macdonald's for tea.'

Amanda felt overwhelmed with sadness. 'Well, there's no reason to be upset; that sounds lovely.'

Emma hiccupped. 'But I'd like to have cake and balloons like children do on TV. It looks fun.' She picked up her spoon and dipped it into her bowl.

Amanda felt her dislike of Helen deepen as she wondered what sort of life Emma had led before they moved into the terrace. 'I tell you what, Emma, how about if we don't call it a party but have cake and balloons anyway? We don't always tell your mommy what happens when you are here, do we?'

Emma burst into tears and slid down from the table to sit by Henry, who licked dregs of porridge from the spoon in Emma's hand.

'Come here, love,' Amanda held her arms out, and Emma climbed onto her lap, making Amanda wince. 'Now why are you crying; isn't my idea about the cake and balloons a good one?' She wiped Emma's tears away but held her close.

After a while, Emma lifted her head, gulped noisily and said, 'Yes, it is, but Harry won't be able to see them, and it's his birthday too.' Tears continued to form in Emma's eyes, but she dashed them away herself and wiped her hand on the tissue that Amanda held out for her.

'I know I've asked you this before, love, but why can't you bring Harry here with you? He could see the balloons, and you could pretend to feed him some cake. Would Mommy let you do that?'

Emma ceased to cry and sat up straight, making the pain in Amanda's knees burn. 'I can't, and Mommy mustn't know I've told you. He has to stay in his cupboard.' Emma's eyes widened until she reminded Amanda of a scared bushbaby. In a whisper, she said, 'I untied his knots once and let him stay out, but I was frightened Mommy would find out and punish us. Amanda could feel Emma's anxiety making her shudder.

'Alright, love, we won't talk anymore about Harry. Have you finished your porridge?'

Emma nodded.

'Well, get down, and you can help me by picking Henry's bowl up, and we can wash up before we do our jig-saw and perhaps sing.'

Amanda quickly changed the subject; she hated to see this lovely child become so upset, and while she gave Emma small tasks to occupy her mind, she decided that something had to be done. When Emma spoke about Harry, she became so distressed that Amanda thought perhaps professional help was needed. This led to her thinking about the previous Friday night when Pat Staples had woken everyone up, including herself and Henry, although they hadn't gone outside. Watching as Pat had put up a tremendous fight not to go in an ambulance until they sedated her and she became compliant was awful. Amanda wasn't sure where she'd been taken and couldn't bear to think what Pat and Eric were going through.

'Manda, can we sing now? I've put the paper in the bin.'

Amanda dried her hands on the tea towel and hugged Emma. 'Come on then, you choose.'

'Can we sing *Away in a Manger*? I love that one, and it's nearly Christmas after my birthday, isn't it?'

'It's not too far away after that, and yes, let do it. Let's see if we can make it perfect for next Friday, and then we can sing it with Robert and Guy.' Amanda sat in her chair and said, 'You start.'

Emma had forgotten her upset as she giggled and went into their routine of, 'No, you start.'

Amanda began to sing, and Emma joined in. Amanda found herself becoming somewhat choked as they sang. She wanted Emma to be happy and felt such animosity for Helen, who she now believed was abusive. She needed to speak with Robert and Guy, sure that they would know what to do so that Emma wouldn't be open to even more abuse. Meanwhile, Amanda thought she should keep quiet.

However, she found it challenging to look Helen in the eye when she picked Emma up unexpectedly at ten o'clock and said, 'I shan't be working at Hamza's anymore. I've just told him I have a job at Tesco. The only problem is it will be longer hours. Of course, I will pay more. Can I rely on you to still mind Emma?'

'Oh, oh yes. I love having Emma here, but why?' Amanda asked.

'I feel uncomfortable with only having a man there most of the time, and Nazia will be returning now her mother has died. I start tomorrow. Would you be able to mind her for six hours each day to be arranged?' I shall be able to tell you my rota a week in advance,' Helen said coldly.

'That will be fine. What about tomorrow and the rest of this week?' Amanda asked stiffly.

'My shift starting tomorrow is ten until four, but it will take me fifteen minutes to walk there, so I'll bring her at half-past nine and pick her up as soon after four as I can manage. Is that alright?'

'Yes, that's fine. Come on out now, Emma; it's home time. I'll see you tomorrow.' Emma appeared from behind the chair, waved to Amanda, and followed her mother out without anyone saying another word.

Later that night, when she went to bed, Amanda rang Robert and told him about Emma's birthday and how upset she'd been.

Robert sighed. 'I hope you're wrong, Amanda, but I have a feeling you aren't. What we don't want to do is make everything more difficult for her.'

'No, I'm not going to say anything to Helen; I just wonder where she comes from and, oh, I'm not sure of anything except Emma's behaviour isn't normal, whatever that means.'

'I'll try and see what I can find out. Try not to worry, Manda. We'll be with you early as possible on Thursday. Now get some sleep, please.'

'I will. Love you, my Robert. Night, night.'

'Bye-bye, love.' The phone went dead. Amanda felt as though a weight had been lifted from her shoulders and slept well.

52

10 Littlebrook Terrace, Thursday 27th September 2012.

'They've made an excellent job of it,' Guy said as he opened and closed all the cupboards in the newly fitted kitchen.

'I love it, but we need to go shopping. I only asked Cathy to buy bread and milk.' Robert looked into the fridge. 'Ahh, bless her, she's bought eggs, bacon and butter too.'

Guy altered the angle of the blinds and looked out of the kitchen window. 'Hey, Lewis is emptying pots and cleaning up out here. Wonder why he isn't at school?' He opened the window and called, 'Hey Lewis, why aren't you studying?'

'Bad throat,' Lewis croaked, 'supposed to be resting, but I was bored.'

Robert went to the window. 'You probably shouldn't be out in this drizzle. Come on in and have a drink,' he said firmly.

Lewis swilled his hands under the tap attached to the kitchen wall, wiped his feet and joined the men in the warmth. Robert helped him off with his damp jacket and hung it over a chair, and then they sat at the breakfast bar where Lewis gratefully cupped his mug of tea to warm his hands.

'Where does your mother think you are? Bet she doesn't know you're out, does she?' Guy asked.

Lewis kept his eyes on his drink as he said, 'No, I'm supposed to stay in bed.' He shuffled his size nines under the table. 'I know what you're going to say, and I will.' He stood up. 'I'm tired now anyway, so I'll go like a good little boy.' He sighed and then grinned as the two men laughed at his hangdog expression.

'Well, we're going to Amanda's now, so begone young man and keep warm,' Robert said, his eyes twinkling.

'If I'm better tomorrow, will you shoot some hoops with me again? Get some exercise like?' Lewis grinned winningly.

'Ok, but it's Emma's birthday tomorrow, so it'll have to be in the afternoon,' Guy said, 'now go on clear off.' He smiled as Lewis ran down the garden and jumped neatly over the wall into his garden.

'Not much wrong with him; he'll survive,' Robert said.

'He's ok. You know I told Manda that we'd go and see her before we go shopping. You ready?'

Robert nodded. 'We need to start choosing furniture too.'

'Indeed. I don't fancy spending too much time sitting on these old garden chairs.' Guy wrinkled his nose.

Robert laughed. 'You must be getting old; it doesn't bother me.'

'Well, you've more padding on your arse,' Guy said and chuckled.

'You saying I'm getting fat?' Robert said and chased after Guy as he headed for the door.

Minutes later, they had barely entered Amanda's house when Emma jumped herself into Robert's arms, planted a smacker on his cheek, then repeated the performance with

Guy. 'Manda said you'd come today, and I was excited.' She skipped along the hall in front of them.

'Let them get in, Emma,' Amanda called as Henry met them, chuffing and pawing at Robert's legs. After petting Henry and hugging Amanda, both men shrugged off their jackets.

'Whew, I think we're welcome,' Guy said as Robert took their coats back into the hall.

Robert folded his body into the chair opposite Amanda while Guy stretched out on the floor with Emma showing him the pictures she'd been colouring. 'Do you know I'm nearly grown-up tomorrow?' Emma suddenly jumped to her feet and raised her arms to the ceiling.

'Yes, we do; it's your birthday, isn't it? How old will you be?' Robert asked, smiling tenderly at the little girl he'd grown so fond of.

'I'll be ten,' Emma said ingeniously, 'won't I, Amanda?'

Amanda howled with laughter. 'Touché. We all know you'll be four. Next year, young lady, it will be school, and you are already clever and beautiful.'

Emma said tremulously, 'I don't want to go to school without Harry, and Mommy won't let him go anywhere.'

Amanda could feel a panicky sensation; there it was again. She looked at Robert, anxiety evident in her eyes. There was definitely something wrong with this lovely child.

'Well, why don't we think about that next year? Why don't we all go to the café, have lunch, and see Maja? Then Guy and I must do some shopping.'

'Can Manda come?' Emma was distracted and smiled as she held on to Amanda's hand.

'Of course. Now let's see what do you eat? Do you like frog's legs? Or how about spiders in honey?'

Emma's expression became horrified. 'Nooo, chicken nuggets and chips, please. But I don't think Mommy will let me go to the café; she says they are bleeding grounds for germs.' Emma's eyes were wider still as everyone burst out laughing. She joined in even though she'd no idea what they were laughing at.

'Don't worry, you have to eat, and today you have to come with us, and I'll tell her so,' Robert said.

Emma looked to Amanda, a question in her eyes. 'Don't worry, love; it will be ok. Come and help me with my jacket.' Robert and Emma helped, then both men tucked an arm on either side of Manda and full of laughter, they slowly made their way across the pavement to the café.

They were seated at one of the two empty tables for a couple of minutes before Alek came from the kitchen and gave two full plates of food to a couple drinking tea.

'Be with you in a minute,' he said and wiped a hand across his red forehead.

'Oh, dear, I wonder where Maja is; it looks like he's doing everything himself,' Amanda said.

They watched as Alek rang up cash from two sets of customers, apologised for the delay and then came to their table. 'Where's Maja? You look rushed off your feet,' Amanda said sympathetically.

Alek rolled his eyes. She's feeling unwell and is staying in bed.' He shook his head. 'It is alright, but,' he held his palms out towards Amanda, 'it's lunchtime, and it is always busy on Thursday. Now, what can I get for you?' He sighed as the bell rang, and a couple came in and sat down. 'Be with you in a minute,' he called.

287

Robert ordered cheese and tomato omelette for each of them and chicken nuggets for Emma.

Guy stood up and placed a hand on Alek's shoulder. 'I tell you what, Alek; I'll make our drinks and take the new customer's orders while you cook if that will help?'

'You are a good man,' Alek said and beamed at his saviour as he went into the kitchen.

Later as they were eating, Amanda said, 'You are a good man. What you just did was very kind.'

Guy smiled lazily. 'Not just kind Amanda, we were all hungry, and I am a problem solver.'

Robert hesitated with a forkful of omelette by his mouth. He looked hard at Guy. 'That's what you do, isn't it?'

Guy smiled again. 'Come on, eat up; we've shopping to do.'

Later, when Helen arrived to pick Emma up, Robert told her in no uncertain terms that Emma had no choice but to eat at the café, and Helen didn't object merely told Emma to hurry up as she needed to get home. Once again, Emma left with a wave of her hand, but she did not speak once her mother appeared.

'Definitely strange,' Robert said when the door closed.

'Let's leave it until after her birthday, and then we can see what can be done. At the moment, I can only see things becoming worse if we challenge Helen,' Guy said.

'I agree. Now let's see if we can find Emma a doll and perhaps something else to play with while she's here. It might help her not to be so obsessed with her imaginary playmate.' Amanda smiled sadly.

Before they left, Guy ran the vacuum around the sitting room and hall while Robert cleaned up in the kitchen. Something that one or other of the neighbours that popped in often did, knowing how difficult it was for their friend who had helped them on numerous occasions in one way or another. When Amanda was settled, Robert and Guy hugged her and heard her begin to tell Henry about her lunch as they closed the door.

Lewis and Penny were shooting hoops on the factory wall. 'I see you're feeling better, Lewis,' Guy said as he laughed, grabbed the ball and put it through the ring. Don't forget our competition tomorrow.'

'Let's have a quid on it. First to twenty wins,' Lewis said and grinned.

'You're on. See you tomorrow.'

53

4 Littlebrook Terrace Friday 28th September 2012

Helen dropped Emma off and said, 'Now enjoy your birthday. I will take you out when I get home, my good girl.'

Emma ran into Amanda's to be met by a corridor of colourful balloons, which led her into the sitting room where more balloons awaited her. Robert and Guy had arranged the surprise for her the previous evening. She ran up to Amanda, hugged her tightly, planted a kiss on her cheek, and said with shining eyes, 'These are for me, aren't they, Manda?' She walked around the room, tenderly touching every balloon she could reach.

'Yes, my love, all for you. Come and open this present, and there's a cake for later.'

By the time Robert and Guy arrived after lunch singing *Happy Birthday* as they walked in the open front door, they found they had been beaten to it by Lily, and Emma was ripping the paper off a gaily wrapped present. After hugs all around, Emma continued to unwrap her gift and looked delighted when a packet of sweets wrapped up in a pretty pink dress fell to the floor.

'The dress is from me and Uncle Greg, and the jelly babies are from Bethany; we hope you like them,' Lily said as Emma held up the dress and kissed it while Lily scrunched the paper up and put it into the bin.

'Oh, I love it. It's the nicest I've ever had; thank you and Bethany,' Emma said with a big smile. Then as Henry sniffed the packet of sweets, Emma pulled them away from him, saying, 'You can't have them, they're mine, and I can share them with Harry.' No one said anything, and Emma shuffled along on her bottom to fetch a pink cardigan from where she'd left it behind Amanda's chair. 'Look what Manda asked Cathy to knit for my birthday, and I have a new jigsaw. Emma went to each person and showed them the picture of cartoon cats on the front of the box, making Robert, Guy and Lily, ooh and ahh appreciatively.

'Guy went into the hall and returned with a birthday bag with party scenes on the front of the paper. He handed it to Emma. 'Open this one, and we hope you like it.'

'More presents!' Emma couldn't believe her eyes when Robert helped her take off the Sellotape closing the bag and then held it while Emma pulled out the box, which contained a baby doll and accessories. Tears welled up in her eyes, and she said, 'I'm the luckiest girl in the world, aren't I, Manda?'

Robert released the ties holding the doll in its box and passed it to Emma, who cradled the present while touching its face and hair gently over and over. 'Thank you.' She kissed Robert and Guy and sat back down on the floor by Amanda's feet, where she continued to hug the doll. Suddenly her face crumpled, she began to sob and allowed the doll to fall face down on the floor between her legs.

291

Amanda leaned forward as Robert picked Emma up and placed her in Amanda's outstretched arms.

'Ahh, it's too much for her. I'll get out of the way. See you. Enjoy the rest of your birthday Emma.' Lily left quietly.

Emma snuggled into Amanda's chest, but eventually, her crying turned to sniffles when Amanda asked,' Why are you upset love, is it Harry?' Emma nodded, and Amanda said, 'Never mind darling, did you ask Mommy if you could bring him with you?'

Emma's reaction startled Robert, Amanda and Guy as she sat up, her face contorted with fury, and she shouted, 'I told you, he has to stay in the cupboard. He's a thing, not a person Mommy says, but he is a person he's, my twin.' She pushed the doll away with her foot. 'And I don't want birthday presents without him, and it's not fair.' All her rage dissipated as she slumped against Amanda.

Robert could see the way that Emma sat was causing Amanda pain. He got up and gently scooped Emma into his arms and sat with her on the chair, making soothing noises until she became calm and the dry sobs ceased.

Guy brought in a pot of tea and a mug of warm chocolate drink for Emma. They watched with relief as she drank while Guy poured tea for the adults.

Shortly afterwards, Guy glanced at his watch. 'I'll be back later, but it's half three, and I promised I'd shoot hoops with Lewis. Ok?'

Robert glanced at Amanda, who looked pale and drawn. 'Yes, but I'd rather stay here for a while. I've ordered Chinese to be delivered here at seven, so we can eat together. See you in a bit.'

'Guy dropped a kiss on Amanda's cheek and whispered, 'Try not to worry, it will be alright. See you later, Emma. Save me some cake, please.' Emma smiled.

Amanda sighed as he left with a wave of his hand. She had come to trust Guy and wanted him to be right, but Helen would be picking her daughter up in about three-quarters of an hour, and she felt terrible allowing Emma to go home when she was still upset. She wondered if it was time she said something to Helen about Emma's obsession with her imaginary playmate.

Guy's head was buzzing. He found it difficult to believe that any child could become so distraught over an imaginary person. Something needed to be done. He waved to Lewis and Penny, who were already throwing a ball into the hoop. 'Ok, let's be having you. A pound for the first one to twenty, you said?'

'I'm going in; some of us have got homework to do,' Penny said pointedly and picked up her school bag.

Guy tossed a coin and caught it. 'Call to see who shoots first.'

'Heads,' Lewis said. Guy tossed the coin again and showed Lewis.

'Ok, you start.' Lewis grinned.

The score was three each when Guy glanced across at number nine and saw a child in the upstairs window. His heart skipped a beat. Emma was at Amanda's. This child had the same curly mop of hair, but it was someone different. The image disappeared, but he knew he hadn't imagined it. Was this child Harry, Guy wondered, had Emma let him loose again because it was his birthday too?

He chucked the ball to Lewis. 'Sorry mate, there's something I need to do. Carry on later.'

Lewis looked puzzled but continued to throw the ball through the hoop while Guy went into number ten and fetched the key to number nine, which sat with others in a drawer in the kitchen.

Lewis scratched his head and said, 'What?' as Guy hurried past him, unlocked the door of Helen's house and went in, leaving the door open. Lewis followed him and leaned against the side of the stairs, amazed as Guy quickly searched around and then took the stairs two at a time. Lewis followed. Guy looked into the main bedroom, in the wardrobes and under the bed. Then into what was Emma's room, where he did the same. Lewis stood in the doorway, eyes wide, wondering if Guy had suddenly become strange as he walked to the large closet in the small room and opened the doors. Lewis heard a sharp intake of breath and a loud exhale as Guy pulled a blanket from the back of a bedside chair and stepped inside the cupboard. He appeared with a small boy wrapped tightly in the blue and white blanket.

'Oh my God, who's that!?' Lewis exclaimed and again followed Guy as he walked carefully downstairs and straight out of the front door.

Guy threw Lewis the key. 'Lock up, I'll see you later. Keep this to yourself for now. Can you do that?'

'Yes.' Lewis turned the key and went into his own house as Guy walked the few yards to Amanda's, knocked and held Harry close until Robert let them in.

Neither of them saw Helen as she turned into the terrace from Singerbrook Road to pick her daughter up from Amanda's, but Helen saw Guy and recognised the blanket.

As soon as she saw the small bare foot protruding from its folds, Helen knew what must have happened, and her mind reeled.

She ran until she was home and found her door remained locked. She must have been mistaken about the blanket, she thought and fumbled to unlock the door. She flew straight upstairs to the small bedroom and found that the cupboard doors were wide open, and Harry was missing. No, no, her brain screamed; it's not too late. Helen leaned into the cupboard, grabbed the sleeping bag and rolled it up before walking steadily downstairs. She picked up her car keys in the conservatory and went quickly down the back garden into the alley.

54

4 Littlebrook Terrace Friday 28ᵗʰ September 2012

Robert's face blanched as he could see that Guy carried a child. 'Harry?' he said, mouth agape.

'Yes, let's get him into the warmth; he's freezing. There was no bloody heating, and he's got very little clothing on either. He's dehydrated and needs water. Some milky chocolate drink would be good too,' Guy said and strode into the sitting room to the chair that Robert had vacated. As usual, Emma had hidden behind Amanda's chair, but she peeped out as Guy sat down.

Only the very top of Harry's hair showed, but Emma recognised her brother. She held onto Amanda's arm and said in wonder, 'It's my Harry, but I shouldn't have let him out. Mommy will kill us.'

'No, she won't,' Amanda said firmly, 'we'll never let her hurt you or Harry again.'

At the sound of Emma's voice, Harry moved for the first time since Guy had wrapped him up. He raised his head and looked at his twin. 'Emma,' he said and smiled.

Emma held onto his hand. 'You can speak,' she said beaming.

The Child in the Window

Robert held a glass of water steady while Harry drained it. Then he did the same with some milky chocolate. A look of wonder came over Harry's tiny face as he tasted the chocolate for the first time in his life.

'Not too much at first, Robert; he may not be able to cope with it,' Amanda advised gazing at the child she had believed was a figment of Emma's imagination.

Guy had opened the blanket enough to allow Harry to sit up and saw just how painfully thin he was. His arms and legs were hardly more than match sticks, and his belly was concave. 'Are you hungry Harry,' Guy asked. Harry nodded and opened his mouth, showing a gap where his front teeth should have been. 'What can you eat, little one? What does your mommy feed you?'

Harry shook his head.

'He needs to go to hospital and let the doctors check him over,' Robert said, 'shall I phone the police and an ambulance now?'

'Not yet. I think Harry should be allowed to enjoy his birthday with Emma before we get the ball rolling. There's going to be a lot of investigation and agencies involved in this. I've checked his pulse, and it's strong, and his breathing is good; he's just malnourished. I think we can afford to wait and give him a little freedom.'

'Harry eats everything I give him secretly, and Mommy gives him porridge and bread and sometimes egg if she's not angry,' Emma said. 'Mommy says the bastard is getting too strong and won't die.' She knelt up by the side of the chair and held on to Harry's hand as though she feared he would disappear if she let go. 'Can you put him on the floor so he can come and meet Henry? He's never seen a really dog before.'

'I don't see why not. You're warm now, aren't you?' Guy asked Harry, who nodded. Guy placed Harry by Emma's side, and immediately Henry came and nuzzled this new creature.

'Dog,' Harry said and tentatively stroked his fur.

'How do you even know what a dog is?' Amanda said.

'Mommy used to let him watch TV with me sometimes if I begged and I was good,' Emma said. 'Harry is clever, but he never said any words before. Can you say Emma again, Harry?'

'Emma, Emma, Emma,' Harry said, and Emma's mouth dropped open.

'Can you say Amanda?'

'Manda,' Harry said and smiled as his eyes began to droop. Guy handed Harry to Robert, who cuddled him while he slept.

'What are we going to do? Helen should have been here to collect Emma by now, and I can't think where she's got to.' Amanda twisted her handkerchief between her fingers. She'd always known something was troubling Emma, but this was more than she could have imagined. Guilty feelings assailed her, and she wished she'd done something sooner. But what? she asked herself.

Amanda and Robert watched as Guy punched some numbers into his phone. He listened for a second, then said calmly, 'I want an ambulance to take two children to the Children's hospital in Steelhouse Lane, a high-ranking police officer and a senior social worker to meet me there in precisely one hour. I will explain when they arrive. He listened for a second or two, then put his phone away.

Robert stared for a minute at the man he loved. 'Just who are you?' he said.

Guy smiled broadly. 'I assure you; you don't need to know any more about me than you do already. I've told you I am a problem solver, and this is another problem. Now, do you want to come with me to the hospital and see what we can do to make these two lovely children's lives easier?'

'Of course. Is that ok with you, Manda?' Robert said as his phone rang. 'Lewis wants to know if he can tell his mom yet about what happened?'

'Yes, he can. He's a good kid. Tell him I'll finish hoops tomorrow,' Guy said.

Robert eased his cramped arms, and Harry woke. He opened his eyes and stared at his unfamiliar surroundings. 'It's ok young man; no one will lock you away anymore, and you're safe. Would you like to eat something?'

'Can we have some birthday cake, please?' Emma said.

'Just a little, but we'll keep it for you. Do you think Harry could eat some?' Amanda said.

'He likes jam sandwiches. Can we please have some of those and some more chocolate drinks?

'Of course. It's your birthday; you are four, but perhaps Harry should only eat tiny bits until he is used to bigger meals.' Guy said and went into the kitchen.

'Emma, Harry has to go to the hospital to make sure he is taken care of properly. It's called a check-up, and I think you should go too. Is that alright?' Robert spoke softly.

Emma nodded. 'What will Mommy say?'

'I don't think you should both live with your Mommy for a while. I think perhaps she is poorly. I know you love her, but—'

Emma cut Amanda short as she said passionately, 'I don't love her; she is spiteful and hurts Harry and me sometimes. I want to live here with you and Harry and Henry.'

Amanda glanced at Robert and raised her eyes to the ceiling. He knew she thought it wouldn't be allowed, and it would be an impossible situation.

Guy came in with sandwiches he'd cut up into triangles and placed the plate on a small table. Then he lifted Harry onto a chair and stood by his side to ensure he didn't fall off while he ate.

An hour later, Emma kissed a tearful Amanda goodbye and made no fuss as Robert took her and Guy carried Harry into the waiting unmarked ambulance.

55

9 Littlebrook Terrace, Friday 28th September 2012

Helen hadn't used her car for over a week, but it started when she turned the key in the ignition. She took the rolled-up sleeping bag off the passenger seat and dropped it into the footwell. She knew she shouldn't carry children in the front seat and, in her scrambled mind, thought that if the police stopped her for any reason, they could prevent her from doing what she must do before she could move on with Emma.

It was four-thirty when she pulled out into the stream of traffic on Singerbrook Road and headed for junction seven on the M6. The traffic was heavy as she approached the M5, and Helen felt the thud as a headache began over her left eye. She hated this junction; last time she'd used it, she'd gone wrong and ended up in Ikea instead of Merry Hill Shopping Centre.

As she approached junction two on the M5, Helen pulled into the middle lane to overtake a slow lorry and realised too late that she hadn't signalled when a car blasted its horn as it swerved into the fast lane. It had happened before, and Helen knew she wasn't a good driver; she hated it. She shook her head, which was now throbbing. Concentrate, for God's sake, concentrate; she took deep breaths to try and slow her heartbeat that thudded in time with the banging in her head.

As soon as she passed the lorry and another car, Helen returned to the inside lane and stayed there until she left the motorway at the next exit and headed for Halesowen. Far from concentrating, Helen drove automatically while her mind wandered into her past, recalling abuse that had been so hard to bear. All the times her father had abused her came flooding back, bringing hot waves of guilt to colour her cheeks. She hated him, but she'd grown to enjoy the feelings that sex gave her.

Helen tried to clear her mind by putting the radio on. It was always tuned to Smooth, and the songs played usually soothed her, but this evening they had the opposite effect. Every time the presenter spoke, she wanted to rip his balls off.

Calm down; you've got a job to do. You have to get rid of it, remember. The voice that often spoke to Helen when she was alone, encouraging her to do things she didn't wish to, now spoke clearly. Just drive faster, put your foot down and let go of the wheel, and it will all be over, it said.

'No, I have it planned; I'm doing it my way.' The Sinatra song played on repeat in her head. *I did it my way… I did it my way… I did it my way.* 'Stop.' Helen screamed and hit the radio button, anything to break the cycle that wouldn't leave her. She heard the song *California Dreaming*, but she didn't listen.

A sign for West Midlands Safari Park flashed into her eyes. Looks interesting, she thought calmly. 'When I've got rid of you,' she glanced down at the bundle, 'I'll take Emma, and we can enjoy ourselves.'

Past the sign for Bewdley and then up and over the bridge across the River Severn, she drove and hoped she remembered the way towards Arley where she needed to be. After going for about ten minutes through the stunning Worcestershire countryside without appreciating any of the views that could be glimpsed between the trees, Helen realised she had missed her turn. She pulled into the Hurtle Hill Farm Campsite and asked how to get back on track.

'Oh, you're not very far out your way, lovee. Just turn around, go to end of the lane and take a left you'll be there in five minutes.'

Helen got back into the car without saying thank you and immediately forgot the woman's existence as she followed the directions. However, when the police showed Helen's photo to the campsite owner, she hadn't forgotten the woman she found abrupt and rude.

As she had done the first time, Helen stopped at several places that she had thought were suitable, but she wanted it to be the place she had chosen initially and continued to stop and start the car more than a few times. Each time she restarted the engine, Helen's head throbbed even harder, and she searched the car for her handbag, which had been left at home. She felt desperate for some painkillers and shut her eyes. When she opened them again, it was dusk. Her headache had gone, but she cursed the rolled-up sleeping bag that she believed was Harry in her confused mind. 'It's all your fault, you little bastard. You'll never live long enough to fool or hurt any woman.'

Suddenly Helen had a flash of clarity. Whose foot had she seen in the bundle Guy had carried into Amanda's house? But as the car engine roared into life, she knew Harry was in the footwell, and she had to kill him, or she could never have any peace. A mile further on, Helen recognised the place she'd picked out where the trees almost concealed the short walk to the river bank. Only a few minutes and I'll be free, she thought as she picked up the bundle from the footwell, shut the car door and, pushing aside a branch, began to walk, clutching her burden to her chest.

'It's the last time, you little shit,' she muttered as she reached the river's edge where the shallow water lapped against some large stones.

Helen stood and looked out across the vast expanse of black water and felt thwarted. She'd intended to throw Harry out into the current but doubted she could launch him that far. She kicked off her sandals and, without further thought, waded into the shockingly cold water, determined to drown him where she thought the current would carry his body out to sea.

Not very far out, the river bed prodded her stockinged feet as her skirt swirled around her body. Helen screamed as the current took her feet from under her, and she fell sideways, still holding tightly onto the sleeping bag. Her mouth filled with water, and she inhaled as she struggled to right herself. Her last thought as the swift current carried Helen and her bundle out into the middle of the river was for her daughter, who she loved.

A little further along the river, a poacher was fishing and had watched helplessly as Helen disappeared under the water. He felt horrified as he realised she had committed suicide holding on to what appeared to be a child. He couldn't believe someone had been so foolhardy as to calmly walk out into the mighty river that he loved and respected.

Tom Graves often poached this stretch of the Severn at night but knew he would be fined if caught. He quickly packed up his gear and walked to the edge of the road, where he could get a signal on his phone. He called his mate who had dropped him there earlier and asked him to pick him up. Then Tom phoned the police anonymously and told them what he'd seen. He was gone before the police arrived at the woman's car and carefully watched the news for days afterwards, hoping to discover who she was and what had become of her. He never heard anything, but it put him off fishing at night in that particular spot forever.

56

4 Condor Drive Monday 31st December 2012.

'Sit still lovely, or I'll never be able to put your socks on, and then your feet will be cold,' Amanda said as Harry grinned mischievously and continued to move his legs.

'Stop being silly, Harry; everyone's ready except you.' Emma placed her hand on Harry's arm, and he stopped moving.

Amanda sat back and smiled contentedly as soon as she'd tied Harry's laces on his trainers, that pictured dragons, which he'd chosen himself and watched him hobble to sit by Henry and Emma on the hearthrug. Henry immediately used his long, pink tongue to slurp Harry's nose, making the little boy laugh. Such a lovely sound, Amanda thought, as she watched the children while they fussed Henry, who obligingly rolled over to allow them to tickle his belly.

It's hard to believe they are so happy and Harry is filling out and becoming stronger every day. It's a miracle, really, Amanda thought as she remembered her shock and horror when Guy had unwrapped the blue and white blanket exposing Harry's underdeveloped body after he rescued him.

Amanda knew that Helen had been mentally ill, but she couldn't forgive her for how she had treated, not just her son, but Emma too. She was glad Helen had died, but whenever the thought crossed her mind, she felt guilty for thinking it. The last three months hadn't been easy, but Amanda thanked the day that Robert had brought Guy into their lives. He had eased the path through every obstacle they'd encountered when the men had decided to adopt Emma and Harry.

Amanda no longer troubled to wonder how or why Guy was so important that he could command such attention and respect. She was merely accepting and grateful, and so was Robert. Her thoughts returned to the present as Guy entered the room in his usual quiet fashion.

'All ready then, I see.' He went to the children, who hugged him fiercely.

'Where's Robert?' Emma asked, gazing expectantly at the door to the large sitting room where patio doors looked out onto a broad, landscaped garden that overlooked an expanse of woodland.

'Obert,' Harry said, echoing his twin.

'RrrrRobert,' Emma corrected him and kissed his cheek.

'He's just seeing the caterers out he'll be in in a minute,' Guy said. 'You look nice, Manda, new dress?'

'Thank you, Guy, and yes, it's the one you and Robert bought for me at Christmas, first time I've worn it.' They both laughed.

'Can we have a biscuit? I'm a bit hungry?' Emma said, looking hopeful.

'And me,' Harry said.

'Would you like a glass of milk as well,' Guy asked.

'Please,' they chorused.

'Come on; you can eat in the kitchen before anyone arrives; no, not you, Henry,' Guy said as Henry's tail banged on the floor.

Ten minutes later, Robert answered the door to Cathy and David with Penny, Lewis and George, who were the first guests to arrive. Lewis proudly carried the guitar that Robert and Guy had given him at Christmas.

'It looks beautiful,' Cathy said as she looked around the entrance hall.

'Wow, are you too posh for us now?' Penny asked Robert.

'Yes, which is why we didn't invite you, you daft bug. Let me take your coats.' Robert hung their jackets in the cloakroom off the hall. Then they all trooped in to greet Amanda and the children. Harry stayed where he was, but Emma came and kissed everyone except George, who frowned at her.

'Take no notice, he's mean,' Lewis told her as she backed away to sit with Harry.

'Come on,' Amanda stood up and seized Cathy's arm, 'I'll show you my palace first. Wide-eyed Cathy supported Amanda, leading her to a door in the corner of the room and into her granny flat. It looked very similar to the interior of number four which she had sold to live with Robert, Guy and the children in their five-bedroom bungalow, and it even had its own small kitchen. 'I never thought I'd leave the terrace, but I'm so glad I have. I love it here, and so does Henry.'

Cathy looked around and sat on the sofa by Amanda. 'I think you're fortunate, but so are they. I'm sure you've helped to make the children settle after everything that's happened in their short lives. I can't believe it even now. I suppose I should feel sorry for her, but I just can't. She may have been sick, but she was wicked.'

'I agree, but she's dead now, and the police who traced her sister, Jean, told us that Helen had always been mentally unbalanced as a child. She said she had no idea Helen had given birth and had never known where she moved to after her husband was killed. And she said she couldn't have Emma and Harry; she'd enough to manage with her own three,' Amanda said.

'I don't know, the goings-on, eh? I miss knowing you're not on the Terrace anymore, and it's weird now Pat has dementia and is in that nursing home. It's Eric I feel sorry for; he's never home. He goes to see her every day, and from what I can make out, she's not pleasant to be with either. Sometimes she has no idea who he is, poor bloke.'

'Well, I'm sorry it's happened to her, but she wasn't the most pleasant person anyway. Never mind, just promise me you'll not become a stranger and make sure Lily and Rita don't either. I don't expect I'll get a chance to talk to them like this when everyone's here. Can you believe it's another year gone? All the changes. I find it hard to keep up.' Amanda turned her head as the chimes sounded in the hallway. That'll be someone else. I suppose we'd better join everyone. Mind you; I'd as soon sit and chinwag with you. I'm not sure I'll make it to midnight.' She laughed.

'You will; get a few drinks inside you; it'll make your arthritis disappear. Come on then. Hold onto my arm,' Cathy said.

'I wish,' Amanda said as she got up slowly and went to meet Lily and Greg, who was dressed in a conservative suit. Bethany and Ryan had already disappeared somewhere with George.

Minutes later, Maja and Alek arrived, followed closely by Hamza and Nazia. As they went into the sitting room, Lily intercepted a look between Hamza and Maja as he looked at her baby bump. Lily had her suspicions about the night of Hamza's birthday, but Alek was so proud that he was becoming a dad that it was an idea worth keeping to herself. If the baby was Hamza's, she hoped Alek would never find out; it would destroy two marriages that seemed to be perfectly happy.

By eleven o'clock, Emma and Harry had fallen asleep cuddled up behind the sofa. Robert decided to leave them there and covered them with a blanket. He stood looking down at his ready-made family and felt glad that this was now his role in life. At Guy's suggestion, Robert had sold his properties as soon as the adoption process began and had happily given up flying to devote his life to Emma and Harry. He hoped that with Guy and Amanda's help, they could forget the untold hell that had been their life with Helen. Once Emma knew that she would never see her mother again, she had told them some of the things that Helen had done, but they could only guess at the depths she had sunk to in order to make her children speak about her with such hate. Something no child should ever know. They reminded him of the *Babes in The Wood*, a picture book his mother had read to him when he was small. After ensuring they were comfortable, he tore his eyes away and returned to the party that was in full swing. A little later, Robert followed Guy as he went into the hall and answered the vibrations of the ingot around his neck. One minute after midnight, when the bongs of Big Ben on the TV died away, and everyone had shouted Happy New Year; Guy kissed

Robert and whispered, 'I'll see you soon, and by the way, when I return, we are getting spliced any way we can.'

'Ok.' He grinned. 'I love you, please take care of yourself,' Robert begged and moments later waved as an unmarked black car whisked his enigma from the drive.

The End

'

Lesley Elliot

Acknowledgements

When I retired from work due to ill health, I wondered what on earth I was going to do to occupy my mind. Well, I found something that I have wished I'd done since my early years. Writing and becoming an Indie author has given me so much pleasure, and I can only hope that my novels have added to your lives my loyal readers. So thank you.

My thanks also to all my friends and relatives, especially Mary Mooney, who has always been my beta reader, for their support.

I cannot finish without mentioning my friends and neighbours who have helped me through these troubled times. Jo, Steve, Britt, and of course Joel, the lovely Cox family. A big thank you to you all.

And, of course, I could not have published anything without the skills of my wonderful wife, Susan.

Warmest regards, Lesley.

The Child in the Window

By the Same Author:

The Copper Connection

In May 1995, life changes forever for twenty-one-year-old Heather Barnes when an abhorrent crime fractures her life. Not willing to rely on the justice system, she vows to exact revenge. Is she strong enough to carry out her plans? Is she smart enough to avoid detection? We follow the highs and lows of her family life and relationships as she grows from a helpless victim into an independent, resilient woman. Will she ever be capable of putting the trauma behind her and finding the happiness she deserves, or will her need for vengeance destroy her?

Sally-Secrets and Lies

Happiness can be hard to find and even harder to hold on to. In February 1916, when Sally Brooks is twenty-five months old, a family argument changes her life forever. Follow Sally's family life and relationships as she grows from naïve child to protective mother, learning about betrayal and loss, friendship and love on the way. Lied to since childhood and unaware of secrets that will cause her heartbreak, will Sally ever be able to make sense of past events and gain the happiness she deserves?

One Child Too Many

Sara Caldicot has an uncomplicated life that she shares with her close-knit family. Her younger sister, Lyn, is spoilt and self-centred, but she has always been loved and protected.

When Lyn becomes disruptive at home, Sara's mom asks her for support. Sara tries her best to help, but in the process, she uncovers a secret. A secret that is so dreadful it threatens to tear the family apart. Can Lyn be made to see sense, or will her selfish actions destroy more than just relationships?

Love and Beyond

Stella is special, but she doesn't find that out until she dies and arrives at the Waystation. There she is given the opportunity to return to her life with the woman that she loves if she agrees to carry out a mission. Find and intervene in the lives of four people to safeguard one who is significant to the future of the world. But there is a problem. If anybody discovers her secret, the deal is off. Stakes are so high that failure is not an option, but even being an angel does not convince Stella that she has the power to succeed.

All of the above books are available for purchase, in paperback and e-book format, at www.Amazon.co.uk.

For more information about the author, please visit www.lesleyelliot.co.uk

The Child in the Window

.

Printed in Great Britain
by Amazon

28444165R00183